JUDITH'S MARRIAGE

First published in 1987 by Credo House
Angelico Press reprint edition, 2020

For information, address:
Angelico Press, Ltd.
169 Monitor St.
Brooklyn, NY 11222
www.angelicopress.com

ISBN 978-1-62138-641-4 pbk
ISBN 978-1-62138-642-1 cloth

Cover design by Michael Schrauzer
Cover image:
Maurice Denis, "Wedding Procession," 1892 (detail)
Source: Wikimedia Commons

Judith's Marriage

BRYAN HOUGHTON

Angelico Press

CATHOLIC
TRADITIONALIST
CLASSICS

CONTENTS

DEDICATORY FOREWORD

I was ordained priest on March 31, 1940. In June of that year I was appointed to Slough, an industrial suburb of London, where I founded St. Anthony's parish in the dormitory to the Trading Estate. In September 1954 I was moved to the parish of St. Edmund at Bury St. Edmunds, the County Town of West Suffolk, where I remained until Saturday, November 29, 1969. I resigned and retired as from midnight on that day. Why? Because on the following morning, the First Sunday in Advent, the New Ordo of Mass was supposed to come into force.

"But surely," one may say, "you were being rather intransigent over a bit of mumbo-jumbo?" Perhaps. But it happened to be the touchstone to a basic issue. This issue was that the new reforms in general and of the liturgy in particular were based on the assumption that the Catholic laity were a set of ignorant fools. They practiced out of tribal custom; their veneration of the Cross and the Mass was totem worship; they were motivated by nothing more than the fear of Hell; their piety was superstition and their loyalty habit. But the most gratuitous insult of all was that most Catholics had a Sunday religion which in no way affected their weekday behaviour. This monstrous falsehood was — and still is — maintained by bishops and priests who, for the most part, have never been adult laymen. Every day the Catholic workman had to put up with the jeers of his colleagues, as the more educated with their sneers. Every night they took their religion to bed with them.

I am not in a position to judge other priests' parishioners. I am, however, in a position to judge what were my own. No words are adequate for me to express my admiration for the conscious faith and piety of my flock, both in Slough and in Bury. This is where the trouble lay. The reforms were based on criticism; I was unwilling to take any action which might make me appear to

7

criticize the wonderful people whom I was ordained to serve. I was perfectly conscious that I learned more about God from them than they were likely to learn from me.

Then there were the converts. I happen to be one myself. The mystery of grace is consequently not absent from my mind. I have no notion of the number I received. A couple of hundred? Perhaps more. They ranged from the highly cultured to, quite literally, tramps. To all I gave the same eternal truths. Perhaps it is pride, but I am unwilling to admit that I deceived them into the Church.

And the marriage converts. This is a breed which is normally despised. I have it in writing in the hand of a bishop. How I admired them! Of course human love has some analogy with Divine Love, or God would not have rooted it so firmly in the human makeup. I suppose I could class myself as an "intellectual convert." What does that mean? Merely that the bankruptcy of my intelligence was filled by God's grace. Marriage converts have more than I to show: their human love looks toward the Divine Love. And they are willing to prove it by an acid test: the creative act. How can anyone despise such people?

Perhaps the reason for my resignation is now clear: I was unwilling to be instrumental in any change which might cause scandal to my wonderful parishioners.

What passes belief is that I know of no book or article published within the last twenty years extolling the virtues and commiserating the sufferings of the Catholic laity. If they dared to remonstrate they were merely told that they were divisive, disloyal and disobedient. Hence the present novel. Its purpose is to show that at any rate one priest appreciates the predicament into which the laity have been put.

I consequently dedicate this little work to my erstwhile parishioners at Slough and at Bury St. Edmunds. It is a small token of my admiration for their loyalty to the Faith and of my gratitude for the example of unquestioning piety which they set me.

Bryan Houghton

I

THE PASSAGE OF EDMUND

Beyond a doubt, Judith Milden was an exceptionally gifted girl. She had won an open scholarship to Oxford in 1953 and was now in her final year at Somerville. Her tutor, Miss Biggs, was confident that she would get a First in history, provided she did a minimum of work. "Judith," she said, "seems uninterested in the two absorbing passions which ruin even the brightest girls: boys and religion."

Concerning religion, Judith had none. Since she had left school she had not darkened the door of a church, except as an inveterate sight-seer. Her father, the chairman of Milden's Adhesives, had no time for religion. In this, as in all things, Lady Milden adhered to her husband.

Concerning boys, Judith totally lacked discrimination. In her eyes they were all equally attractive, but their only real use was to provide a dancing partner. Dancing was her one addiction. She did it very well. Provided the young man was a reasonable dancer and did not talk too much, he was marvelous.

It must be admitted that in this, as in much else, Judith was quite exceptional. The chatter among her girlfriends of their diverse conquests, of the details of their experiences in fornication, did not even nauseate her. Perhaps, in an odd way, she envied them their self-satisfaction and wished she could be as normal as they, but it did not really interest her. She had no high-falutin ideals of sexual purity, neither had she the remotest fear of sex, or of anything else for that matter, but it all seemed the maximum of fuss for the minimum of pleasure. Besides, she had a highly developed aesthetic sense, and from the copious descriptions of her friends it seemed a singularly unaesthetic pastime. Of course she would marry some day. He would be a supremely good dancer. She might allow a child or two; that would obviously depend.

9

Scarcely had she returned to Oxford for the summer term in 1956 when she had to go up to London for a dance. It was rather a grand affair. She and her cousin, Millicent, had been invited. Judith was to stay the night at Milli's flat. It was Milli who was doing all the organizing and finding the boys.

Milli was the only child of Sir George Milden's elder sister. She was twenty-six years of age, had just qualified and was working in a London hospital. Her father had been killed in the war. Her mother had died quite recently, and Milli was still occupying the rather large flat in Chelsea which, as a matter of fact, she could easily afford.

With her usual competence, Milli had found Judith a handsome boy with golden hair, brilliant blue eyes and a delicate aquiline nose. In spite of being tall, he was as straight as a poker. Judith was not inspired by willowy youths. He was also attractively ancient: about twenty-seven, she thought. In fact he only had one drawback: he was a wretched dancer. However, she managed to drag him around the floor a few times; and he was not possessive, so she was able adequately to indulge her addiction with more accomplished young men. His name was Edmund Something-or-other. Judith already knew Milli's boy, one Timothy Bradfield, the brilliant young gynaecologist at Milli's hospital. At least he was not all that young, in his middle thirties, balding and tubby, but a beautiful dancer.

Judith enjoyed herself. She was scarcely tiddled but agreeably tired when they left shortly after two in the morning. Milli had arranged everything. The boys drove them home in appropriate sports-cars. They had a final whisky in the drawing room. Then Milli announced: "Let's go to bed. Judi, show Edmund the way. I'll put the lights out in the hall. Come along, Tubby."

Edmund was horrified. He knew well enough that Milli had no morals, but he had not expected her to organize his night for him. His immediate reaction was to bolt without a word. But he stopped. Surely this charming Judith was not as corrupt as her cousin? If he bolted he could never know. He would automatically equate Judith with Milli: a couple of bitches from the same kennel. He had no intention of sleeping with Judith, but he did hope that she had some moral fibre and that refusal would eventually come from her. It was obvious that Milli had engineered the situation, but how far was Judith a willing accomplice?

Judith was completely in a maze. She walked automatically to her room, Edmund dutifully following. She switched the lights on. Obviously, while she had been waiting in the drawing room before going out, Milli had tidied the bedroom. Her own little cotton pyjamas had vanished and a frothy short-length nightdress taken their place. A pair of men's silk pyjamas was laid over the back of a chair.

Judith was a virgin. She had always presumed, however, that this juvenile state would end one day. She felt a bit piqued that Milli should organize it all for her. But then, she probably could not have organized it herself, and Milli was always so competent.

Edmund made some fatuous remark about it being a very beautiful room and sat down at the foot of the bed. Judith did not know what to do. "Yes, it's not Milli, but her mother who had the taste. Did you know her?"

"Well, I met her a few times."

"It's funny that we have never met before."

"No, not really; I don't belong to your cousin's set." Then silence.

Judith wished Edmund would help her along a bit: kiss her, hug her, do something. No, he just sat on the bed. Bravely, she tried again: "Did you enjoy yourself this evening?"

"Yes, because I met you. I think you are very charming and very lovely. But generally speaking, I dislike vast gatherings. The best way to meet nobody is to meet everybody. We could have had a lovely evening together had there been a couple of hundred fewer people about." That was a bit better, but it was not much.

Judith knew from her girlfriends that stripping was an important part of the process. Perhaps that was what Edmund was waiting for. She went over to the dressing table and took off her odd bits of jewelry and her rather glamourous evening dress. She sat down and started to comb what she knew to be her magnificent head of hair. In the mirror of the dressing-table she could see that Edmund was watching her intently. But he still remained silent and did not move. Couldn't he help her in some way? Was she doing something wrong?

She got up, went to the bed and sat directly on Edmund's left, so that their thighs touched. He would only have to lift his arm to hug her. He did not. He took her right hand into both of his. He looked straight into her eyes and said very gently — he had a beautiful voice — "You don't want to really, do you?"

"No," she murmured. Her lower lip started to quiver violently. She burst into tears.

It was then that he took her into his arms, hugged her, kissed her. Eventually, he said in the same soft voice: "I knew you didn't...God bless you, Judith. You are as good as you are lovely." Then: "I must go now."

Judith found the strength to say: "Thank you, Edmund! You are so kind, so kind. I shall never forget you."

She let Edmund out. She waited to hear his car disappear down the street. She had never remembered feeling so happy as she fell off to sleep.

It was about ten when Milli appeared in a dazzling kimono carrying a tray of tea and toast for two. "Good heavens! Has Edmund gone already?"

"Not exactly, Milli, because he has never been."

"The brute! I knew he was R.C., but I did not think he was an eunuch. Poor Judi, I do apologize. Tubby's a very different kettle. Here, take the tray while I tell you..."

Judith's thoughts were miles away while Milli revealed Tubby's unconscionable vulgarity.

II

THE CRUCIFIX

Judith had intended to spend the afternoon with her parents in Hampstead, but she rang them up to say that she had got to get back to Oxford. The fact was that she felt too happy to risk the spell being broken. She wanted to be alone. The hedonists who talk about the joys of experience know nothing of the joy of inexperience. It was a revelation to Judith: how deep it is, how secret, incommunicable, inexpressible.

Judith got back to her rooms at Somerville at about five in the afternoon. She was fond of them. Her bedroom was a bit poky, but the bedspread was her own, a beautiful piece of Italian cut-velvet with bold acanthus leaves in deep red on cloth of gold. Mother had given it to her for her twenty-first birthday three months ago, along with lots of other pretty things. There were photos in old-fashioned silver frames: Daddy coming away from Buckingham Palace after receiving his knighthood for making sticky bombs during the war; Mother looking frightfully funny when she was presented at Court; her elder brother's wedding photo; Milli looking frightfully smart even though she was wearing academic dress for her doctorate. Yes, Milli: humph! Judith had an enormous admiration for Milli, but she was out of place. She slipped the photo into a drawer.

The study was very respectably furnished by the college. She had had the chintzes renewed herself. The books, some of them beautifully bound, were of course her own, as were the odd bibelots: a fine Sevres group of Diana, inadequately clothed for the chase, surrounded by sniffing hounds; an early Florentine bronze inkstand of Narcissus looking at his reflection in the ink, and the like — good things, in fact, which had stuck to Milden fingers during four generations in the glue trade. Apart from the books, however, there was only one thing in the room which she

13

had bought herself. At the time she had thought it wonderfully clever and technically perfect. As she looked at it that evening, over the mantlepiece, she discovered that she no longer liked it. Truth and beauty are more hidden than that. It was the reproduction of a recumbent female nude by Picasso. Overnight her taste had changed. She climbed onto a chair and took it down. She slid it behind the cupboard. Great art it was, but it lacked joy because it lacked innocence. She felt too happy for such company.

During the week she did her best to satisfy Miss Biggs with the pedigrees of the barons in the Barons' War and other such, but her heart was not in it. The real problem was to find something to replace the Picasso over the mantlepiece. There were plenty of beautiful things, but they were not sufficiently gay; plenty of gay things which were inadequately beautiful. If only she could ask Edmund, he might be able to help. With a nose like his, he must be terribly refined; and it was he, after all, who had given her the unique experience of her life: the consciousness of the beauty of innocence.

She wished she could remember Edmund's surname — Wickham or Wexham or something — but it had not registered when they were introduced. She had had no idea that he might be more than a dancing partner. Anyway, it was up to him if they were to meet again. He knew her name all right because he had asked if she was connected with the glue people. He also knew where she was at Oxford. If worse came to worst, Milli could be relied upon to arrange a chance meeting. But Judith did not like that idea; it would be the last resort. Not only was Milli out of favour, but she could never be made to understand that the motive was innocent. Poor Milli, she was good and kind and generous to a fault, competent and intelligent, but she really was a . . .; no, that was a harsh word: she was sexually amoral.

Friday was a perfect May day. Clouds were riding high like great galleons in a deep blue sky. She and a friend, one Pamela Playfair, decided to take a bus out to Dorchester and go for a walk. They got to Dorchester but did little walking. Pamela was a great collector of Staffordshire dogs; there were a couple in the window of a junk shop. While Pamela haggled, Judith rummaged round the place.

Lying on top of a nondescript chest of drawers was a polychrome high-relief in wood of about 1520. It represented the Crucifixion, with baby angels catching the blood of Christ from the five wounds in lovely little chalices. In very bold relief in the foreground were the Virgin and St. Bruno. The background was some hill town in low relief. It was fairly large: about four feet tall and three feet wide.

Judith was staggered. She would have looked at it with care in a museum. To find it in a junk shop was simply past belief. "How much is this thing?" she asked.

"It's a lot of money, Miss. I had to pay £50 for it myself. I could not let it go under £60. I had to get it down off the wall and transport it. But seeing as you're young, you can have it for £55."

"Yes, I'll take it. Where did it come from?"

"There was an old lady who lived at Shellingham. A real lady she was. She was one of them Roman Cath'lics and had an oratorio, as they call it. She died and her effects was all sold. Lor', the price some of the furniture fetched! Dealers came all the way from London and Reading. But nobody wanted the religional stuff — out of fashion nower days. I'm a God-fearing man m'self and I says to m'self I won't come to no 'arm if I give £50 for Jesus. So you can 'ave 'im for £55."

There was a certain amount of ringing up Judith's bank, but eventually the girls emerged carrying the high-relief between them, with Pamela dangling a couple of Staffordshire dogs around her neck.

As they got back exhausted, they happened to pass Miss Biggs. "Oh! You must come to my rooms later, Miss Biggs, and see what I've bought. It's a North Italian polychrome high-relief of the early Cinquecento. There are some marks on the back, but I have not had time to decipher them. It's marvelous!"

Eventually the girls got it upstairs, and with the help of Bill the Boilerman fixed it firmly to the wall over the mantlepiece.

Judith sat back triumphant and contemplated her acquisition. It was not exactly gay and innocent: a corpse nailed to a bit of wood. Yet, in an extraordinary way, it was: not merely the

Virgin, the saint and the baby angels collecting the blood, but even the corpse, pinned out like a butterfly. Certainly if Christ had to be killed there was no other way in which it could be done. He could not have been electrocuted, guillotined, hanged or garroted. Perhaps that was what had determined the time of his incarnation. Apart from an unopened Bible, Judith had never owned anything religious before. The crucifix's impact was un-dulled, as strong in its way as the impact of Edmund.

Later that evening Miss Biggs knocked at the door. She was a very distinguished old lady. During the past forty years some of the brightest girls in the country had passed through her hands. She knew everything. She knew everybody. "What a beautiful thing, my dear," she said after closely examining the crucifix. "It is quite unsuitable for a college room, but magnificent it is. Curiously enough, I have seen it before, but I cannot remember where. How did you come by it?"

"I bought it in a little old junk shop in Dorchester."

"In Dorchester? Let me see...Yes, of course! It was over the altar in the Dowager Lady Stanningfield's chapel at Shellingham. Her niece, the present Viscount's sister, was here just before the war. The old lady had no children, so I suppose her belongings were sold. She came from an old recusant family, perhaps the most distinguished of them all — you failed to mention them in your rather skimpy essay on the Barons' War — people called Rougham, descended from..."

Judith jumped. Yes, that was the name: Edmund Ruffam, spelt Rougham. Miss Biggs rambled on, a mine of information. When politeness permitted, Judith asked as innocently as she could: "And do the Roughams still exist?"

"Dear me, yes! I had the pleasure of meeting her brother, Brigadier Rougham, at Lady Stanningfield's. He must be an old man now, but he still lives at Rougham Castle, which must be among the grandest of our Stately Homes."

"So the crucifix really comes from the Roughams?"

"Quite certainly, my dear. I now recall it well. The only inconvenience of lunching with Lady Stanningfield was that guests were expected to parade in the chapel afterwards to recite the Angelus."

Yes, Milli had said that Edmund was R.C., so it was more than likely that he was a member of the recusant family. That then, she thought, as she looked at her crucifix, was Edmund's background: a baby angel suckling at the wounds of Christ.

Later, in the Senior Common Room, Miss Biggs remarked: "So that's the end of Judith Milden, quite the brightest and most charming girl I've had this decade. She has been bitten by religion, and I suspect there is a boy."

III

MASS

Judith spent a great deal of Saturday looking at her crucifix. She was hypnotized by it. Of course one must not allow oneself to be influenced by coincidences. They do not mean anything; they just happen. However, it was rather absurd to be studying mediaeval history and never to have attended Mass. After all, apart from ruins, it was the only thing that had come intact from Imperial Rome, through the Dark and Middle Ages down to the present day. As an historical phenomenon it was unique. She could write brilliant essays for Miss Biggs on religious movements in the 12th century but had never looked at the reality in the identical shape under her nose. It had nothing to do with Edmund. She was being objective; it would help her understanding of history. She found out the times of Mass at St. Aloysius's for the next day, Sunday.

Inevitably, both as an educated young woman and as a student of history, Judith knew something about Catholicism: papal infallibility, cardinals, the Real Presence, confession, indulgences and the like — things which seemed completely divorced from reality. But such knowledge does not help very much in practice. In the first place, being unused to church-going, she arrived for Mass far too early. There was nobody there to give her a cue. You had to do something or other with holy water. She dipped her glove in but decided that you were probably meant to take the glove off. She put her hand in but had forgotten to bring a towel and none was provided. She waggled her hand about until it dried. Genuflecting in front of the tabernacle: that ought to be easy enough. Yes, but which knee, right or left? After much thought, she did both, one after the other. Then came the insoluble problem of where to go. If only the church had been full she could have stood inconspicuously at the back.

But it was empty. To stand would be terribly conspicuous. The wretched building had no convenient columns behind which to hide. Then, were the seats reserved? Was there a special pew for non-Catholics? She was on the point of leaving when a boisterous family barged in, blocking the only exit; coppers were given to the older kids and sticky sweets to the younger. Behind them was a motley crew filling the little courtyard. She recognized a girl from Somerville whom she particularly disliked, so she could not push her way out for fear of meeting her. She followed the boisterous family and sat directly behind it.

What turned out to be rather less than half the congregation had piled in when a bell was rung and a diminutive boy emerged from the right followed by a priest. Judith was well-acquainted with vestments from splendid pictures by Rubens, and with birettas from 17th century engravings. Naturally, these did not prepare her for how immensely comic they looked on the gaunt figure of Father Philip McEnery, S.J.

The priest gave his cap to the diminutive boy, spread his tools on the altar, turned his back on the people and started off at high speed in incomprehensible Latin.

Judith had always imagined that Roman Catholics had a special grace or charism — whatever the word was — enabling them to understand Latin. Perhaps they had, but it was quite certain that they were not using it. Nobody was paying the slightest attention to the priest, just as the priest was paying not the slightest attention to the congregation.

In front of her, the older children were rolling their coppers about the floor while the younger ones filled their mother's handbag with sticky sweet-papers or used the bench as an improvised trapeze. All this without the parents taking any notice whatsoever, except when the father gave the youngest a good clout for climbing up his back and landing, over his head, on the bench in front. Dad was far too occupied in arranging little pictures of saints in a much-thumbed book called, Judith could see, *The Garden of the Soul*. Mum sighed spasmodically as she rattled, very literally, through the Rosary. Much the same was going on all round her.

However, all these good people must have had a vague consciousness of what was happening at the altar because they all followed with unbelievable discipline a sort of sacred gym of breast-beating, cross-signing, kneeling, sitting, standing and the like. Exhausted by over five minutes of gym, the congregation collapsed into the benches while the priest put on his cap and ascended the pulpit. Judith steeled herself for a sermon; she had always abominated them at school. She need not have worried. Although in the vernacular, it was clearly a part of the liturgy: a list of events which nobody could possibly want to attend, a ticking-off about money and a long catalogue of totally unknown dead people for whom one was asked to pray. The priest returned to the altar, having duly given his cap to the diminutive boy.

Then things seemed to start in earnest. The priest began fiddling about with his tools in complete silence. Dad started to clout his children at regular intervals. Something was up. From her mediaeval studies, Judith recognized the *Sanctus*. There was a surge onto knees; she could hear the click in the old folks' joints. There was another bell and even the smallest child in front of her disappeared under the bench. Then there were six bells and the elevation. Judith knew what it meant: it was the consecration, the Real Presence. There fell a silence like the primeval silence before ever the world came to be. It was colossal.

Anyway, so it went on, all utterly inhuman, out of this world. Long before the end, people started surging out. Perhaps it was etiquette for the priest to be first aboard and last off the ship, like a sea captain. However, Judith waited. Eventually the priest collected his tools, put his cap on and, preceded by the diminutive boy, went out as he had come in. The boisterous family gathered itself, looking radiantly happy and chirping like sparrows. They went. Judith stayed.

So that was Mass. Certainly it had been nothing like her preconceived notion as to what a religious ceremony ought to be. It was not in any sense a community service; everybody seemed to be doing exactly as he liked. There was no question of "improving" anybody. Neither were there any of those ghastly, smug prayers which used to make her writhe at school. Their memory haunted her yet: "Let us pray for the United Nations and all who work for peace," "Let us pray for racial justice in South Africa," "Let us pray that industrial conflicts should find a Christian solution" and so on. They had probably contributed to Judith's irreligion more than the influence of her father. But at Mass nobody or nothing had been prayed for at all, apart from the list of unknown dead "whose anniversaries occur about this time." No, that was not quite true: right at the end when the congregation was surging out there had been some Hail Marys followed by some incomprehensible prayers.

Yes, that was the Mass: aboriginal Christianity. Judith sat there completely shattered. Thousands upon thousands of people had died to defend or deny THAT. The Wars of Religion had always been completely incomprehensible to her, people getting killed for abstract arguments concerning grace and good works. She could see it now. The wars had nothing to do with grace or good works: they had to do with THAT. It was for or against THAT that people had been willing to die. The rest was just rationalization.

In the sharp light of a first impression Judith could see the problem clearly. It had nothing to do with particular theological arguments; it concerned the whole orientation of man's outlook. Was religion centered on man or was it centered on God? She hunted round in her mind until she had found the correct terms. Was it theocentric or anthropocentric? Was the basic religious act one of adoring or one of begging? The Mass gave a peremptory answer: the religious act was theocentric; it was an act of adoration. All those strange folk, including the boisterous family in front of her, were not begging for peace or justice but, quite unselfconsciously, were attempting to adore. The object of their adoration, too, was perfectly clear: it was the Real Presence.

In practice, the Real Presence came as a bit of a shock to Judith. She had naturally met a number of apparently sane R.C.'s. She had always taken it for granted that by the Real Presence they must mean something other than a real presence. They must attach the notion of reality to their supreme symbol; "symbolic reality" would be a better term. It was the same with "transubstantiation";

she took it for granted that sane R.C.'s must mean that the significance of the bread and wine had changed; in ordinary language it would be "trans-signification." But the experience of one Mass had disillusioned her. It was abundantly clear from their whole attitude that those pious Papists, groveling on the floor with rosaries, *Gardens of the Soul* and sticky sweets, believed quite literally in the Awe-ful Presence.

The insignificance of the priest also surprised her. She had always understood that Catholicism was priest-ridden. But the priest seemed to be no more than a mere craftsman, of much less personal importance than the chaplain at school. All the priest did was turn up with his little mate and lay on the Body and Blood of Christ as the plumber lays on the water. He picked up his tools and vanished once the tap of Eternal Life had been turned on.

By this time Judith was alone in the church apart from the priest. A moment ago he had been decked out in lace and silks. Now he knelt, a black shadow, at the altar rails. Yes, Judith could see how it was: he had enacted his part, the gay moth fluttering round the Light of the World; inevitably he had scorched his wings and was again no more than a mournful caterpillar.

It took enormous courage. Judith went up to him and said: "Father, I want to become a Catholic."

IV

TO LOVE OR NOT TO LOVE

It was on the following Tuesday that she received the letter.

Dear Judith,

I find that I shall be in Oxford next weekend. Will you lunch with me on Sunday at the Randolph? I shall be in the lounge at any time after 12:15. I apologize for giving you such short notice. Please do not bother to answer. I shall understand perfectly if you are unable to come.

Best wishes,
Edmund Rougham

Actually, she and Pamela had promised to go to a party with some boys at Christ Church. Pamela would have to find someone else. She had known it would come, but it was frightfully exciting when it did. Twelve-fifteen at the Randolph; that presumably meant he was going to the 11 o'clock at St. Aloysius's. She would have to avoid that one. It might be safer not to go at all. No, she would have to go; the poison had entered her blood. She would go at eight.

As Miss Biggs had foreseen, she got nothing out of Judith that week. Apart from the fact that she was walking on air, Judith had to attend instructions with Father McEnery on Tuesday and Thursday. At last Sunday came. Judith dutifully went to the eight o'clock Mass. She felt far too gay to pay the slightest attention, but she was sufficiently wide awake to notice a curious phenomenon: it made precisely no difference if she were attentive or not. The Mass was so far above human affairs that her thoughts, her attitudes, her longings added or subtracted exactly nothing. She pushed her way out at the earliest possible moment as though she were a hardened Catholic, utterly satisfied at having done nothing. There had been two presences, God and Judith; there could not be more.

She was not a vain girl, but Judith knew by instinct that her hair and her arms were recognizable, fractionally different from those of other girls. She brushed the former with considerable care. She wore a sleeveless dress. Punctually at 12:30 she arrived at the Randolph. Edmund was waiting for her in the hall. She skipped toward him and flung her arms round his neck just as she had a fortnight before and kissed him, in front of everybody — which in fact consisted of two flunkeys, the receptionist, and a very retired colonel and his wife. "Come along, Edmund! Let's go and eat straight away to avoid the crowd."

Having settled the difficult matter of the menu, she said, "Edmund, tell me about yourself. All I know is that you are very kind and that you can't dance."

She had been right: he was 27. His father was a retired brigadier who lived in moth-eaten grandeur in the ancestral home, Rougham Castle, near Royston in Hertfordshire. His father had married late in life and Edmund was the only child. He had been educated at Beaumont and Trinity, Cambridge. He had taken his degree in modern philosophy, but had stayed on to get a B. Sc. in economics. He was working at the Treasury, where his main occupation was to prepare unlikely answers to M.P.s' improbable questions. He shared a flat in Chelsea with another bachelor.

It was not wildly exciting, but he was of the family Miss Biggs had talked about, and it was his aunt, presumably, who had been the previous owner of Judith's crucifix. But she was not going to let on about that. "And what are you doing in Oxford?" she asked.

"I suppose I really came to see you," he said rather awkwardly.

Judith appreciated the compliment but did not quite believe it.

"Thank you so much! But then, what are you not really doing in Oxford?"

"Yes, there was an excuse, in case you did not want to see me. You see, one of my aunts used to live in the neighbourhood. She died about six months ago and her heir sold most of her stuff. But some of the things weren't really hers at all, but belong to my father. Ronnie — that's the heir: a certain Lord Stanningfield, who is abroad in the diplomatic service — asked my father to collect his stuff, which Ronnie had obviously kept. I came down yesterday to see exactly what there was. Actually, Ronnie has been a bit of a chump. Among other things, he sold for ten quid a crucifix which had been in our family since before the Reformation. It must be worth over a thousand, even had we wanted to sell it, which we did not..."

Judith gulped. It was very lucky that Miss Biggs had prepared her for it or she would inevitably have exclaimed that she had got it. As it was, she expected what she heard. She had no intention of getting rid of her crucifix. It was hers, wasn't it? Or was she Its? She let Edmund continue.

"...but he had the sense to keep the pictures and drawings. There is a lovely Virgin by Girolamo Genga and some fascinating drawings. I must show them to you one day."

Judith was delighted with the last sentence. It meant that today was not the last day.

After lunch they went for a walk, hand in hand, through the beautiful city, past the Sheldonian, the Radcliffe, St. Mary's, the High, through the Botanical Gardens, round Christ Church Meadows. Of course the inevitable happened. As they approached Meadow Buildings, Pamela, who was at the party, saw them from a window.

"Good heavens, John! Look who's there. I have never seen him before. Who is he? And I always thought Judith such an open creature! She's as close as an oyster. Never even mentioned him. Look at them: all ecstatic, hand in hand. They're in love."

As a matter of fact, Pamela was probably right, although neither Edmund nor Judith knew they were. After all, they had only met twice. True, there was an extraordinary intimacy between them, such as might have taken months to develop in the ordinary way. It was the intimacy of innocence.

Certainly the word "love" never crossed Judith's mind in connection with Edmund. At least partially this was because romantic fiction had given her the idea of love as implying passion, desire, longing, yearning. When a girl was in love she became soppy and pined and moped and probably ran away from home. Several had done it at Somerville. But Edmund evoked no such grand passion. Quite the contrary, in his company she felt at peace, confident and, above all, secure. Of course, Edmund had the enormous advantage of being male, and Judith liked men; but that did not qualify him of necessity for "love."

Anyway, when he had driven off and she had got back to her rooms, she sat down in front of her crucifix. And it was hers; and no Rougham was going to snatch it from her. She had had a lovely day and felt thoroughly happy. Somehow she would have to justify herself for two little bits of deception, however. Why had she not told Edmund about the crucifix? Why had she not told him that she was becoming a Catholic? She did not really know. She only knew that she could not. Somehow, it would have been unfair: to mention the crucifix would have been unfair to her; to mention religion unfair on him.

Edmund's position was a little more complicated. He had suffered the usual vicissitudes of puberty, but had been protected by the strong emotion of shame with which nature balances the sexual appetite. Moreover, he had been much helped by his spiritual director at Beaumont. "One should always look at things from above, not from below," he used to say. "Take a God's-eye view instead of a worm's. Thus, to call man a 'rational animal' is absolute nonsense: he is a 'creative creature.' In nothing is this clearer than in sex. Animals merely reproduce themselves, whereas humans force God to create immortal souls. With us, sex is so sublime that it is mighty difficult not to debase it. Keep it sublime, my boy, or you'll land in the ditch." Edmund had kept it sublime.

As he grew up, however, he realized that he was a very good catch. Not only would he be the head of an historic family, but the sole heir of Rougham Castle with its untold treasures and extensive acres. Perhaps he became a trifle cynical as doting mothers pushed their daughters at him. Men loved girls all right, but girls seemed to love things. It was well worth becoming Mrs. Rougham of Rougham Castle, even if it meant putting up with Edmund. He did not blame girls for this. He merely thought it a part of their psychology. Woman was instinctively a mother and wanted to provide the best possible nest for her chicks. The male seemed quite secondary. Such a view made him rather diffident of the fair sex.

Obviously, he had met a number of charming girls to whom he had been genuinely attracted. But in almost every case the nascent flame had been extinguished by a premature use of the bellows: instead of kindling the flame, it had blown it out. He was willing to admit that it must be awfully difficult for a girl to know exactly when to turn the heat up or down, on or off. Doubtless they did so instinctively, but it did not always seem to work.

This is where Judith came in. When he asked her, "You don't want to really, do you?" had she answered "Yes," he would have acted as he had previously on a similar occasion: spanked her soundly and walked out. But her "No" was so desperately sincere. He could still hear the intonation of her voice. It was that ghastly Milli who had arranged everything. Then she had been so gauche at getting undressed and had taken so long fiddling with her hair that she obviously was not used to the situation. He felt quite sure that she was a virgin.

Moreover, he was not a "catch" in Judith's eyes. She probably did not even know his name. If she did, it would mean nothing to her. Even in the 20th century, the great recusant families form a closed circle outside the normal social run.

But that was one of the troubles. He would marry only a Catholic; and he knew that Judith was not one. His religion meant much to him, and he simply could not conceive not sharing it with his wife. The marriage would somehow be incomplete, no matter how successful in other respects. That simply would not do. He had not even told her that he was a Catholic. She might have gathered it, however, because it had somehow cropped up that he had been to school at Beaumont; but she might never have heard of it. On the other hand, he could not broach the subject of religion until he was certain of his ground. But he could not be certain until she was a Catholic! There was a vicious circle there which needed sorting out.

Then, it was well known that the Mildens were immensely rich. It was true that the Rougham estates were worth some vast sum on paper, but they absorbed nearly as much money as they produced. The Roughams had land but the Mildens had cash. This presented another problem. His father, whom Edmund loved and admired, was perpetually rubbing it in: "Marry a penniless virgin. That's what your dear mother was. Happiest marriage in the world!"

Besides, he could not fail to notice, young as he was, how many marriages came unstuck in which the wife was richer than the husband. The alternative seemed to be for the husband to become a poodle. On the other hand, Judith must have acquired tastes and habits far beyond his means. If she did not bring some money with her, he probably could not afford her — at least until his father died, which God forbid. That, too, would have to be sorted out. It was all very difficult.

During the rest of the term Edmund only turned up at Oxford on three Sundays. On each they went through the same ritual: lunch at the Randolph and the walk through the Meadows. Curiously enough, Judith never invited him to any of the Commemoration Balls. The reason was not that he danced badly, but that if she brought him she would have to introduce him all round. That she could not bear. There are intimacies which only grow in silence. As for Edmund, he was deeply attracted to this mentally rather dominant but physically frail creature. This in itself surprised him, as he had always been attracted to healthy, hearty, vivacious girls. Judith was refined and elegant, all right, but the attraction was not purely physical. Anyway, he could not help noticing that her company completely satisfied his craving for femininity. Just as Judith felt secure in his company, so did Edmund feel at rest in hers. Yes, he could let himself go and fall in love with her. In fact, he did love her. No, he must not. He could not, until the problems had been sorted out.

In the same month of June, Judith took her finals. To her gratified surprise and Miss Biggs's disgust, she got a perfectly good Second.

V

RELIGION

During this fatal month of June, the month of her finals and of Edmund, Judith's principal occupation was religion. She acquired the habit of daily Mass, getting up at some unearthly hour of the morning. She found history unbelievably trivial beside the writings of the great mystics. She devoured Teresa of Avila, Francis de Sales, Augustin Baker and the rest as others do thrillers. Nothing was beyond her digestion. Then there were the two instructions a week from Father McEnery.

Fortunately, Judith kept notes on her instructions, so it is possible to know exactly her reactions. They fill thirty closely-written pages of a copybook. A few extracts will not come amiss.

Tues. 6 p.m. Went to Fr. A poppet. Incredibly masculine: smells male. Must have been frightfully handsome: hatchet face, curly white hair, black eyes. Room full of books, papers, dust. Lots of pi pictures, but no taste. Furry bedroom slippers. Beautiful hands: more sensitive than decisive.

"And what, my dear young lady, is your name and what is your religion?"

"My name is J.M. and my religion is School Religion: attending chapel, singing hymns and giggling."

"And what is the religion of your family?"

"Father is an unbaptized Baptist and thinks all religion bilge. Mother is an Anglican and goes to church when she wants to annoy Father. My brother, John, is rather pi and goes to Evensong when he is in the country."

"And what has decided you to become a Catholic?"

"I don't know — but there are sort of pointers: a) I bought a crucifix and I want to know what it is really about; b) I met a boy who is very, very kind: he's R.C.; c) I attended your Mass: it is out of this world."

They sounded a bit thin, so I added:

"d) I am doing mediaeval history: full of popes, bishops, abbots, saints and scoundrels who took religion seriously. They cannot have built those vast cathedrals and abbeys just for fun. What's it all about?"

"Perhaps they did build them for fun. Life is colossal fun if you get the hang of it. To do so, you have to hang from God. You cannot hang upwards. It's what the materialist tries to do: he gets flat feet. Anyway, here's a one-penny catechism. It costs three pennies, but I'll give it to you. It contains everything you need to know. I'll blurb about it, give the colour, but the outline is all there.

"You know, the mediaevals did build those vast cathedrals for fun. Of course the glory of God entered in, but even that is funny: that such weird little creatures as you and me should be capable of glorifying God! And fun did enter into it directly. You have only to look at the monstrous gargoyles, comic carvings and ribald frescoes which survive. Today you see Salisbury in austere grandeur: a skeleton. When it was alive, it was full of comic incongruities; it was fun.

"However, you want to become a Catholic and that is very serious. The fun will come after you have been received: it is a manifestation of the true religion but not its justification. Of necessity its justification is its truth.

"Yes, truth. Some atheistic philosopher — I rather think it was Nietzsche — maintained that he had found only one intelligent remark in the Gospels: 'What is truth?' And this was not said by Jesus, but by Pontius Pilate. Exactly: the real problem in religion is not God at all, but man. How far can man attain to truth? The atheist reduces man's capacity to nil; the Christian expands his capacity to the Ultimate — God. In a nutshell, the problem is reductionism against expansionism. Either you reduce truth to acknowledging a phenomenon or you expand it to recognizing its ultimate inference. Am I, Philip McEnery, a mere phenomenon in front of you signifying nothing? Am I a mere idea in your mind with no objective reality? Or am I a real, objective phenomenon who am propounding ideas which have a real, objective value, whether they be false or not? If you accept either of the first two reductions, there obviously cannot be a true religion because there can be no truth. If you accept the third, then there must be a true religion, because false ones can only be false by opposition to the truth. The atheist, in fact, is not a fellow who doesn't believe in God, but one who doesn't believe that man is a rational animal. The agnostic is not a fellow who is uncertain of the existence of God, but one whose only certainty is nothing. Got it, girl?

"Anyway, you have got all the answers there for three pence. What I am trying to do is to broaden, expand your outlook so that in one colossal gulp you can swallow the truth — and thereby arrive at certainty: the Faith. Then everything will become significant. The universe, about which everybody moans and groans will suddenly become alive, significant, magnificent — and enormous fun."

Quite different to what I had expected. Very persuasive. I was familiar with "reductionism." It even exists in history: the most exalted, heroic human acts are reduced to economics. "Expansionism" is new to me. Certainly I had never thought of it as the justification for religion. But it fits — quite literally in the age of the "expanding universe."

Curious, too, how the colossal "expansion" of knowledge thanks to the physical scientists is neatly negatived by the total "reductionism" of the philosophers. I am thinking of Wittgenstein, A. J. Ayer and the logical positivists — the only ones I know.

Yes, I do believe that I can know the truth and attain certainty. I do believe that I have a duty (if that is the right word) to expand to my uttermost limit — even if this means submitting to God. So help me, God!

"I was talking about truth, wasn't I? I shall continue to do so, even at the risk of boring you. If Pilate asked the only intelligent question in the Gospels, it was provoked by Christ's most fundamental assertion: 'What I came into the world for was to bear witness to the truth.' It is difficult for us post-Christians to grasp, but this one statement has totally altered the religious psychology of mankind. You are a mediaevalist, but I imagine that you know more about ancient history than most. You must be well aware that the pre-Christian left the matter of truth to his philosophers, to Socrates, Plato, Aristotle and the like. The criterion for his religion had nothing to do with objective truth. He employed the criteria of sociology, psychology, poetry, art. Rather like your schoolgirl religion — going to chapel, singing hymns and giggling — the pre-Christian's religion was a series of acts which had to be done, not a series of dogmas which had to be believed. It was a sort of white magic when it was not a sort of black magic...

"You will have noticed that the ancients produced a vast

mythology, but no theology. The Christians promptly relegated mythology to the lives of the saints and produced a vast theology, unique in human history. In its sheer bulk, it is vaster than the vastest cathedral. And its only object is to get at truth. Yes, truth is both a Christian ideal and the sole justification for Christianity.

"But that is where the trouble lies. Truth of its nature is exclusive and universal. That two and two make four excludes every other number is as true in Timbuctoo as it is in Oxford, and was as true in the beginning as it is now and ever shall be. In fact, it is truth which is 'catholic,' that is, 'universal and exclusive.' The term is applied to the Christian religion merely because it claims to be true.

"You will also have noticed that there was complete ecumenicity among all ancient religions except one: that of Israel, because it too claimed to be true. The sad corollary of this basic fact is that wars of religion and religious persecution are post-Christian phenomena. The first purely religious persecution in history gave us the early Christian martyrs. In your mediaeval studies, you will have come across the Church as persecutor. Today it is the Church which is persecuted in one half of the world and soon will be in the other. I mention all this because in your penny catechism you will find the 'Four Marks of the Church.' They are given as: One, Holy, Catholic and Apostolic. What they mean is that the Church is exclusive, heroic, universal and unalterable. And that in turn boils down to this: you will have to admit that the religion is true. Got it?"

I suppose I have "got it." The trouble is that I do not in the least want to be uncompromising and heroic. What on earth have I let myself in for? But he said another thing which I had not thought of:

"Never have people known more or believed less. Why? Because to believe is 'to know lovingly'; indeed, in English the two words have the same root, 'lieve-love.' The trouble is not that people don't know the truth, but that they are incapable of loving it. They are so hard and selfish. You will have to become sufficiently soft, girl, to believe and belove.

"Girl — I can never remember your name; you must pin it on your frock or hang it round your neck — we must now get down to the fundamental truth: that there is a transcendent God, personal, infinite and eternal, who has created all things *ex nihilo* — out of nothing."

He was very convincing about the Five Ways: causality, movement, contingency, perfection and design.

"However, they are all variations on the same theme: there cannot be a specific, contingent being unless there is Being as such, absolute and transcendent — God. Mind you, there are those who deny the validity of the Five Ways. What they are denying is not the existence of God, but the significance of the universe. Be chary of them. They are reductionists, as incapable of awe and wonder at the creation as they are of love in belief...

"You know the intelligent atheist — and such exists — is really a pantheist. He is obliged to apply to matter the attributes of God. To him it is the cosmos which is self-subsistent, infinite and eternal. He has the notion of God all right, but thinks of it — instead of Him — as being immanent, as being the universe, instead of transcendent, as outside the universe. The inevitable result is fatalism; everything is as it is because it cannot be otherwise. Since God is nature, nature determines all things. Hence the mechanical determinism of Darwinian evolution in biology and of Marxist communism in history; they are equally ugly twin sisters. All things move in the inexorable circle of an Eternal Return — unless they are going down a bottomless drain. There is no purpose, no hope.

"In Christianity it is exactly the opposite. There is no fatalism because everything depends on the will of a transcendent God: Divine Providence. Everything has purpose; everything is wanted; everything is alive. The creation is so wonderful, so extraordinary, so specific that one should adore it as a manifestation of the Transcendent God. You find this attitude expressed as sublimely in a man as emaciated as St. Francis of Assisi as in a man as fat as G. K. Chesterton.

"Moreover, since the First Cause is transcendent, there is nothing to prevent Him creating millions of secondary causes, each in its more or less restricted field: angels, men, elephants, fleas, cabbages, pebbles, atoms — what you will or what He wills. Everything is stupendous.

"What I am trying to explain is that the whole of Christianity depends on the transcendence of God. It is not really a question of this or that dogma. They all fall into place logically enough once transcendence has been accepted. The atheist, pantheist and agnostic have their feet more or less firmly rooted in eternal mud. The Christian hangs from heaven — upside down. It may be an uncomfortable position, but you can see everything. Quite literally, you get the hang of things..."

Apart from his general theme, there were a lot of obiter dicta, e.g., "If you can imagine God, you quite certainly have the wrong idea of Him." Well, I did vaguely imagine God — as a vast piece of cotton-wool in which the world was kept cosy. Now, dear God, I cannot imagine you at all, so perhaps I am beginning to believe in you.

After these introductory talks, Father McEnery followed the catechism more closely and became more conventional. However, he dealt specifically with Judith's "pointers," as her notes show.

"You told me, girl, that you had bought a very beautiful crucifix and you wanted to know what it was about. Very well, it is proof of the truth of Christianity. In all other religions man is more noble than God. God eternally enjoys the beatitude of his own infinite perfection, yet He expects miserable creatures to love Him disinterestedly and to suffer nobly. Alone in Christianity is this not so. God becomes incarnate precisely to do as man what He cannot do as God: suffer. The personality of the man who is dying on the cross is the personality of God. He does not ask you to do what he is unwilling to do Himself. Indeed, your suffering nobly borne, your disinterested love, are justified by his. Nothing is more terrible than unrequited love; and no love goes more unrequited than that of God. Love your crucifix, girl, from the summit of your soul to the depth of your heart...

"Next, you said that you thought Mass was 'out of this world.' It is. It is the ultimate proof of God's omnipotence. People talk about 'Almighty God,' but they invariably imagine that they can help Him along a bit. They cannot. By comparison with the Mass, the creation is a mere bauble. One can conceive any number of other creations, but one cannot conceive another Mass. What is it? It is the last will and testament of God incarnate. Now look at your crucifix. It represents the most inconceivable of all crimes: deicide, the killing of God. But in his will, what did God possess that He could leave? Exactly nothing; He had even been stripped of his garments. All He owned on earth was his body and blood. So that is precisely what He left. Yes, but that body and blood are the physical evidence of the most inconceivable of crimes — the killing of God. Exactly, and we have now come to the node, the central point of Christianity. God, omnipotent and transcendent, turns the evidence of the most inconceivable crime into the guarantee of salvation for the criminal.

"Such is the Mass: the sacrificial presence of Jesus Christ; the salvation of mankind through the ultimate in crime.

"There, my dear young lady *(I noticed that he was too moved to call me 'girl')*, I have tried to explain the Real Presence and the Sacrifice of the Mass. You must forgive me, I cannot. You will have to go. There are things one cannot talk about. But come again. God bless you!" *He was obviously quite exhausted. I know he gives four or five instructions a day.*

Dear Jesus, yes, I do believe and belove your sacrificial presence. It is an ultimate, an "expansion" beyond which one cannot go. Therefore, it must be true. Poor Father McEnery! I well understand him. But also, poor me!

Later in the proceedings, Father McEnery got round to the third of Judith's "pointers."

"You told me that one of the reasons why you asked for instructions was because you had met a very kind young man who turned out to be R.C. Is he still about? Is he still kind? I am delighted. He has certainly found a very charming girl.

"You will have listened to me enough to have realized that Christianity is a very odd, very revolutionary religion. It has changed the whole outlook of mankind on God, religion, truth, creation, purpose — and all this in quite unexpected ways, as God might do it, but not as man would. It is the same with sociology.

"Jesus repealed all the positive laws of the Old Testament and only introduced one new one. It is an example which I wish our governments would emulate. But this one reform was so revolutionary that it has affected everything — sociology, politics, economics, the lot. One can gauge how Christian is any society by how far it adheres to or rejects the two facets of this reform: the indissolubility of marriage and the sanctity of the procreative act. I shall deal first with the procreative act."

He was really frightfully helpful. We are supposed to know all these things by instinct, but instinct gets outpaced by human ingenuity in evil. I had heard most of the terms, of course, but I really had not a clue how they all worked. He was wonderfully clear and explicit.

"Abortion is the deliberate murder of the totally innocent and totally defenseless, whom the parents, moreover, have an obligation to protect.

"Direct contraception in the act is a sin all right, but at least it is done and over. Sterilization in its umpteen forms is a different matter. But they now have invented the Pill. Apart from the fact that the only 'safe' ones are abortifacients, its use is a constant and cold-blooded state of sin, even if no act follows or the couple happen to be sterile. Morally, you cannot fall much lower than that."

Indeed, he explained the degrees of responsibility and moral significance of the lot. Normally, we simply do not look at things that way. I am so grateful.

What surprised me, however, about his attitude was that, rigid in principle, he seemed rather liberal in practice. It is the exact opposite to home, where we are puritanical in practice although liberal in theory. It was not Mama who explained menstruation to me but our old cook, Bridget, who was R.C., incidentally. Anyway, Father McEnery's general line was quite clear.

"Without the sexual urge, we might be damned for egoism; without sexual sin, we might be damned for pride...Sexual sin is damnable when it no longer humiliates...Lying is not right merely because all children lie; the same applies to sexual sins. Indeed, I sometimes think that the definition of an adult Christian is one who commits adultery...But even if we fall, we must keep the standards high. It implies very low standards if we always practice what we preach...Unfortunately, sexual sin often interferes with religious practice, although avarice, hatred and envy don't. Yet, when the ship is sinking, it is unwise to throw the wireless overboard...Chastity is the most angelic of virtues, but its opposite is not necessarily the most diabolic of vices...Do not imagine that the Church condones sexual sins; she condemns the lot. But sex is a matter in which one must exercise great patience with others — and sometimes with oneself."

Anyway, the net result is that, instead of feeling vaguely ashamed at being a virgin at 21, I am both surprised and grateful. Surprised because, knowing so little about sex, I could have done absolutely anything with a perfectly clear conscience. Grateful, because the loss of one's virginity is an irremediable loss. As Father said: "Virginity should never be lost; it should be exchanged for marriage." I am so grateful, so grateful. To Edmund, of course, but above all, to God.

The good Father waxed quite lyrical about marriage; it was obvious that he was a celibate priest!

"Of their nature, all contracts are revocable, either by a mutual agreement or by factual breach of contract. Christian marriage is not a mere contract, but a sacrament. It establishes, by God's grace, the relationship of husband and wife on exactly the same footing as God's Providence establishes the relationship of father and mother, son and daughter and the rest. Its only limitation is death, which does not apply to your other relatives...Curiously enough, relationship is an entirely human phenomenon. No mother is more solicitous of her baby than a cat of her kittens. Yet, once the kittens are severed, the relationship vanishes. Not so with human beings. It would be quite as fair to call us 'related animals' as to call us 'rational animals.' I spend a week every summer with a third cousin once removed, and the poor devil has to put up with me because I am indubitably his cousin. Well, husband and wife is a relationship, but on a rather more formidable footing: day and night for 365 days in the year. You said that your young man is very kind. I hope he is; but you must be determined to be even kinder."

He was very interesting when he ascribed the hegemony over the world of the comparatively poor, barbaric and small European peninsula to the social cohesion, continuity, stability and drive engendered by monogamous marriage.

"And the hegemony has disappeared along with monogamy. It was shattered in the divorce courts."

He wound up with two typical remarks:

"Nothing — and certainly not the sins of the partners — is sufficient reason for breaking the divine institution of indissoluble marriage." *And:* "Inside or outside marriage, it often requires heroism to obey the Sixth Commandment. That is why it is worth obeying. It is the only opportunity most of us get in life to be heroic."

Dear Father McE. must wear magnifying contact-lenses: he sees everything as colossal and dramatic. I do not want to be heroic. I simply want to love and be loved; to give and receive fidelity; to support and be supported. Is that unreasonable? God has made me far too fragile for much heroism. If He expects it, He will have to supply the strength.

Such are some relevant samples of the instructions taken from Judith's notes. They covered the immense fields of both the natural and the supernatural, fields as closely interwoven as the warp and woof in a length of cloth. There can be no doubt but that they had a profound influence on Judith. Not only did she learn much which she simply had not known, but whole new vistas were opened to her. It was the process of "expansion." And her assent to truth was no longer a mere question of knowledge, but became one of believing and beloving. It was this change in attitude which constituted her conversion.

As with every other convert, her act of faith was not composed of a series of assents to this and that doctrine, but was a surrender, unconditional and absolute, to the Faith as such. However, a convert she was and inevitably remained. This does imply a psychological difference from the cradle Catholic. The cradle Catholic has to learn the dogmas and assent to them just as much as the convert, but the attitude is absorbed imperceptibly along with the process of growing up. Not so with the convert. It is precisely the attitude which changes, and the convert knows when and why. In fact, the convert is conscious of the motives for conversion in a way which the cradle Catholic rarely is. This must be borne in mind in the story of Judith's marriage.

Judith was received into the Church on June 28th, 1956. Two strangers were her witnesses. She made her first, poor, faltering confession. On the following day, the feast of Saints Peter and Paul, a retired bishop was found to confirm her along with half-a-dozen other converts. She received the Body of her Redeemer. As she walked away from St. Aloysius's all alone, the whole world seemed to have changed. Even the paving stones under her feet were dancing.

VI

REVELATION

Conversion is so intimate an affair between God and oneself that it had never struck Judith that she should tell anybody about it. Obviously, she could not tell Pamela or all Oxford would know. It was not that she minded, but it would be so awkward. People would not be sure whether to send greeting cards or condolences.

Edmund was more difficult. It so happened that the last of his spasmodic visits occurred on the Sunday before she became a Catholic. She tried to act exactly as she had before, but could not quite manage it. She did not throw her arms around him and kiss him; she waited for him to kiss her. She felt a certain reserve although she felt terribly happy. It was a question of being fair. How could she tell him without appearing to throw herself at him? She felt sure enough neither of him nor of herself to do that. She longed to do so as they said goodbye, but it would not come out. She returned to her rooms and cried a little in front of her crucifix. She felt soppy. Perhaps she was in love.

But the real problem was Daddy and Mother. Actually, it was Father McEnery who first mentioned it: "Have you told your parents that you are under instruction?"

"No, not yet."

"Well, you should, you know. We are supposed to honour our father and mother, and the least you can do is warn them of the impending disaster."

"But I am not absolutely certain it is impending. Then, I must try and think out how it will hurt them least. Daddy is the trouble. I love him very, very dearly. But he positively hates religion. It might be all right if I were becoming a Buddhist, but to become a Papist is the red flag to the bull."

"Tell him, girl; and the sooner the better."

But it was not as simple as all that. It was no use writing to Mother. She would be diplomatic: "George dear, as you know, Judith takes after me and has adopted some quaint religion or other — a sort of Buddhism, I believe. Don't get upset. We're all going the same way anyway." Besides, Judith knew that her father loved her as deeply as she loved him. That she should write to her mother instead of direct to him could only add fuel to the fire. So that would not do.

Several times she started a letter: "Dearest Daddy, As you know, I love you dearly and would not hurt you for worlds. But there is something I feel I must tell you..." But it would hurt him; it was pure hypocrisy. Besides, it was an invitation for Daddy to turn up at Oxford and have flaming rows with all and sundry, including Father McEnery and Miss Biggs. She would prefer the row at home.

Fortunately, an occasion presented itself when she could tell him face to face. Tubby Bradfield's divorce had at last come through and he was to marry Milli, the co-respondent, on the second Saturday in June.

The ceremony (if such it can be called) in Caxton Hall was to be private with no more than the inevitable witnesses: Sir George and Lady Milden on Milli's side; Tubby's father with his wife and his mother with her husband — divorce being an hereditary disease — on Tubby's side. Judith thanked God that she did not have to turn up to that. But she would have to attend the reception at the Dorchester. Actually, she wanted to. She was very fond of Milli and admired her enormously. Her faults were obvious, even flamboyant, but so, in Judith's eyes, were her virtues, notably her unstinting generosity, her fearless determination and immediate grasp of realities. Milli was tremendous, even if she was wrong. And her wedding provided Judith with the ideal opportunity for telling Daddy that she intended to "Pope." If he was willing to preside at his niece's marriage to a divorced man, he might in fairness be induced to swallow his daughter's conversion. Besides, he could scarcely blow up in public at his niece's wedding. It would give him time to get used to the idea.

But things did not pan out that way. Daddy was constantly

surrounded by an impenetrable guard of honour made up of perfectly dreadful people. She could not get at him. When finally she could, he had shipped sufficient champagne to be in a belligerent mood. She did not want to provide the spark which might make him explode. She saw Mother all right, but in the milling throng she seemed even more helpless than usual.

Like everything which starts, the reception ended. Nothing had been said. Judith escaped back to Oxford.

In the week following Milli's wedding, Sir George, accompanied by his wife, set out as usual for his annual inspection of the South African and Australian subsidiaries of Milden's Adhesives. They were not expected home until July 28th. This was the obvious time when Judith should have written to her father. She did not. It was not out of malice, but because the idea never crossed her mind. She had failed to tell Daddy at Milli's wedding, so it would have to wait until his return.

Judith left Oxford well after the end of the term. There were books to sell, people to see, things to pack. She took her time. As her parents were not home yet, she spent ten days in Essex with Pamela, who was consequently the first person to know of her conversion. Pamela immediately suspected that the "boy in the Meadows" must have been an R.C. She was, of course, right — as women always are; but probably for the wrong reasons — as also women always are.

Judith had sent a few crates home, full of books, Diana, Narcissus and the like, but only arrived herself with two trunks of clothes and her crucifix on August 2nd, just in time for dinner.

Daddy and Mother were at home and expected her. She had the trunks taken upstairs, the crucifix into the drawing room. She dutifully and lovingly kissed her parents.

"Good heavens, Judith!" said Sir George. "And what's this you've brought home? It looks good enough to me. Early Cinquecento I should say. Almost a museum piece — like the religion it represents!" He laughed.

Judith did not take him up immediately. In fact, it was only after dinner, when the butler asked the time people wanted to be called and have their breakfast that things began to move.

"And would Miss Judith like to lie in tomorrow," he asked.

"No, thank you, James. I shall be out early. I shall not need calling and shall be back by 8:15. The usual, please: my tea mixture, toast and honey."

When James had left the room, Sir George asked: "What on earth are you doing tomorrow morning?"

"My dearest Mummy and Daddy, there is something I have been wanting to tell you, but the occasion simply hasn't arisen. It has made me wonderfully happy, but I fear that it may upset you. That is really why I have delayed telling you. I have become a Catholic and want to go to Mass before breakfast."

There was a dreadful silence. Lady Milden did her best: "Yes, dear, but be sure you put a woolly on. Even in August it can be chilly on an empty stomach."

More silence.

At last Sir George spoke, very calmly as he sipped his brandy.

"Judith, I doubt if you could have done anything which would cause me more displeasure. You may have thought that because I never talk about religion I am indifferent. Insofar as this is so, it is my fault. I am not indifferent. I despise all religions except one, Roman Catholicism; it I hate.

"I hate it because it is the most religious of religions, carrying escapism from the realities of the world and human needs to the uttermost limits. I hate it because it is uncompromising, whereas reality is one long compromise with the possible. I hate it because it exalts suffering instead of relieving it. I hate it because of its claim to be universal when in fact it is outrageously exclusive. I hate it because it looks backwards and never forwards.

"Its two pillars are bald, unverifiable statements which it calls dogmas; and an appeal to the superstition of the ignorant, which it calls sacraments.

"When the world is clamouring for social justice, what does it do? It talks about private sins! Instead of stretching out the hand to help their neighbours, Catholics clench the fist to beat their breasts. You have only to look at the slums of Naples and the bogs of Ireland to see how it works. It creates poverty and ignorance because it thrives on them.

"I need not mention confession except to say that it is a poor specimen of humanity who cannot face his own acts and asks forgiveness for what he cannot undo.

"You say you are going to Mass tomorrow, and I suppose nobody can stop you. I have had to go dozens of times for weddings and funerals. The intolerable mumbo-jumbo and mystification of it all! Is there any attempt to instruct the people or make them perform intelligible human acts? No! Are there any prayers which might crystalize the people's consciences on human needs? No! Any uplift, any hope? No! What is there then? The adoration of a corpse! It is the religion of death.

"Yes, so much is it the religion of death that it denies the very process of life — evolution. And I am not merely talking about the superficial evolution of matter. I am talking about the only evolution which could possibly justify religion: the evolution of man to God."

There was a good deal more along the same lines. What staggered Judith was that her father might have listened in to Father McEnery's instructions and turned them inside out. The facts in both cases were the same but produced diametrically opposite reactions. Precisely what made the religion lovable to Judith made it hateful to her father. It suddenly struck her: yes, the difference shows exactly what they mean by "grace" and the "gift of faith."

She tried to interrupt a time or two: "But Daddy, you know, there is a reverse to the coin." But she was promptly squashed: "I have tossed it and it always comes down tails." Later she tried again: "Just suppose, Daddy, that Catholics did suddenly veer round and say that God was point Omega in the evolutionary process; that the social virtues were the important ones; turned the Mass into a ceremony of uplift; became compromising, ecumenical and forward-looking, would you believe in it then?"

Sir George paused for an appreciable time. He had not expected the question. But he was both a very intelligent and a very upright man. "No, Judith, I should still hate it. In the last resort, I hate it for what it is, not for what it says and does."

"That is very deep of you, Daddy," said Judith perfectly

sincerely; "and I suppose it is the same with me. I love it for what it is..."

Poor Judith! She was very ill-prepared for it all. At worst she had expected benign disapproval but, in her heart of hearts, she had hoped for loving admiration. She was not exactly getting it.

After Judith's last intervention Sir George became a bit more personal. "When were you received?"

"June 28th, Papa."

"You never had the courtesy to let your mother or me know. I hope your new religion will not affect your manners in other ways. Presumably you were under instruction from a priest for some time. He clearly skipped the commandment about honouring your father and your mother. And it never crossed your mind to consult the wretched people who begat you, educated you, have given you everything you have?"

"Father, how can you be so cruel?"

"It is you, Judith: how can you be so cruel? But then, your new religion goes hand in hand with secretiveness and deceit. I doubt if you would have bothered to tell us had James not brought up the question of breakfast. Incidentally, Gertrude, the kitchen-maid, is a Catholic. She is the only person in this household with whom you share your religion — and you won't do that for long: she is dirty and dishonest.

"That brings me to another point, Judith. You are well-bred; you have a good home; your mother and I have lavished all our love on you; you have received the best education the country can give. Moreover, under normal circumstances you could expect to be among the richest heiresses in the land. You could have married whomsoever you liked. Who do you think is going to marry you now? Nobody but a fool would saddle himself with a Catholic wife to give him a baby a year which he cannot afford to keep. Who is going to pay for them? I suppose you think I shall provide as I always have provided. Well, you will have another thought coming."

Another thought also struck Sir George. He paused a moment, then: "Tell me, is there a boy in this?"

Judith was in a very awkward position. She was not at all sure whether or not there was a boy in it. On the one hand, Edmund did not even know that she was a Catholic. On the other, would she have become one had he not left her her innocence at Milli's? She was being accused of deceit, so she must try to be scrupulously truthful: "Well, in a sort of way, rather indirectly, I suppose there is."

Sir George meditated. Then he asked in a tone of voice which, had she not been so desperately hurt, Judith would have recognized as showing sincere, if misguided, paternal concern: "And tell me, Judith, are you pregnant?" As it was, Judith took it as the final insult. To have the intimacy of innocence slung back at her was more than she could bear. She looked calmly into her father's eyes and said with a slight sneer: "Why? Was mother when you married her?"

Sir George immediately congealed: "How dare you suggest such a thing of your mother!"

"Because, Father, you suggest it of her daughter."

The rest of the conversation did not take long. Judith was ordered out of the house then and there — "and take that thing with you," Sir George added, giving a little kick to the crucifix. Judith slapped him across the face — yes, her own father — and walked out of the room to ring up Milli.

As she knew, Tubby and Milli were at home. Yes, they could put her up. The two trunks and the crucifix were piled into the car, and Judith was safely delivered to Chelsea. Inevitably, her bedroom was the one associated with Edmund.

The tragedy of the break between Judith and her father was heightened by the fact that both thought religion was at the bottom of it. It was not. Judith could have put up with any amount of criticism and jeering. What had made her revolt was the implied accusation against Edmund. The precise reason why she loved him was because of the innocence of their relationship. And, by the way, yes: she did love him. It was her father who finally convinced her of the fact.

It was exactly the same with Sir George. After he had let off steam and been as rude as he knew how, he would inevitably have accepted the fact that his daughter, whom he genuinely loved, had become a Papist. What was unpardonable was the accusation that Mary had been pregnant before marriage, because it so happened that she had been. It was away back in the winter of 1928. Young Milden had had to face Mary's father, Mr. Justice Turncliffe. The old boy was warming his bottom in front of the fire. "Yes, young man, it is not the first time this sort of thing has happened. The best families have their quota of illegitimates. For my own part, to procure an abortion is illegal and I shall have nothing to do with it. On the other hand, I am the last person to interfere with any decision which may be taken between a future husband and wife. It is their concern. I hope I have made my meaning clear."

He had. Mary was aborted and in due course wedded. Her two children were conceived in wedlock. John was born in March 1931 and Judith nearly four years later, on February 11th, 1935.

At the time, it had seemed inevitable. Nevertheless, it was something which Sir George bitterly regretted. He could not forgive himself. He knew of no God to forgive him. There was only one thing to do: forget it. He succeeded. It had not crossed his mind for more than twenty years until Judith accidentally brought it back, with all its pain, all its remorse. He knew it was not Judith's fault, but he simply could not bring himself to see her: she would be a constant reminder of the one thing he must forget.

He cried bitterly though tearlessly when he went to bed that night. It took all Mary's calm and patience to lull him off to sleep.

Well, there it was: the arrogance of innocence and the remorse of guilt. And Judith had left home like the soppiest, heart-sick girl at Somerville.

VII

THE WEDDING

The great thing about Milli was that she was so matter-of-fact. Judith had Poped; so what? It was still fashionable in the 1950's and lots of lads and lasses did it. She did not believe in it herself because it had too many taboos, but some people seemed to thrive on them. She presumed that it gave them an extra kick to break them. Of course it was a different matter with people of Uncle George's generation. To them Rome was the Scarlet Woman, the red rag to the bull. Even so, it was a bit fierce of Uncle to pitch Judith out, but it would all come right in the end. So that was that. Naturally enough, Edmund never crossed her mind. Why should he? Equally naturally, Judith was very reticent about the whole episode.

As she went to bed, Judith felt very sorry for herself. She loved her parents. It was true that she had never been very close to her mother, but she idolized her father. It was he who had cast her out. Father McEnery had said that heroism was one of the marks of the Church, but she did not want to be heroic quite so soon. She hoped that she might dream of Edmund. How she wished she could run to him! That was one thing she certainly could not do. In due course she'd get Milli to let him know where she was.

After Mass next morning at the Holy Redeemer, she felt much better. With Milli's help she managed to hoist her crucifix up over her bed. Then she went to Sotheby's to see if they would take her on immediately. Yes, they would be delighted to. There were going to be some large sales of drawings in the winter; the cataloguing was behind-hand and anybody who could read and write would be welcome. She could turn up the next day.

Mother rang up in the early afternoon to discover how Judith was. From the tone of her daughter's voice, Lady Milden knew she was all right. She was not such a fool as to exhibit emotion or

offer advice. That would come later. Daddy seemed quite un-
changed. He had merely said that he would settle any outstanding
debts and make Judith an allowance of £100 a month until she got
married. Judith said that she had no debts and was starting work
the next day. She would have loved dearly to refuse the £100 with
hauteur but she thought better of it: it was the last link with
home and should not be broken.

It was on August 15th, because it was the feast of the Assumption of Our Lady, that Judith decided to go to the early Mass at
St. Mary's, Cadogan Street, instead of to Holy Redeemer. In her
usual way she paid no attention to anybody or anything. She
trickled up to Communion with the crowd. As she passed the
communion plate to the person on her right, she noticed the hand
that took it. Oh, oh!...It was Edmund's. She waited at the altar
rail until he had gone, then slipped down the aisle and out of the
church to avoid him.

He knew she would. He was waiting for her in the porch. For
the first time it was he who enfolded her in his arms. He kissed
her very delicately, first on the forehead, then on the lips.
"Judith, Judith, you owe me an explanation for this wonderful
event."

In those distant days, Communion was still taken fasting.
They went to a cafe for a cuppa and some rolls. Judith did a lot of
talking, but explained very little. She had been received into the
Church a long, long time ago; yes, away back in June. She also
explained that she had quarreled with her father and been
disinherited. Naturally, she failed to mention that he, Edmund,
had been involved. She also kept religion out of it: she did not
want to appear too heroic, neither did she wish to throw herself
at Edmund. Anyway, the chancellor got no answers from the
Treasury that morning, and Sotheby's catalogues remained in ar-
rears.

The rest is reasonably obvious. As far as Edmund was concerned, the two obstacles preventing marriage with Judith had
miraculously disappeared: her lack of religion and her wealth. She
was to spend that very weekend at Rougham Castle to meet his
parents.

To Judith's rhapsodical eyes, Brigadier Rougham and his wife were the most charming people she had ever met. They were both as grand as where they lived and as simple as the way they lived. The house was built of red brick and had been erected in 1556 when the then-Mr. Rougham was Comptroller to the Household of Mary Tudor. It was E-shaped and simply vast. The central projection of the E was the only part of the mediaeval castle that remained. The rest had been razed to the ground by Henry VII because the then-Rougham had fought for Richard III at Bosworth. The rubble from the ruins had been used to make the splendid terrace on which the present building stands. The great hall was full of wonderful portraits of bygone Roughams: the Blessed Gregory Rougham having his guts rolled out of him like macaroni; Cardinal Rougham in the late 17th century, with great, fat cherubs supported by diminutive wings carrying his coat of arms; Father Rougham, the dubious Jesuit involved in the Gunpowder Plot; two full-length and beautiful Rougham women, the Venerable Caroline and Mother Agnes, prioress of the Convent at Bruges; a pair of Gainsboroughs representing the Lady Anabella, daughter of the first Duke of Blackwater, and her husband, who had made a vast fortune in the West Indies; their Regency grandson, who had lost it — and so on.

It was all quite magnificent. Room after room cluttered up with the junk of ages — and what junk! Women are usually rather fond of "things." Judith was no exception; she was fascinated. The only trouble was that there was no staff. True, at 8 a.m. a posse of women with their brooms at shoulder-arms marched up the drive, but they were immediately lost in the vast building and never seen again. Even the cook was a daily. She turned up at the appropriate time, cooked a hot dinner and left a cold lunch for the following day. Mrs. Rougham was the parlormaid and the Brigadier the butler. Both performed their duties with complete good humour and consummate lack of skill. The set-up was exactly opposite to her home in Hampstead, where in a rather restricted area one was constantly tripping over servants. Judith was enraptured: never had she seen such grandeur and such simplicity combined.

It was on the Saturday evening of the third weekend which Judith and Edmund spent at Rougham that Edmund told his father what was already obvious: he wished to marry Judith. He also repeated what little Judith had told him at breakfast on August 15th about her quarrel with her parents. On the Sunday evening the Brig asked Judith into his study. At least, that is what it was called, but instead of books and files, all it contained was a vast array of weapons.

"Well, Judith, as you know, my boy wants to marry you. I'm delighted. Couldn't have chosen better. But it's your family I'm worried about. You've got a father and mother like everybody else. Edmund tells me you've quarreled with them. But you see, I cannot have the newspapers announcing the engagement without your father having had his say. You follow me, Judith?"

"Yes, I suppose that is true."

"Can't you make it up with your father?"

Judith just shook her head.

"What's the quarrel about anyway?" the Brig asked.

"I simply cannot tell you. I have not even told Edmund," she replied. This was perfectly true. As Judith saw it, the quarrel had been about religion on her father's side, but really about Edmund on hers. She wanted neither to act the heroine over Edmund, nor to reveal her father's bigotry. She felt that there was nothing she could do about it.

"That's awkward," said the Brig. "I suppose you have no objection to my writing to your father? It does not matter if you have. If you won't write, it is obvious that I shall have to."

This was the letter:

Dear Sir George,

My only son, Edmund, has told me that he wishes to marry your daughter, Judith.

Judith has stayed several weekends at the Castle. I know of no girl whom I should prefer my son to marry. May I congratulate you and Lady Milden on how you have brought her up?

Judith tells me, however, that, for reasons which she refuses to explain, there is a rift between you and her. I asked her to write to you herself; she said it was impossible.

But marriage is a public act, particularly in our walks of life. I cannot allow my son to announce his engagement to your daughter without your consent.

If, as I sincerely hope, you give your consent, there are a number of matters to be decided: what settlement on your daughter you expect from us; what allowance you may wish to give her; where and when the marriage is to be celebrated — and the like.

Moreover, you will certainly want to meet my son. He is a fine physical specimen, as we Roughams usually are. Fortunately, he has also inherited a little grey matter from his mother. He works at the Treasury where, the undersecretary assures me, he is doing particularly well. Since he is my only child, he is the sole heir to the Rougham estate, which is not inconsiderable.

I write also on behalf of my wife, who would like very much to talk about her Edmund and your Judith with Lady Milden.

Obviously, you would be welcome if you and Lady Milden would care to come to the Castle. However, my wife and I should be delighted to call on you at Hampstead if that is more convenient to you.

Believe me, my dear Sir George...

The answer came by return post.

Dear Brigadier Rougham,

I am in receipt of your letter of Monday.

In answer to your immediate question: since I have no means of preventing the marriage, I have no objection to its being announced in the press.

Concerning the other points you raise:

1) I have no intention of seeing my daughter again. I therefore see no point in meeting her future husband. I only hope that Judith will prove a more loyal wife than she has a daughter.

2) What settlement you wish to make on your son's wife is no concern of mine.

3) I shall give no dowry to Judith; neither has she any expectations out of my estate. At the moment I allow her £100 a month until marriage. On second thought, I feel it would be mean to cancel this merely because she marries your son. You can tell her that the allowance will continue to be paid — not, however, by me, but direct from the International Glue Corporation.

4) I am not interested as to where the marriage will take place; I am, however, as to when. I feel sure that you will have the courtesy to let me know of the date well in advance, so that my wife and myself can go on a business trip to Australia, where I have considerable interests.

5) What you say about our respective wives is certainly true. They will arrange a get-together and natter no matter what we may say. I have consequently told my wife to get into touch with yours.

I cannot end this letter, my dear Brigadier, without saying how delighted I am for Judith's sake that she is marrying into so distinguished a family. I only hope, as I have already said, that she does not cause you the disappointment which she has given me.

Yours sincerely,

So that was that. It shook the Brig a bit. He would dearly have loved to know what the quarrel was about. It never crossed his mind that religion might have something to do with it.

He had only just shown the letter to Lucy when Lady Milden was on the phone. That very afternoon Lucy popped up to London, and the two mothers met.

At dinner that evening the Brig said to his wife: "Milden seems to be a quaint cove: absolutely hates his daughter."

"Talking to his wife this afternoon," Lucy replied, "I got the opposite impression. She seemed to think that Judith was the only person he really loved, and consequently the only person who could hurt him — which she certainly has succeeded in doing. I did my best to discover what the quarrel was about, but Lady M. nearly burst into tears. All she said was that it was nothing remotely discreditable to Judith."

"Curious, isn't it," said the Brig; "you cannot imagine how a flimsy strip of a girl like Judith could hurt a tough old hide like Milden."

"The answer must be that the flimsy strip is much tougher and the old hide softer than meets the eye," said Lucy with much penetration.

"You know, Charles (for such was the Brig's name), we have only met Judith at three weekends. I think she is wonderful, and I would not have Edmund marry anyone else. But there is something heroic about that girl. Our Edmund is in for a tough time. Everyone is not so lucky as to marry a soppy creature like me."

"Why do you think I married you?" asked the Brig innocently enough.

"How dare you call me soppy!"

"Come along, give me a kiss."

The wedding took place on Saturday, February 9th, 1957, at 12 noon, the latest hour possible in those days for a Nuptial Mass. Judith had spent the night at Pamela's, whose parents lived not all that far away, near Dunmow, in Essex. Judith wore a sleeveless white satin dress with an ample skirt, over which was a sleeved lace mantle with a long train. She looked very lovely but, at least until she arrived at Rougham church, she felt less radiant than she looked. Why was not Daddy going to be there? What had she done wrong? He was willing to give Milli away to a divorced man in a registry office and propose the health of the bride and groom, but he could not turn up at his own daughter's wedding because it was R.C. It was monstrous, unfair, beastly! To what depths of prejudice could Daddy sink!

Judith was given away by her elder brother, John. Pamela and Ronnie Stanningfield's eldest daughter were the bridesmaids. There was nothing particular about the Mass except that the parish priest, Father Cromer, preached a jolly sermon. It is strange how doleful the clergy usually are on such occasions. The reception, of course, was at the castle. Luckily, it was not raining, so umbrellas, mackintoshes, waders, galoshes and other accoutrements usual at a February wedding were not required. The five hundred yards from church to castle were done on foot, processionally, in the cold, bright light of the winter sun. Edmund and Judith led the way. Edmund duly lifted his wife over the threshold. He had never lifted her before. Gosh, she was light! And half of that must be clothes! He had married a soul which scarcely had a body. As he let her down in the great hall, surrounded by portraits of bygone Roughams, his whole being went out to her. Before, he had only loved her as something extrinsic. From that moment he became in love with her; he had become intrinsic to this frail creature, his wife. He did not say "I love you," as he had said many times before and which now seemed an impertinence. He kissed her and said: "I thank you," and his eyes were moist.

At the reception, the Mildens were inconspicuously absent because nobody expected them to be present. Rougham is a very self-contained community which might have resented an invasion by too many foreigners. As it was, apart from John and his wife, Tubby and Milli, Pamela's parents and a few girlfriends with their boys, there was nobody on the Milden side. The Rougham guests were legion and formed a splendidly heterogeneous collection. The old recusant families were represented from all over the country and eyed with great suspicion by the local nobility and gentry. There were those who shot pheasants and those who poached them; obvious members of the professional classes and people who were obviously not; wild farmers and solemn traders; the whole heavily diluted by tenants and estate workers of every shape and size. Like everything about the Roughams, it was grand and simple.

As far as Judith was concerned, her brother John was an absolute brick. Not only did he give her away, but he proposed the toast. He first apologized for the absence of Sir George and Lady Milden, unexpectedly detained in Australia. He read a charming telegram from them which he had sent himself that morning. He sang Judith's praise as brothers usually don't. He wound up as follows: "Edmund, in the odd thousand years that your family has lived here, think of the contributions it has received from outside. As we look round this hall, we not only see the portraits of many former chatelaines of this great castle, but also the present chatelaine, your gracious mother. I am confident that in Judith, the Mildens will not contribute less. Not only have we something new and living to contribute in the form of my sister, however, but something very old, which has always been yours and which represents your living faith."

At this juncture John's chauffeur pushed his way forward with a large object covered in white satin. "Take it between you while, my lords, ladies and gentlemen, I give you the toast of the bride and bridegroom."

With some difficulty Edmund removed the satin covering. "Good God! It's the Rougham Crucifix!"

VIII

THE BLESSING

The honeymoon was spent in Rome. To Judith it was a double honeymoon, that with Edmund and a delayed one with the Church.

She had been to Rome before, but had only seen it from the outside. Heaven alone knows, that was glorious enough! But now she was seeing it from within. She owned it. It was hers. From the graffiti in the catacombs to the dome of St. Peter's, from the first Christian carvings in the Lateran Museum to Bernini's St. Teresa, they were all made for her, not as mere works of art, but as an expression of her religion.

His frail bride ran Edmund off his feet. She darted from shrine to shrine as a bee from flower to flower. Doubtless the beauty of the flower attracted, but she sucked the ambrosia which fed her soul. No matter how splendid, everything is flat when seen from without. From within, it not only has the three dimensions of reality but the fourth, of life.

As the Roughams were a distinguished recusant family which had produced a martyr in the 16th century, a cardinal in the 17th, a venerable in the 18th and, moreover, since Edmund and Judith were newlyweds, a private audience with the Pope had been arranged for them. Unfortunately, they had not known this when they left England, and had not brought the appropriate clothes — a long-sleeved black evening dress for Judith and tails for Edmund, even though the audience was for 10 o'clock in the morning. They had to hire them. With a tuck here and there, Judith's dress was vaguely presentable, but Edmund's tails were green with age, shiny from cleaning and cut to encompass some important gentleman of more than twice Edmund's girth.

"The Pope must think it awfully funny," said Edmund, "every day to see different faces emerging out of the identical kit."

"I suppose," Judith answered, "he looks upon the laity much as we look upon the priest. It's the same old vestment no matter who's inside."

Anyway, they got there on time and were duly placed in a small antechamber, scarcely more than forty feet each way, through which the Pope was to pass. They did not have to wait long. At a sign from a rotund monsignor they fell on their knees. Pope Pius XII appeared.

He was not as tall as he looked in his photographs, but quite as emaciated. The eyes were black and burning. Was it zeal, was it anguish? He had a trick of looking through you, not focusing on you at all. The fine, aquiline nose was not unlike what Edmund's might become at his age. But the mouth! At rest it seemed shapeless and melancholic, almost fish-like, but it could twist into any shape and would suddenly give a smile as innocent as a baby's. Lastly the hands, the most beautiful Judith had ever seen. Edmund had fine, aristocratic hands, but they were not as beautiful as the Pope's.

He came up to them where they knelt, fingering some little cards which doubtless gave him details about the people to whom he was giving audience. His English was quite fluent although it had an unexpected American accent.

"Mr. and Mrs. Rougham. You come from an old recusant family." His eyes unfocused and he looked into eternity. "Your family must have suffered much. You have the *Beato Gregorio* among your ancestors. It is easy to bear suffering oneself, from moment to moment. But to suffer in your wife, in your children, hopelessly, from generation to generation, this the English Catholics have done. They are dear to the Sacred Heart of Jesus and to ours.

"Mrs. Rougham, you are a newlywed. We shall say a special prayer that you are fruitful in children who can bear suffering, who do not flinch at the Cross. Men have stopped looking at the Cross. Priests will turn it out of their churches. You look at it. Teach your children to look at it.

"The persecution of Catholics is finished in England, by the mercy of God, but to suffering there is no end. You will find the enemy within the Church, not without. We see it coming from our exalted position on the summit of the Rock. We can see far from where we stand. You will suffer more than your ancestors, Mr. Rougham, but they must remain an example to you. There is only one nobility in man: suffering nobly borne."

He suddenly broke off, refocused on them and gave them his most beautiful baby-smile. "Is there anything special you would like to ask of us?"

Of course they had prepared nothing. They had even forgotten the rosary they had especially bought to be blessed. But Judith was terribly moved and said quite spontaneously: "Yes, Holy Father! You spoke of the Cross. At home we have a crucifix which has been in the family since before the Reformation. In front of it each generation of Roughams has prayed. In a strange way it was the cause of my conversion. I want you to bless it; really bless it. It isn't physically here, but that is what we want you to bless. It has baby angels catching the Precious Blood from the sacred wounds."

The Pope's mouth twitched into a series of strange shapes. He unfocused. There was an appreciable pause. Then: "We do bless it. The arms of that crucifix will ever be outstretched in suffering and in mercy over you. The mercy of God is so incomprehensible to man that it makes us suffer. Yet mercy it is. The angels' little cups of mercy have to be drunk to the dregs in suffering. You will do it. I know you (he dropped into the singular) although I have never seen you before. And you have all my affection, although I shall never see you again. For your part, whenever you are at home, we (he reverted to the plural) command you once a day to fall in front of your cross for just one minute in silent adoration, and we grant you a plenary indulgence at the hour of death.

"Now we impart our Apostolic Blessing..."

He laid his hands lightly on their heads. The baby-smile reappeared as he said: "Goodbye, Mr. and Mrs. Rougham — and teach your children to cling to the Cross." He passed into the next antechamber.

Judith and Edmund picked themselves up. They had been

kneeling the whole time. They joined hands and waited in silence until they were escorted out of the Vatican into the brilliant midday sun of a cold and clear February day.

"Gosh, what an experience!" said Edmund, which was all either of them could say.

IX

BIRTH AND REBIRTH

The chancellor did not pay Edmund a very princely salary for preparing his statistics for him. Edmund, moreover, refused to sponge off his father, so he could not afford a new home. The other bachelor moved out and Judith moved into the flat in Chelsea. That was about the only change except that the crucifix was hoisted over the bed and the other bachelor's room was turned into a living-room.

Sir George's allowance and, for the first six months, Judith's small salary from Sotheby's were positively useful. Judith was very good at her job. She had an astonishingly accurate memory and rarely had to look up twice a collector's status or a watermark. She soon got to recognize the chalks and inks used. Her triumph came when she identified from the curious quality of the black chalk a genuine Sodoma which the pundits had turned down as a fake Vinci.

In mid-July she missed her period. She was wildly excited. But early in October something went wrong. She lost blood. She was constantly dizzy. She became delirious. The clever doctor was called in. Judith was suffering from colossal blood pressure. A specialist would have to be consulted immediately. Far the most able was a young Mr. Bradfield. This, of course, was Tubby, Milli's husband. He duly appeared.

As far as Judith was concerned, she was living in a nightmare. Edmund sat sneering at her bedside, occasionally calling Tubby in to suck her blood while Milli jabbed pins into her. Lucy, dressed as a nurse, attempted to choke her from time to time. She tried to scream to wake herself up, but could not. Then she would click back to normal, press Edmund's hand, feel immensely tired and go to sleep.

For all that, she was much more conscious of what was going

60

on around her than people seemed to think. She was well aware that Tubby wanted to abort her baby. During one of the more painful nightmares, she still knew that Tubby had said to Edmund: "Look at her! You're killing your wife for your bloody religion." Poor Edmund!

When Judith came out of the nightmare, she just had the strength to say to him: "Don't let them kill your baby." He kissed her again and again; she slept deeply and well.

Milli was at her wit's end. Here was this boor Edmund killing her little cousin. She had tried everything. She had even induced Tubby to bring a Catholic colleague along to attempt to knock a little common sense into the fool. As a matter of fact, the colleague had been very persuasive.

"You see, Mr. Rougham, it is the well-known principle of double-effect. Mr. Bradfield has no intention of killing the baby at all. He is merely removing it to save the mother. In this process, the baby will, unfortunately, die; but it will not be you or Mr. Bradfield who has killed it. It will be nature, or, as we should say, God's providence."

"But, Professor, you are not going to attempt a Caesarian or something at this stage, are you?" Edmund asked.

"No, Mr. Rougham; the baby is not viable and it would probably kill your wife."

"Then there is no double effect. It is direct killing of the baby — and you cannot do it. We are not certain either way whether Judith will die, but we should be certain that the baby would. Oh! But Professor, that is all hair-splitting. Just look at the situation as it affects me, since I have got to make the decision — as Judith cannot. If I refuse, Judith still may not die; but if she does, I shall be left with the memory of a wonderful woman who loved me to the end. If I consent to the abortion, Judith may live, and I shall be tied for life to a woman who hates and despises me, the man who begat her child and killed it. It would be worse than her death to be hated by Judith, whom I love more than my life. Cannot you see, Professor, that this is a human, not a medical problem?"

"Mr. Rougham, when the situation is looked at from your

angle, you are right," said the professor, who turned and walked quickly away.

After the professor's failure, Milli did not know which way to turn. Somehow the baby must be aborted. It was obvious. People did it without any reason at all, and in this case there was every reason under the sun. This dam' Popery was the cause of the trouble. She simply could not understand it. It was a remote chance, but she could think of nothing else: perhaps Uncle George could do something. She rang him up.

"Uncle George, Judith is dying. That Popish boor, Edmund, won't allow her pregnancy to be terminated. It is the only possible thing. Couldn't you make peace with Edmund on condition that he was sensible? Or you might even persuade Judith; she has sane moments."

"Thank you, Milli. Young Rougham has written to say that his wife is very ill. I thought it was an excuse to get round me. I had no idea of the real nature of the situation. Thank you, Milli; thank you! I shall be around straight away."

"Uncle George, you're a marvel."

Sir George tiptoed into Judith's room. Edmund stood behind him. Judith could see them all right and she smiled. Her father's lips started to move, but she could not hear him; there seemed to be a thunderstorm going on. She was so happy to see Daddy. She went to sleep. When she woke up — thirty seconds, a couple of hours later? — he was still there. Her mind was quite clear and she was sufficiently rested to talk.

"Kiss me, Daddy." He did.

"Can you hear me now?" he asked. She nodded. "My darling child," he continued, "be determined to live and be determined to save your baby. You must save your baby, Judith. Do you understand me?"

Of course she did! And with Edmund and Daddy behind her, of course she would not give in.

Sir George spent an hour with Edmund afterwards. The G.P., Milli and Tubby were all rung up. Sir George was not in the habit of mincing his words. An additional nurse was procured; so was Lady Milden. Within no time, a mass of useless but necessary luxuries started to make their appearance. It was not the financial help, however, which altered the situation, but the change in the psychological climate.

There was a general shift as to who was what. Judith, from being just a poor creature, became a heroine; Edmund was no longer a Popish boor, but a man of principle supported by common sense; Tubby went from being the Supreme Pontiff to a not noticeably successful technician. The G.P. and Milli disappeared into the oblivion from which they should never have emerged.

It is doubtless an exaggeration to say that all disease is psychological. Nevertheless, it remains true that the human is an unit, and his hates and fears, disappointments and frustrations will produce a physical effect as surely as shame will make him blush. Nobody can say whether the emotional upset due to the break with her father expressed itself eventually in Judith's toxaemia — or whatever it was called — but what is certain is that her condition began to mend as soon as was mended her relationship with her father. She lasted out until, on March 7th, 1958, the baby was happily produced by caesarian section, a bit premature but weighing nearly six pounds and lively enough. It was a little boy.

Who could express the joy of Edmund and Judith? The same miracle had happened as when Eve bore the first child ever to be. The whole universe had been enriched by a new personality, distinct from all others, yet made in the image of God, someone who had not existed before, but was endowed with immortality. He was to be baptized Richard, since that had been the name of both his great-grandfathers, Rougham and Milden. Although he was brand new, he incarnated a tradition. God had given him existence through the medium of a family.

Edmund and Judith did not have to explain their own joy: it was a fact as natural as the rising of the sun and the setting thereof. What passed belief was the happiness the birth of Richard brought to Grandpa George. Of course, they did not know his story; nobody did except Mary. It was as though he had been exorcised, as though the child he had killed had been reborn in Richard and the crime of his youth forgiven.

To Sir George, that funny little pink baby was the sign of his redemption; he had certainly done everything in his power to prevent its abortion. And there was Richard, alive, in front of him, along with Richard's mother, his own dear daughter, Judith. It was beyond belief. It was a miracle. His whole character changed. From hard and dominant he became kind and considerate. Lucy Rougham had been right: there was a basic softness under the tough old hide.

He bought a beautiful Regency house for his grandson in Walthamford, just over the border in Hertfordshire from Essex, so that Richard could grow up among trees and Edmund could easily get to both the Treasury and to Rougham "to visit your dear parents." Incidentally, he made peace with the Brig with astonishing humility and simplicity. He even apologized to Judith: "My dear child, I was wrong, blinded by prejudice and my own follies. How easy it is to blame others when it is we who are wrong. I am sorry. You have married a man far above what I might have chosen for you. As for your father-in-law, he is the greatest gentleman I have ever met."

Unfortunately, the house at Walthamford was in poor shape, and would require at least three months to put in order. In the meantime, old George lunched or dined in Chelsea rather more often than was convenient. He could not keep away.

It was after dinner one evening, when they were talking as usual about the baby, that Edmund revealed his little story. "I had had an awful day. My work at the Treasury was suffering terribly. I had given the Chancellor some figures so grossly absurd that even the opposition noticed it. There was a bit of a hoo-ha in the press. I tried to sort that out. When I got home, not only was Judith in a poor way, but Tubby had sent some blasted professor round to see me. Of course he gave me the usual clap-trap about abortion, but I was so sad and tired and muddled that as near as a toucher I gave in. After the professor had gone, I went into the bedroom and fell on my knees in front of the crucifix as I always do. It was a moment of peace in my utter misery. Suddenly, for no apparent reason, the words of the Pope's blessing sounded in my mind as though shouted through a microphone: 'The arms of that crucifix will ever be outstretched in suffering and in mercy over you.' Up to that moment I had felt sure that Judith would die. But no: the suffering was but the herald of mercy, of mercy beyond my hopes. I did not go to the Treasury the next morning; Judith was too ill and I too tired. That was the morning you turned up, George. I shall never forget it. You were the instrument of mercy. It was you who changed the whole situation."

"Thank you, Edmund. You cannot conceive how your words console me. But what did your Pope say?" Sir George continued. " 'Those arms will ever be outstretched in suffering and mercy,' was that it? Yes, my dear boy, I believe him. And it is not only you who have suffered and received mercy. Indeed, perhaps some of your suffering has fallen as mercy upon me. Come, let us go in front of your crucifix."

They went. Edmund's and Judith's bed had been pushed further along the wall to make room for Richard's cot, which was now directly under the crucifix. They knelt. Was it in front of Richard or the Cross? Of both: one was the expression and the other the source of God's mercy. George and Judith cried; Edmund just felt immeasurably happy. After a few minutes on their knees, each in turn kissed Richard. It was very emotional, sentimental, superstitious. But such is the noblest layer in the mud of which man is made.

"You know," said George when they had returned to the living room. "I am not a religious man. As you doubtless remember, Judith, I kicked that crucifix. Yet, since the birth of Richard, I do believe. You can call it subjective and sentimental as much as you like, but it is based on an experimental certainty: the mercy of God revealed in our baby. Yes — and I accept whatever consequences can be deduced from that one certainty. At the moment, I am not particularly interested to discover what the consequences are, because I already possess the certainty. I accept what your Pope said, that there is no mercy without suffering. That is the justification of Popery: the redemption of man by the suffering of God. It is obvious once God has revealed it and man has experienced it. And I imagine that all men would if they bothered to look.

"As I said, my dear children, I am not a religious man, but I am a practical one. What is to be done about my recognition of God's mercy manifest in our baby? I want to be buried exactly as Richard will be. I shall instruct my executors to bury me as an R.C., in the religion I not only despised, but hated. I think I hated it because of its claim to be changeless in a changing world. Like a fool, I always pictured tradition in my mind as looking backwards. But since the birth of Richard, at last I realize that tradition is precisely looking forward, giving to the new life — to Richard — the incalculable accumulation of knowledge and wisdom which has been handed down to us. Therein, Edmund, lies the strength of your Church. It lies less in your possession of the traditions which it has received than in the guarantee to hand them on to the end of time. That you, Edmund, should be buried as were your forefathers is less significant than that I can guarantee to be buried as will my grandson. Tradition is an insurance for the future, not a bill for the past. How right you Catholics are!"

It must be remembered that Sir George Milden was talking in June 1958, when what he said appeared true to the point of being trite.

He continued: "I suppose one day I shall have to see a priest, but for the moment I wish to enjoy my certitude. I am a tiny bit frightened that by too much talk he may make me doubt. Besides, I have another funny sentiment. Since Richard was born, I feel that I have completed my life although I am only fifty-six. But now I can depart in peace."

He did. A fortnight later, on July 5th, 1958, Sir George Milden had a stroke during a board meeting. According to his instructions, he was buried as a Catholic. The only Catholic relatives or connections at the funeral were the Roughams, from the Brigadier down to Richard in his carry-cot. Judith brought him along since he owed his life to the grandfather he would never remember, and the grandfather owed his faith to the baby.

As he himself had said, Sir George was a practical man: whatever he had determined was done immediately. He had altered some of the settlements in his trusts. He left a modest allowance to Judith and, out of respect to Brigadier Rougham, who disapproved of a wife wealthier than her husband, a substantial estate to Edmund.

He died the day after he had the stroke, having been baptized *in extremis.*

X

HOLY CROSS

As far as Tubby was concerned, the birth of Richard was not the end of the business. The fact was that Judith was quite unsuitable for bearing children and should be sterilized at the earliest opportunity. Another pregnancy might be fatal. He had raised the point with a certain amount of diffidence in March, but after Sir George's death he became insistent. The technician reverted to being the pontiff.

It so happens that in this Tubby had a reasonable case, far better than in the matter of abortion. Judith possessed a damaged womb. She hemorrhaged from time to time. She suffered spasmodic pain. It is perfectly clear that, just as one cuts one's fingernails, one can mutilate the part for the benefit of the whole. Judith's womb was sufficiently detrimental to her general health to warrant mutilation — at least, so Tubby maintained.

That was not how it appeared to Judith, however. She admitted that such mutilation was justifiable, but that did not mean it was justified. To her there was a fairly wide margin between what was positively wrong and positively right. She would not have criticized any friend who had done it, but she would have criticized herself. It represented a lowering of the standards. She would not be mutilated, even if she could.

What worried her in the situation was something quite different. She had no right to beat her neighbor's breast. Could Edmund stand the strain which she would be imposing on him? She broached the matter with enormous delicacy. Of course he could: he would do anything for her! After all, he had no right to her; she should have died. Then, if the strain became too great, there was always the "safe period."

In the meantime and apart from his parents' marital problems, Richard existed. Judith would dearly have loved to suckle him, but she could not. How she envied the Blessed Virgin! Doubtless she had suffered the Seven Sorrows, but why was there no devotion to her seventy-times-seven joys? Not the least among them was to give suck to God. However, Judith enjoyed feeding her child, albeit artificially. He was so selfish, the little brute. If time or temperature were the least bit wrong he complained as poor Edmund would never dare. If both were passable — he never paid compliments — total satisfaction, a foretaste of the beatific vision, radiated from his whole being.

What she liked best was cutting his minute little nails; they were so perfect. The Blessed Virgin must have kept Jesus's nails. They will be found one day, the most cherished of all relics. Judith also cut Richard's eyelashes in the hope of making them grow stronger. How wonderful, wonderful, wonderful it all was! And to think that the greatest of all miracles was reproduced millions upon millions of times, and that every mother had experienced it, be it in the African bush or Buckingham Palace. The democracy of God! And people talk of women's rights. Yes, woman has a right which no angel has: she can reproduce the image of God. It was wonderful, all right. And to think that they had tried to abort her Richard! "Yes, you selfish little beast, not only did they want to kill you, but they wanted to prevent me from partaking in the only joy which humans share with God: that of creating. Richard, my love, my love!" Curiously enough, it was the advent of Richard which gave Judith her first glimmer of devotion to the Blessed Virgin. As with many converts, it had been something new and strange to her. But now she could appreciate the uniqueness of the position of Mary, who alone among mortals, could love God as her baby and her baby as God.

With what anxiety Judith waited for Richard's first recognizable word! She repeated constantly the Holy Name in the hope that it might be "Cheshoo." Or would it be Pa or Ma? It was not. As clear as a trumpet and with the determination of a dictator, his first word was "no." Judith did not even remember pronouncing it in his presence. Whatever philosophers may say, the human certainly has one innate idea, that of the negative: NO! She could not help feeling that instead of writing his *Grammar of Assent*, Newman would have been more realistically employed in writing a *Grammar of Dissent*. But that is enough about Richard; he is already running ahead of schedule.

It was at the end of July, 1958, only three weeks after George's death, that Edmund and Judith moved into the house he had bought for them. It was called the Dower House, because that is what it had been on some large 18th century estate. The main house had long since vanished, but the land had only been developed since the war. A vast London County Council Housing Estate had been dumped on it. But the Dower House had not been touched. Although on one side it was only twenty yards from the road and consequently the new estate, on the three others it stood on five-and-a-half acres of its own land jutting into the forest.

Judith was also fortunate enough to acquire an admirable domestic, one Signora Giacinta Cacciacapri, a widow of only about fifty in years, but a good seventy around the waist. Her two sons were married and employed at Hatfield, not too far away. In theory Giacinta was supposed to keep the place clean, as it was not small, while Judith did the cooking and looked after Richard. In practice, however, Giacinta did the lot, as she thought Judith's cooking inedible and, from double her maternal experience, felt that the poor girl had not a clue as to how to spank a baby. Giacinta was in fact a marvel. The only trouble with her was that she had forgotten Italian and had failed to learn English. She was both more voluble and more incoherent than Richard.

The only drawback to the house was one which George could scarcely have been expected to take into consideration: it was not within easy distance of a church. The friary at Woodham was the nearest but it was nearly five miles away by an awkward road. It was perfectly all right for Sunday but was inconvenient on weekdays — and Judith lived for her daily Mass.

Fortunately, when the new estate had been built, the London County Council had scheduled a site for a church and presbytery which the diocese had acquired. This, via a footpath, was not more than five-hundred yards from the Dower House. Nothing had been done about it from lack of funds. When Edmund came into a considerable fortune from his father-in-law, he could think of no better way of spending it than to indulge the passion of the testator's daughter — to build a church for Judith in fact. This involved endless negotiations with the diocesan and local authorities as well as with architects and builders, but it was eventually completed to everyone's satisfaction and as Edmund had conceived it. Since it has been considerably altered, it is worthwhile describing it as it used to be.

It is not an unoriginal building. In shape it is oval. Its main axis, between porch and altar, is the short diameter. From the outside this makes the building appear much larger than it is, owing to the breadth of the facade which curves round the long diameter. A square porch juts out on the west front with four Ionic columns running through two floors, of which the lower is the main entrance and the upper, with three arched windows between the columns, the organ loft. On each side of the porch the oblong recedes with three enormous windows either side, practically the height of the building. Except for a porch, which has a high entablature carrying four baroque statues of saints — unidentified, but with plenty of drapery being blown about by the Holy Ghost — the whole is covered by a single aluminum dome with a charming lantern in the centre, surmounted by the Cross.

If the exterior is impressive, the interior used to be positively beautiful. Upon entering, one sees immediately opposite and across the short axis — consequently quite near — the sanctuary. It stands in an elliptic, half-domed apse. There are no side aisles to interrupt the view of the High Altar. To the right of the apse, balancing the windows to the south of the porch, is a side altar, the font and a confessional; the same to the left, except that the pulpit replaces the font. On the north and south tips of the oblong are side entrances surmounted by oval windows. Each section of the building — between apse, side altar, font, confessional, side entrance, windows and so on — is marked by an Ionic pilaster supporting a wide frieze and deep cornice, from behind which the dome springs up, deep blue in colour. The pilasters are stone yellow. The rest is white. The building is immensely light, although, looking at the altar, no windows can be seen; they are all behind one. The church can seat three-hundred comfortably, with standing room for another hundred at least. The organ loft is rather large, being the full size of the porch. Not only is there a three-manual and pedal organ, but there is room for a small orchestra and a fair-sized choir. This was a point on which Edmund was most insistent: "The Church's principal contribution to the culture of our country seems to lie in organizing football pools and bingo. Just for a change we might have an occasional Mass by Haydn or Mozart."

The presbytery and parish hall, which latter has never been built, were invisible from the main front although both were attached to the church; the presbytery to the south of the sanctuary, the hall to the north.

If Edmund looked after the building of the church, it was Judith who took care of its furnishings. Not only had she worked at Sotheby's and was consequently acquainted with the trade, but her friend Pamela was still working at Christie's. Sooner or later everything gets sold in London, from Japanese inros to Eskimos' pants. It was Judith who had bought the four baroque saints for the entablature of the porch from the most dishonest dealer in London — but at a price arranged by Pamela. She bought a brace of Bavarian confessionals decorated with palm trees to represent the oasis of the thirsty soul. She got a pair of charming Louis XVI side altars at Christie's. For their reredos she procured from Sotheby's a couple of beautiful paintings from the much-underrated Genoese, Piola. One represented Doubting Thomas touching the side of Christ; it would do for the Sacred Heart altar. The other was of Pentecost with the Blessed Virgin in the middle; it would do for the Lady altar. The altar rails for the High Altar came from the balustrade to the old Waterloo Bridge.

Some other parishioners by the name of Waddington, who had once owned a private chapel but could no longer afford the upkeep of a big house, supplied chalices, ciboria and a monstrance; quite remarkable sets of Venetian vestments, candlesticks, altar linen and much else. The presbytery was built and furnished to the last detail for two priests and a housekeeper.

Alone the parish hall had been left until a parish priest had been appointed and could be consulted.

There remained the High Altar. The altar itself presented no problem. The Brig would give a fine French inlaid marble altar dated 1776, the twin, it was said, to the one in the cathedral at Viviers in the Rhone Valley. It had been erected in the chapel at Rougham after the Catholic Relief Act of 1791, but had not been moved to the new church in the town, built in 1830, directly after emancipation. That was splendid, but what reredos should it have, and what crucifix?

As Judith and Edmund were discussing it together one evening, Judith had an idea: "You know, dear, it has been wonderful and, apart from the work you have put into it, I suppose we have had no change out of £200,000. But, in a way, we have made no personal sacrifice. We have never had the money. It has passed straight from Daddy's estate to architects, quantity surveyors, structural engineers, builders, plumbers, electricians, art dealers and the rest. True, we could have had it but we have not taken it. That is already much. But the Brig has actually parted with his very own altar at Rougham. We have parted with nothing."

"Judith, my love," Edmund interrupted, "I see exactly how your mind is working. You want me to part with the Rougham Crucifix, which you gave me along with yourself as a wedding present. Well, I won't part with either." Brave words, but of course he did.

The Brig was further induced to give a Queen Anne overmantle from one of the umpteen disused rooms at the castle. It had a fine broken pediment and superb fluted columns. Those who saw the completed High Altar had to admit that in spite of its diversity — the French rococo altar, English palladian reredos and early Cinquecento high-relief — it was among the most beautiful expressions of religious art in the country. Naturally, the church was dedicated to the Holy Cross.

Thanks to Judith's drive, Edmund's competence and George's money, the first Mass was celebrated at midnight on Christmas, 1960. The church was served by Franciscans until such time as the bishop could appoint a parish priest. This occurred in the following March, 1961.

Edmund and Judith had never been in the least apprehensive as to whom the bishop might send because in those days the personality of the priest simply did not matter. In this Age of Mass-Unproduction — of presidents, chairmen, directors, managers, executives, planners; of boards, committees, commissions, seminars, courses — the priest was almost the only surviving craftsman. He planned nothing but did something. He would be well-versed in the theory and practice of his trade. He would baptize, catechize, forgive sin, lay on the Body and Blood of Christ, marry and bury, all perfectly competently, were he zealous or lazy, enchanting or boring, sinner or saint.

In fact, however, Canon Slattery — for such was the style and name of the first parish priest of Holy Cross — was a sweet old boy, with that soft, recessive amiability which is not uncommon in aging priests. He was only sixty-eight, but had had some disease or other which had shrivelled him a bit. At his prime he must have been fairly corpulent, which doubtless explained his being made a canon, but now his skin, like his clothes, hung loosely about him. He had perfectly white hair, white skin and was meticulously shaven. He looked like a benign albino toad. The bishop had appointed him because he thought that Walthamford would be a nice little parish, well-within the canon's physical capacity.

Of course it turned out otherwise. Scarcely had he started rootling round the place when the Catholics began to emerge from their lairs. Judith had a real shock when she saw at Mass nearly a quarter of the people with whom she had dealings in the neighbourhood — including the charming postman and the ghastly little fellow from the tobacconist's who had given her the wrong change more than once. It was just like the Alpine meadows bursting into bloom as the snow melts. Give them their Mass and all these dark and hidden people would suddenly start burgeoning.

The real trouble, however, was catechizing the masses of children who turned up from nowhere. In this Judith was really useful. She had acquired some pre-catechetical practice on her own Richard. She loved doing it. The only thing which the young human understands naturally is religion. That two and two make four is so silly that it is not worth remembering; that c-a-t spells cat is so arbitrary as to be insignificant; but that God is, and is at once everywhere and nowhere, that's worth knowing. Even the toughest atheist, when he was a little fellow, understood exactly what was meant by God. It takes millions upon millions of pounds of education to make man impious. Atheism is the most expensive commodity in the world.

As a matter of fact, Judith knew this from her own personal experience. When she was five or six years old, an Irish cook had taught her the Hail Mary in the privacy of the kitchen — an example of Popish proselytism which would have earned her the sack on the spot had it been known. In moments of great stress — when she had been caught stealing sweets or had bitten John for beating her at ludo — Judith used to recite it secretly behind the sofa in the drawing-room. It had required the most expensive education England could provide to make her an agnostic.

To return to catechism at Holy Cross, Judith took two classes, one for the nine- and ten-year-olds on Saturdays at 10 a.m. and one for fives and sixes after the 9:30 Mass on Sundays. It was a bit of a bind, but infinitely rewarding. The general scheme was, of course, the old penny-catechism. Although Father McEnery had never taken her through it, she had found it an admirable little book. It supplied the one thing which is required of religion: certainty. Nobody is able to believe and doubt at the same time. With a minimum of intelligence and imagination it gave a wonderful series of hooks on which to hang the vast tapestry of the Faith.

She handed the seven- and eight-year-olds over to the canon, who thought it best that he himself should deal with first confessions and Holy Communions. Judith was delighted at this arrangement. Like most converts she had found — and indeed still found — confession very difficult. This, she realized, was because in the adult, sin is inextricably tied up with the emotion of shame, with which it really has nothing to do. One can feel ashamed of a virtuous act and delighted at a successful sin. But shame only begins to sprout and flourish in the human conscience at some time between the ages of seven and ten. Judith did not wish to contaminate the children under her care with her own difficulties and scruples — or lack of them.

Anyway, the parish of Holy Cross started off, as had every other parish since the dawn of Christianity, with absolute certainty in faith, with unquestioning hope and boundless charity. This, of course, was in 1961-62, in a parish rather off the beaten track under the care of an aging and devout priest.

NEW LIFE AND RENEWAL

As has been said, after Richard's birth Judith and Edmund practiced total continence. This lasted for a little over two years. They did not find it anything like as difficult as they had expected, possibly because the habit had already been acquired during Judith's long illness. In July 1960 however, at Edmund's suggestion they tried the safe period. As far as their experience went, perfectly safe it was, in spite of what some of Judith's friends swore to be true. Nevertheless, it had considerable drawbacks. All the charts and temperature-taking removed spontaneity from the act. It reduced to nil the "giving" value in the expression of love and seemed to turn it into self-satisfaction. Then, when the mutual desire was perhaps strongest, intercourse could not take place. On the other hand, when neither of them wanted it, they felt obliged to have it because it was safe. It was this last aspect which was the least satisfactory. Its only positive advantage was that it implied discipline, a quality which neither Edmund nor Judith despised. Nearly a year later, however, in May 1961, they reverted to total continence. For them, at least, they thought it preferable to the safe period. There was real sacrifice instead of false indulgence. But after the false indulgence, both found it hard to make the sacrifice. Moreover, to be absolutely honest, Judith wanted another baby. Time had dulled her memory more than it had Edmund's as to how near death she had been while carrying Richard. Anyway, the pundits had been wrong: she had produced Richard and was herself alive. It was ridiculous to mould one's life on the dictates of doctors whose gift of prophecy had proved false. But the determining factor was that Richard was now three. Luckily, he was a good-natured little fellow, but it was clear to Judith that he was getting spoilt. Not only was he the apple of his parents' eyes, he was the only grandchild of the

Brig and Lucy. Fortunately, Mary Milden had John's two children to fuss over, but there were still too many eyes glued on Richard. Lucy was the worst. She was convinced that the only toys suitable for Richard were ones twice his size. Richard not only had a bedroom and playroom, but a storeroom as well. It was getting out of hand. What was needed was a baby girl. Continence was consequently jettisoned soon after the safe period.

It was not, however, until July 1962 that Judith conceived. Tubby Bradfield was consulted straight away, when his techniques could be of some value instead of too late. Tubby was a firm believer in his own trade: the body controls the mind, not *vice versa*. Judging by his appetite, it was probably true in his own case. Thus, the more pills people took, the better they would be. Judith rattled with them. They seemed to work. She was really very well and carried quite easily. The only trouble was that Tubby was adamant on rest.

Rest was a bit of a nuisance, as it was one of the few things of which Judith was incapable. She did her best. What she most regretted was having to give up her daily Mass and catechism classes. The latter she handed over to Mrs. Larkin, the postman's wife, who had had umpteen brats of her own. Judith admired her, nay, loved her, and felt that if she did not know how to catechize children then nobody did. Judith had never seen better brought-up children than the Larkins'.

The obligation to rest altered Judith's life completely and was a great penance to her. The employment of a nursery maid to look after Richard and of a daily to help Giacinta and of a part-time gardener was highly disagreeable to her. She felt that it cut her off from the realities, the important things in life. It threw her back onto herself, her own ego, far too much. However, she was willing to put up with anything for the sake of the new life which was palpitating within her.

Those sorts of changes were obvious enough, but there was another which was most unexpected. Out of loyalty to her new religion, Judith had always subscribed to every Catholic periodical which came her way. *The Tablet, Universe, Catholic Times and Herald, Month, Downside, Blackfriars, Novena* and the rest. Of course she never read them because she did not have the time. However, it consoled her to see that English Catholicism was churning out such masses of stuff for every type of outlook. On the rare occasions when she happened to glance at one of them she felt filled with pride. *The Tablet* under Mr. Woodruff was a masterpiece of intelligent journalism; *The Universe* really was universal, with writeups about centenarian nuns in Java or Brazil; *The Catholic Times* pontificated less than the non-Catholic variety; Bedoyere in *The Herald* was usually intelligent although sometimes unintelligible; *The Fireside* was indeed homely and *Novena* pious — and so on.

Now, in October 1962, Judith felt that the most rewarding way in which to rest would be to read the Catholic press. She had scarcely even glanced at it over the last year. Here was the opportunity to make amends and do it justice. This was at the beginning of October 1962. On Thursday the 11th Pope John XXIII was to open the Second Vatican Council.

What an event! Even on the physical side, what could be more magnificent than to see over two-thousand bishops in mitre and cope playing their allotted part on the stupendous stage of St. Peter's, Rome? Bishops of every race and culture would manifest their unity in faith with the fisherman of Galilee who lay buried beneath their feet. No political or financial power in the world could remotely compete in producing such an assembly. Pope John was right: the mere fact of the council proclaimed the uniqueness of the One, Holy, Catholic and Apostolic Church of Rome. Such were Judith's sentiments when she started to read the Catholic press by way of rest and recreation.

At first she was no more than surprised at the press's general attitude. It appeared to be in complete agreement that the Church, the Immaculate Spouse, needed a face-lift and a change of clothes. It had never crossed Judith's mind that anybody should wish to change the Church. That all Catholics, from the Pope to herself, should beat their own breasts was one thing, but to beat the Church's breast was quite another. And if the Immaculate Spouse was to be rejuvenated and become fashionable, who was to be the plastic surgeon and the dress designer? With a woman's sure instinct she felt that Cardinals Frings, Döpfner, Lienart, Suenens and Alfrink were unlikely to prove successful in spiritual *haute couture*.

She also discovered that the council was not to be dogmatic but pastoral. By the end of October she became aware that "pastoral" had nothing to do with the sheep, but was concerned exclusively with the pastors. The sheep did not count. They were an ignorant, superstitious gang of totem worshipers who would do what they were told anyway. The only virtue of which they were capable was blind obedience, and the blinder the better. The pastors were different. Up till now, bishops had only had rings on their fingers; they should also have rings on their toes. Collegiality was in the air. As for priests, instead of being mute ministers of the Divine Sacrifice, they should become Managing Directors of the Catholic Assembly Line. Did Judith already foresee the queues standing for Communion? It is not impossible: she was highly intelligent and had a vivid imagination.

As a convert, she was particularly interested in the emphasis placed on ecumenicity. She had presumed it to mean that from henceforth Catholics could treat the Separated Brethren with common courtesy instead of being virtuously rude. But it seemed to mean something quite different: that a change in structure and Agreed Statements of adequate ambiguity would make Catholics protestant and Protestants catholic; thus would reunion be achieved. Neither faith nor grace entered the problem at all. This really did puzzle Judith in a big way. Even more odd than her own conversion had been that of her father. He had denied the Faith on identical grounds which had made Judith accept it; what had converted him was the birth of Richard. As far as Judith was concerned, structures and statements had nothing to do with reunion. She even felt (but here she was doubtless unfair) that ecumenists were not really interested in the reunion of the churches; this was merely a handy lever to create a new church of their own at the cost of destroying whatever was upright, noble and true in Catholicism and Protestantism alike.

However, it was only toward mid-November that the press really started to annoy Judith. She felt that it was not the bishops

— not even Alfrink, Suenens and Co. — who were running the council. It was the mass media. Even the Catholic press had ceased to provide nice, homely little publications of parochial gossip in order to become instruments of propaganda. The media were running Alfrink, Suenens and Co., not *vice versa*. Now, both Judith and Edmund mistrusted the media. There was no television or radio in the Dower House in spite of Giacinta's moans and groans. Neither was any national newspaper delivered. The Catholic press and the local rag were allowed in precisely because they were in no sense mass-media; they had no pretension to informing and forming public opinion.

In this matter Judith was doubtless prejudiced. She had a theory about the media of communication in general. The invention of printing had inevitably given rise to Protestantism with the worship of the printed Bible. On the continent the Renascence became a bit confused since Virgil and Boccaccio were printed as well. In the 17th century the pamphlet produced the Fronde in France and the Commonwealth in England. In the 18th, the Encyclopedia produced the Age of Reason and the Revolution. In the 19th the daily paper was responsible for representative democracy. The invention of the telephone coincided with the European Civil War of 1914-1918 — which is still going on in backward-looking Russia. The silent film produced Mussolini, a political version of Charlie Chaplin. There was great art and something rather endearing about the silent films as there was about the Duce. The talkies and wireless begat Adolf Hitler, the Greatest Shouter of all times. The result was disastrous. Now, with television we must be prepared for an even more terrible result: total tyranny of body and soul.

Television was Judith's particular bugbear. Glued to it, the human ceased to be a rational animal and became a reception box linked to the goggle box. Instead of an independent, vital, responsible person, man was transformed into a machine to receive sensation and impulse. From positive he became negative. He no longer had to use his imagination even for a dirty thought. His judgment was conditioned by how the screen put the problem. No action was required of him other than moral indignation as the screen suggested. Judith felt that the real world, flesh and devil presented her with sufficient problems without her having to contend with the World, the Flesh and the Devil, all with capitals of monumental magnitude, as presented to her by the goggle box.

Such was Judith's prejudice. But in all fairness to her, Vatican II did nothing to dispel it when, at its first session in 1962, the only two *schemae* presented were those on liturgy and the media of communication. It looked as though the assembled Fathers thought they were much the same thing: the media were the new form of liturgy and the Mass was one of the media.

As has been said, Judith started off by being surprised at the Catholic press, then puzzled. She only became frankly annoyed when she learned of Archbishop René Stourm's presentation to the council on November 23rd of his *schema* on the media. Admittedly she was young and had had little experience, but never had Judith read such drivel. Inevitably he trotted out the statistics: a thousand television stations feeding a hundred and twenty million sets, wasting umpteen billion human hours and increasing at some appalling rate each year. Then came the claptrap: "The Church must recognize that modern man is nourished, educated and formed by these media." They were "a providential means for transmitting the Christian message more rapidly, more universally and more effectively." It did not seem to strike the archbishop that they might be even more suited to transmit the anti-Christian message with equal rapidity, universality and effectiveness. But the crowning clause ran: "The duty of seeing to it that danger to public morals and social progress (sic) do not result from a perverted use of the media...is vested in the civil authority" — in the state! Of all institutions! So the state is given the right to decide what constitutes public morals and social progress — which are lumped together as though they were in some way equivalent. Old Joe Stalin must be cheering in his grave. And the media can preach abortion as much as they like, provided the state decides that it is conducive to "social progress." It is past belief. It justified to the hilt Judith's theory that television would lead inevitably to total tyranny of body and soul.

Actually, Judith felt that the restlessness among the clergy, evident from the Catholic press, was due principally to their being conditioned by the media. A priest or nun who had been perfectly happy in 1947 was no longer so in 1962. What had happened in those fifteen years? They had bought a television. That was the means by which the spirit of worldliness had invaded cloister and presbytery. Perhaps television should be prohibited in monasteries, convents, presbyteries and bishops' palaces to preserve some independence of mind among clergy and religious. Doubtless, Archbishop Stourm was too busy watching television to have time to consider such a proposition. Judith wrote a beautiful hymn in the archbishop's honour, of which the last verse ran:

The sword will not slip from my hold,
Nor shall I leave unturned a stone
Until religion is controlled
By telescreen and microphone.

In fact, by the time the first session of the council closed on December 8th, Judith's hackles were up. She felt that an immense opportunity had been lost. Instead of proclaiming the Church as One, Holy, Catholic and Apostolic, the council was making her appear divided, permissive, ecumenical and evolutionary. It was busy undermining the very marks by which the Immaculate Spouse was recognizable to man.

Yet it would be premature to say that Judith felt herself to be in direct opposition to the council. In the first place, she had not lost confidence in the bishops. They were there to preserve the integrity of the Faith and the traditions of the faithful. They could be trusted to do their job. It was true that a sizable number of them seemed to be sufficiently stupid to wish at all costs to appear intelligent. But surely that could not apply to the majority? Besides, no matter how stupid, most of them must have a modicum of humility.

Then there was Pope John. The ridiculous "personality cult" was rather frightening because it was so clearly engineered by the mass media. Nevertheless, Pope he was, and to Judith's mind one Pope was worth a gaggle of bishops. Besides, he had splendidly strong, square peasant's hands. They were exactly the opposite to those of Pius XII, but they were just as valid and trustworthy. After all, the gentry are only big peasants and the peasants little gentry. In both cases it is direct contact with the land, with God's creation, which creates nobility. Judith was never quite sure whether the Brig was the most humble gentleman or the greatest peasant she had ever met.

But more important than bishops or Pope was Edmund. Now, at this early date, Edmund had none of Judith's misgivings. He was positively optimistic concerning the council in particular and the state of the Church in general. This optimism naturally reflected back on Judith. She presumed that she could not see the wood for the trees. It helped her enormously. If Edmund could laugh at Archbishop Stourm it would be silly of her to cry.

Obviously they talked to each other about these things. It was after Christmas, in January 1963, that Edmund said to Judith: "I can well understand how these bishops annoy you. As a convert, you are in love with the Church as she stands. She has given you the only fundamental certainties you have in life. For any bishop to criticize her is not merely impertinence, but must of necessity undermine the Church's credibility. Not only are you wedded to the Church's faith, but to every detail of its external expression, since you could only get to know the Faith by how the Church manifested it. This seems to me absolutely fair. But myself, as a cradle Catholic, do not look at things quite in that light. Perhaps I take both the Faith and its expression too much for granted — which, of course, you don't — but my first and natural reaction is to bow to the Church's visible authority. The Faith as such is unalterable, but I am perfectly willing to accept whatever external expression the visible authority wishes to give to that faith.

"I think that the problem could be formulated in this sort of way. We agree that the Faith is transmitted to us by the teaching, testimony and authority of the Catholic Church. Fine! But if the visible authority in the Church wishes to change the expressions in which the Faith is formulated, there are two possible reactions. The first is yours: what must be preserved at all costs is the Faith. But to change the symbols by which it is known and recognized can only lead at best to confusion and at worst to a change in belief. One must therefore be prepared to fight the visible authority to guarantee the integrity of the Faith. The second is mine: what must be preserved at all costs is the authority of the visible church, even if it means accepting ambiguous or inadequate expressions of the Faith — especially as we are in no position to judge the presumed ambiguity or inadequacy.

"I see and understand your reaction, darling; but obviously I prefer my own. Why? At this moment of time, anyway, in January 1963, the council has in no way formulated the Faith inadequately or ambiguously for the simple reason that it has not as yet promulgated a single decree. All that has happened is that a number of bishops have got so hot under the collar that their mitres are unable to contain the steam. But even if the council does make some pretty rum pronouncements, my own reaction will still be to save the authority of the visible church."

"Edmund, darling, how wonderfully clever you are," Judith replied. "You put the problem so plainly. I suppose I am frightened of the impossible: that a gang of bishops will use the authority of the Church precisely to destroy it — autodemolition, suicide. But at the moment you are quite right. I have jumped the gun. I am angry at what people have said instead of waiting until something has been done. Nevertheless, wouldn't you admit that there might come a point at which the faithful would have to resist the fallible, human legislation of the Church because it was not in harmony with her infallible faith?"

Edmund hesitated. "I suppose in theory such a situation could arise, but it would be well-nigh impossible to formulate a concrete example."

"No, it would not," Judith rejoined. "It would be perfectly easy. You don't read the Catholic press, apart from Woodruff's beautifully balanced articles. I admit that you are right at the present moment, but I also think that we must be prepared for the worst. Here and now, before creeping paralysis sets in, we should decide at what point we shall draw the line."

"Yes, I agree," said Edmund. "At the Treasury millions of pounds are wasted merely because nobody decided at the start when a given operation should end. But give me your examples."

"Easy! I'll give you three for a start, although I could give you a dozen: the jettisoning of the Immemorial Mass; recognition of the validity of all ecclesial ministries or orders — notably Anglican and Lutheran; the licitness of artificial contraception. There you are."

Edmund roared with laughter. "Of course, if that sort of thing happened, every Catholic would have to protest; but it's impossible. You seem to forget that the Pope and bishops are just as much Catholics as you and I."

"That's the trouble, Edmund: it is not I who forget it, but they. Also, I do not say that these things will come about by positive legislation; they will come about by failure to enforce any condemnation. However, for the moment you have set my mind at rest. Only, instead of the Catholic press, I shall read P. G. Wodehouse and the Bible. They won't annoy me."

"Yes," said Edmund, "and we have decided at what point protest might become inevitable."

Edmund's optimism was not mere wishful thinking. It was derived from his personal experience. As far as he was concerned, the council had already achieved its object. It had managed to transform the Scarlet Harlot of Rome into an English Blue Eyed Boy. Never in the whole course of history had a pope received such universal acclamation as John XXIII. Although Catholic emancipation was now a hundred and thirty years old and Catholics had got killed in both wars like anybody else, they were still considered a bit odd, to be "left-footers." They represented a very thin scum at the top of society, such as the Roughams, and the thick lees at the bottom of society. But all the good wine was solidly non-Catholic — apart from converts, who were mistrusted by both sides. Thus there was not a single Catholic on the boards or in upper management in any of the companies controlled by Milden Adhesives. Neither were there any in the upper regions of the Treasury apart from Edmund himself.

It was at the Treasury that the new atmosphere struck Edmund so forceably. Until some time in early 1962 it was impossible for any of his colleagues to mention religion in his presence. It would have been impolite, since he was known to be the odd man out.

After that date it became a normal topic of conversation and, as Edmund was the only person who knew anything about it, his religious pronouncements carried almost as much weight as his statistics. It even affected the Supreme Boss, the Chancellor of the Exchequer himself.

It was only a week after the recorded conversation with Judith that Edmund was summoned into the chancellor's presence. Edmund liked the man, although he was not generally as popular at the Treasury as he was in the country. "Hallo, Rougham! You Papists seem to have got hold of the right fellow at last. If he put up for election in this country he'd sweep the board. Bloody good idea, that council. Makes him look good. He's grasped the essence of democracy: look good. And I like that expression about 'fresh air.' Makes him sound English. Foreigners always live in a fug. Don't know what he means by this 'immunekissity' or whatever it is. Damned if I'm going to become a Papist. But it's the right spirit. Incidentally, I called you in to thank you for those graphs. One can grasp graphs in a tick instead of wading through wadges of gore-blimey literature. Thanks. And that last speech you wrote went down a treat; exactly what I wanted to say, but I couldn't have put it across like that. Here are some notes for another. By the way, doesn't your dear old dad own Rougham Castle? Never seen the place. Why don't you invite me and my missus down? We love old places. They make one feel one's got somewhere. What about the Whitsun weekend? According to my diary, that's from drinks on Friday evening, May 31st, to after lunch on Monday, June 3rd."

Edmund made some rapid mental calculations. The Brig and Lucy could certainly manage it. Judith's baby would be two months old. It was indeed possible.

"Very well, Rougham, you get your mum to write my missus and we'll have a grand old time. All social engagements go through the missus. I'm just a political machine. You've never met my missus? She's trumps. A real educated lady. Deputy-head at a grammar school in Jarrow until I swept her off her feet. That's been my real success in life. Your mum won't have to blush about my missus no matter what your dad thinks about me."

In due course the Right Honourable the Chancellor of the Exchequer and his missus were invited by Brigadier and Mrs. Rougham to spend the Whitsun weekend at Rougham Castle. They graciously accepted.

In March Edmund was appointed one of the five assistants to the permanent undersecretary. It was astonishing: he was only thirty-four. The next youngest assistant was forty-eight. The reason for the sudden promotion was clear: the chancellor wanted to have a small nucleus of personal advisers in the ministry. He disapproved in principle of importing his own friends so he chose from among the civil servants those on whom he felt he could rely. Edmund was among them. Yes, but would it have crossed the chancellor's mind to appoint a ridiculously young Papist to his inner circle a couple of years previously? Almost certainly not. Now, it was the obvious thing to do: a bit of "immunekissity," as he called it, looked good. Incidentally, he was no fool and was never more deliberate than when he got things wrong. The proposed visit to Rougham Castle was to cement the personal relationship between the chancellor and his young *protégé*.

Thus was Edmund confirmed in his optimism concerning the general impact of the council, no matter what misgivings Judith might have concerning details.

XII

DILEMMA AT ROUGHAM

Judith did not really have too bad a time while carrying her baby. However, at the end of February she had a hemorrhage and her blood pressure shot up. Tubby gave her even more pills and, as he was taking no risks, moved her into a hospital. He performed a perfectly successful caesarian on April 4, 1963. It was another little boy — "George" — after his maternal grandfather.

Three days after the caesarian, on the night of Palm Sunday, April 7th, Judith again developed some sort of toxaemia. It was nothing like as bad as it had been before the birth of Richard. Besides, she was in the hospital and Tubby was on the spot. It left her, however, extremely weak. When she and George were movable, which was on April 26, they were sent down to Rougham Castle, where Lucy had found a retired midwife who would be delighted to look after both. Edmund and Richard were left at the Dower House under the competent protection of Giacinta. They came down to Rougham for the weekends. Richard had started school in January, of which more anon.

Unfortunately, Judith was by no means strong enough to sit through Mass even if Lucy drove her the few hundred yards from the castle to the church: she tended to feel sick and faint in the morning. But the parish priest, Father Paul Cromer, was very kind and solicitous. He brought her Holy Communion on Wednesday mornings. He also called round for a chat and a drink at about 7 p.m. on Tuesdays after his rounds and on Fridays after Benediction. The fact was that Cromer was a bit of an intellectual and found that his parishioners were more interested in ploughing their fields than in ploughing through books. Judith had the immense advantage of being someone out of the parochial rut, of the opposite sex, educated, always available since she was house-bound and well-supplied with his favorite sherry.

Judith, of course, knew him in the indefinable way in which a parishioner knows a priest: both very intimately and very distantly. He was aged about forty-five. Rougham was his first parish, to which he had been appointed in 1955. It was he who had assisted at Judith's wedding and preached a jolly sermon. He was remarkably handsome — which always helps. He had inherited from his late father, a doctor in the Indian Medical Service, a magnificent East Anglian physique, and from his mother, a Portuguese from Bombay, jet black hair, deep bronze skin, wonderfully refined features — and his religion. Judith liked him. He was easy to talk to and well-informed.

It was on his second visit, Friday, May 3rd, that he started to open up. He was miserable at Rougham, a square peg in a round hole. The bishop had only sent him there out of jealousy for his ability. However, the council would put an end to all that. As in any other profession, the priest would have some say as to how, where and when he practiced. Indeed, the clergy were forming an association to protect their professional interests.

"Don't be silly, Father," said Judith after several minutes of Cromer's moan. "You don't belong to a liberal profession. You belong to a craft — the priestcraft. Admittedly, it is a divine one, but it is still a craft. You have the power — or *Kraft* in German — to give to men the means of salvation, be you intelligent and charming or stupid and boring, whether people want you or whether they don't."

"So you too, Mrs. Rougham, think I am just a machine and that my personality, with its loves and hates, its ambitions and fears, its longings and loathings, simply does not count."

"I don't like the word 'machine,' Father. Had you said 'tool,' I should have agreed. Insofar as you are a priest, you are a tool and no more. Insofar as you are Paul Cromer, your ambition, love and longings should be centred on your instrumentality, on being the perfect tool in the hand of God, even if you are only utilized in the wilds of Rougham."

"No, no!" Father Cromer expostulated; "Christ came that we should have life 'more abundantly,' so that our personalities should flower and fructify in charity — not in order that we

DILEMMA AT ROUGHAM 91

should be reduced to a sort of ecclesiastical spanner. Not even a machine, a tool!"

"Yes, Father. But how can we have life 'more abundantly'? 'Unless the seed die' there is no life at all. Only if it dies can it yield an hundredfold. Surely that is the basis of the spiritual life? Isn't that what you preach week in and week out in a thousand forms from your pulpit? Anyway, I hope you will be able to bring me Holy Communion on Wednesday. You see, whatever may be my feelings for you as a man, as a priest you are the instrument through which I communicate with God."

At dinner Judith mentioned that Father Cromer seemed very unhappy about Rougham and asked if there was anything that could be done about it.

"Nothing apart from a miracle," said the Brig. "He was as happy as a lark until eighteen months ago when he wrote a dam' silly article in the *Clergy Review* — he showed it to me. He then became a theologian and discovered that the Church was infallibly wrong. A bit later he got another article published in some left-wing rag. He is now a sociologist and has discovered that socialism is Christianity in practice. His next article will doubtless prove that Heaven is a concentration camp and th sooner Christians are dumped into one the better...No, don' write to the bishop. I am probably the only person round here who hasn't! You don't have to listen to his sermons, my dear. But it does not really matter what he says; he still gives us the Mass and the sacraments, which is all that matters. Anyway, where is the bishop to send him? He cannot do any harm here because we all know him. At a new place, people might take him seriously."

On the following Tuesday Father Cromer arrived a little earlier and came to the point straight away. "I have been thinking, Mrs. Rougham, of what you said about priestly instrumentality, but it simply does not work. It falsifies the Gospel message, the whole Economy of Salvation. It reduces the priesthood from a social to a personal level. You do not really need a priest for your personal salvation. Taken individually, you are as much the Church as is the Pope. You constitute the People of God as much as he and the

People of God are a 'priestly people.' I shall bring you Holy Communion tomorrow, yes; but what is to prevent you from celebrating here, on this table, the *anamnesis*, the memorial of Christ's love? No, the priest is not a personal chaplain multiplied by the number of people to whom he administers. He is the ecclesial leader of the social group.

Up till now, Mrs. Rougham, we have only had half — and the lesser half — of Christianity. We now have to preach the Whole Christ. That is to say that we must preach the social as well as the personal dimension of our religion. And it is the social dimension which justifies the existence of the priesthood. The individual needs no priest because he is one. It is the group which requires a priest, minister, president, chairman or what you will, to guide the People of God in their quest for social justice and for the liberation of all men from the tyrannies of class, race, social and economic inequality which history has piled upon their shoulders."

"That must be a quotation," Judith interrupted, "from one of your articles. The Brig told me about them. But I suppose that at Rougham you don't get much help from the People of God — I mean the Knights of St. Columba, the St. Vincent de Paul, the Catholic Women's League, the Children of Mary and the like?"

"Don't talk to me about the Catholic laity," Father Cromer continued. "They are hopeless, steeped in personal religion, totem worship, catechetical clap-trap, tribal custom, prejudice of class and race. As for those lay organizations, I have managed to suppress the lot — at least I have driven them underground. They were all run by your in-laws anyway. The laity took their orders from Brigadier and Mrs. Rougham as though they were on the parade ground. And all they were interested in was charity: seeing to it that Mrs. Dogsbody's brats had shoes, that the Whistlebottoms got transport to Mass, that some old codger had wood for the winter. And this when injustice on a vast scale was staring at them from all over the world: the Yanks bombing innocent Asians, apartheid in Rhodesia and South Africa, Franco in Spain, dictatorship in South America and unbelievable poverty in the Philippines! They simply were not interested in justice, only in their wretched little charities. I hate charity. Well, I stopped all that."

Father Cromer paused for breath and Judith burst into laughter: "Father, you are a dear!"

"Why, what have I said?"

"You're wonderful! But cannot you see that there are vague inconsistencies in what you say? Last Friday you were all against being a tool; it was the personality which counted; you yourself wanted to flower and bear fruit as a person. Today, not only does the personality disappear into the group, but you proclaim your hatred of the most personal of all acts — charity, the movement of the heart. What you want is the most impersonal of all virtues, justice; a virtue so abstract, so cold — just ice, in fact — that judges have to put wigs on their heads to keep them warm. You know, Jesus spoke a lot about charity but not much about justice — in fact, off hand, all I can remember is his lavish praise of the unjust steward. I suppose you hate the Sisters of Charity. You would like to found the Sisters of Justice. A gay gaggle of girls they would be, in peaked cap and coat and skirt, with a briefcase full of forms. Then you are indignant that your parishioners should do what they can. You want them to be indignant over matters about which they can do nothing. If a beggar comes to your door dying of starvation you doubtless feed him with a pamphlet on the advantages of rationing. He needs justice, not charity!

"You have got things upside-down, my dear Father. You first explain to me how I, a laywoman, am just as much a priest as you and that there is no reason why I should not celebrate the *anamnesis* as you call it. You then describe how the laity are utterly incompetent at their own job of being laity, of dealing with the problems of the society in which they live; and that is what justifies your ministry. Cannot you see that all you have done is to reverse our roles? You make the laity priests and the priests laity. It somehow makes it appear as though your contempt for the laity is only equalled by your hatred of the priesthood."

"You are absolutely unfair, Mrs. Rougham," Father replied. "Irrespective of the words I used on the spur of the moment, what I was getting at was that Christianity is a social as well as a personal religion and that this has been too often forgotten."

"What you mean by 'social religion' would need very careful defining, my dear Father. At the moment this is all I will say: as far as I know, Christ made one social reform only. It is fantastic, almost preposterous. It is never easy, even if it brings untold happiness. Sometimes it requires heroism. It has had astonishing results — even the overwhelming wealth of Christendom, due to social stability and certainty in heredity. It is monogamy and the sanctity of the procreative act."

"But Mrs. Rougham, you must remember that two-thousand years ago..."

"Keep quiet! And to safeguard such an astonishing social reform," Judith continued, "He required even more of his special friends: celibacy in the ministers of his sacraments and virginity in his ministers of prayer — because that is what nuns are. You can talk sociology to your heart's content, my dear Father, provided monogamy is your theme."

"Judith — may I call you Judith? To me Mrs. Rougham means Mrs. Brigadier. Judith, you are superficial and cruel..."

"You are not all that profound and charitable yourself. But have another sherry. Then I must get ready for dinner. However, I have a little problem, Father. You tell me I can celebrate the *anamnesis* as well as you. Do you believe in the Real Presence? Is there any point in your bringing me Holy Communion tomorrow?"

"Don't worry about that, Judith. I intend to do what the Church does. My consecration is valid even by your standards. As for myself, 'symbolic reality' seems the best term available, but I have not been able to work out what it means."

"My poor Father! So I shall receive in certainty what you give me in doubt. You had better go or I may be sick."

Judith felt desperately sorry for Father Paul Cromer. He was obviously a good man who had lost his way. It was difficult to see how he could ever find it again. He upset her far less than the press had done. In her eyes he was not — could not be — the cause of the new outlook, but the victim, indeed the first victim she had met. Her heart bled for him. Although she had contradicted and laughed at him, she had kept a very kindly attitude and tone of voice. But had she offended him? Would he come again?

He did. The faithful hound came sniffing round on the following Friday. He was a glutton for punishment. This time he started off on another track.

"From what you were saying on Tuesday, Judith, I think the trouble is that you are not taking a broad enough historical view of the problem facing Christianity. You look at it only as it affects you personally, not in its socio-historical context. It is surely undeniable that in the last century-and-a-half the Church has lost ground insofar as she is a social institution. Indeed, she has been on the defensive ever since the Middle Ages. First she lost the educated classes and then the workers in a massive way. It started with the alienation of the scientific world at the time of Galileo, which has continued right down to the present day. Then at the beginning of the last century she lost the industrial workers, from the management through to the proletariat, since the whole Industrial Revolution took place outside her jurisdiction or cognizance. And now even the artisan in the town and the farm-hand in the country are falling away from her.

"But there is hope. A compensatory factor is at work. For about a hundred years — rather more: since La Mennais — a new Catholic intelligentsia has gradually been taking shape. At last it has become coherent and self-conscious; it is adult. It has forced the council on the Church and by the same token will force its views on the council. No longer will the Church appear as the last refuge of conservative obscurantism. No longer will scientist or scholar have to blush at being a Catholic. The new Catholic elite accepts their findings and will work from their hypotheses. It is the same with the proletariat: the worker-priest will espouse the cause of the workers, will crystallize their aspirations and vindicate their claims. The Church will no longer dominate as she has attempted to do since the age of Constantine. She will guide and educate, as Jesus did himself."

"My dear Father, how absolutely marvelous!" Judith replied. "You express yourself with wonderful clarity. Neither do I deny the intentions of at least some of the new elite, including yourself.

What I do deny are the facts. You say that the Church has progressively lost the educated classes and the workers. Let us look at a reality which we can both verify: your own parish. You know it better than do I, so correct me if I'm wrong.

"First, concerning the educated classes. At the turn of the century the Roughams were their only representatives. Now, among sizable landowners there are the Fitchfields, Stubbingtons and Worseleys; among the professionals, to whom you are so keen to belong, there are two doctors, of whom you received one, and a dentist, whom you also received; one of the three vets and the wife of another; one of the four solicitors and again the wife of another. Oh! I was forgetting old Lady Snares, J. P., who was received by your predecessor. You have the schoolteachers. The nuns at the convent are educated women. They came in about 1925, didn't they? There is that young surveyor and his family. Yes, and the wife and children of the accountant — charming people. Good heavens! I could go on forever. Rougham is a hotbed of Catholic culture.

"As for the working classes, you can tell by your parish school. I remember Lucy saying that it was opened in 1910 with thirty Catholic children out of fifty pupils aged between five and fourteen — it catered for 'further education.' What have you got now? About a hundred-and-eighty Catholics on roll from five to eleven-plus, and you send the older ones to Royston. And I doubt if the total population of the area has more than doubled in the period.

"But you brush all these splendid — and sometimes heroic — people aside as being steeped in personal religion, totem worship, tribal custom, class prejudice and the like. You maintain against the evidence of your own parish that Catholicism has failed merely because you do not happen to like the way in which it has succeeded. Why? Can the reason possibly be because the religion has succeeded although the priests have failed? Anyway, your new Catholic intelligentsia has absolutely no roots, no more among the educated than the uneducated classes. You are its sole representative in this parish and you know it. If the council has been engineered and run by a few disgruntled priests like you, my dear Father, heaven help the poor laity like me!"

"Yes," said Father Cromer, "in a way I agree that religion has succeeded and we priests have failed. But we have failed because of our blind obedience to the ecclesial structures instead of to Christ. The council will change all that precisely because it will be run by the new elite. We alone have a positive program and the necessary organization. But you need not be frightened of it, Judith. It will provide a wonderful renewal of fellowship and partnership, both in religion and in society. You just wait and see. But you must discard your prejudices, inevitably strong in a convert."

"Dear me! I was forgetting that I was only a convert and a marriage one at that: the dregs. But tell me, what do you think is going to happen to all your cradle totem-worshipers and tribal customers here in Rougham?"

"With any luck, most of them will lapse physically as they already have spiritually," Father Cromer replied without a qualm. "We shall then be able to start again from scratch with a new ecclesial group, conscious of the whole Christ, in which personal commitment will be centered totally on the group: a new, living church in fact."

"So you will start again from scratch? Well, it is certainly true that you will have to scratch Rougham from your new, living church."

"I wish you would not harp on Rougham. As I said, the trouble with you, Judith, is that you fail to view the problem facing Christianity in its broad socio-historical context. You reduce it to Rougham or even to your own personal sentiments. I suppose it is the feminine outlook."

Judith again roared with laughter. "Father, you are tremendous! Not only am I a marriage convert but a sentimental female as well. Yes, sentimental I am: I love my religion with my whole being. And cold, unloving intellectuals like you, Father, have no more right to trample on my sentiments than to change the object of my love. I am a convert as well. But tell me, Father, was I received or deceived into the Church?"

"At least you cannot blame me. Who did?"

"A Jesuit called McEnery."

"I wonder if he is the man who has just been sent out to Bombay to stir up the Jesuit province?"

"I don't know; but if so, he would certainly do it. However," Judith continued, "you have not answered my question: did he receive me or deceive me?"

"No, he did not exactly deceive you, but he gave you blinkers which you will find it difficult to shake off."

"Thank you, Father. So his blinkers did deceive me. And I suppose you harnessed with identical blinkers all your converts here at Rougham. Now you tell us to remove them. Cannot you see that in doing so you have lost all credibility? But I don't want to be nasty. For once let the female leave personalities alone. You accuse me of harping on Rougham. But your intellectual church exists only between the pages of books, whereas the physical church is compounded of thousands and thousands of Roughams. If we widen the spectrum from Rougham to England, we do not get a different image. By the 19th century, you say, we had irretrievably lost the intellectual elite. The evidence points in exactly the opposite direction. From Cardinal Newman to the present day, never in the history of the Church has there been such a galaxy of intellectual elitist converts, with Faber, Manning, Patmore, Wilde, Baring, Chesterton, Dawson, Knox, Waugh, Greene, Ross-Williamson and a host of others who do not spring to mind. As for the proletariat — as you insist on calling those less educated than yourself — you only have to look at the rise in infant baptisms. Be a dear and get a couple of Catholic Directories from the library. The Brig files the very old ones in the North Wing, but bring this year's and the oldest available. They are on the bottom shelf to the right of the fireplace."

Father Cromer did as he was told. He came back with the directories for 1955 and 1963. They contained the statistics for two years before publication, that is, for 1953 and 1961.

"There you are," said Judith. "Infant baptisms in 1953 were 90,936 and in 1961 they were 129,469. Incidentally, I notice that converts had increased by twenty percent in the same period, from 11,900 to 14,174. Thus your catastrophic loss in the working classes amounts to an increase in infant baptisms of 38,533, or over forty percent in eight years. It is fantastic. And don't try to shrug it off with Irish immigration and national averages because

I happen to know that they scarcely affect the issue. It is not your logic, my dear Father, which is at fault; it is your facts."

"But England is in a rather special position. You are still being parochial. Look at France which, from the Eldest Daughter of the Church, had become a mission land — 'Pays de Mission' — in the 1940's. You can scarcely deny that."

"I deny it absolutely, Father. After the persecutions of the Revolution followed by Napoleon's strangling grip, the revival of Catholicism in France during the course of the 19th century will one day be accepted by historians for what it is: among the most glorious pages in the Church's history. From Gueranger and Lacordaire to St. Therèse and Charles de Foucault, passing through Montalembert, Le Play, La Tour du Pin, Albert de Mun, Abbots Cabrol, Chautard and Marmion — and I cannot remember a tithe of them — why, it is simply fantastic! Then, after the violent persecutions around 1905, when all ecclesiastical property was confiscated, just look how rapidly it picked up: half a dozen *Instituts Catholiques* re-bought, refounded and refinanced; the same with seminaries, colleges for higher education, village schools, monasteries and convents, bishops' palaces and parish halls — the lot. The effort of French Catholics between 1910 and this year of grace to restore the shattered edifice of their faith's physical expression was quite as prodigious in its way as was that to build their stupendous cathedrals in the Middle Ages. Such are the facts, Father. Moreover, not only is the pocket the most sensitive organ in the human frame, but the French are not notorious for lack of thrift. And it was in the early 1940's, in the middle of this splendid effort, that a couple of disgruntled priests dare publish their book on *La France, Pays de Mission*. The little swine! But, as clergy, they were at the receiving end; they had not had to pay and count the cost."

"Judith, you are being absolutely horrid. It is all pure casuistry. You are incapable of looking at the principles involved."

"I am not half as horrid as I should like to be. Unfortunately, words escape me. Yes, it is casuistry: I am looking at the facts which contradict your theories. And don't you dare say that it was the final fling of the *bourgeoisie* to keep its grip on the masses.

There was an equally magnificent flowering of the Catholic elite, and this quite irrespective of political outlook. Even at Rougham I suspect that you have heard of Leon Bloy, Péguy, Claudel, Maritain, Bernanos, Mauriac, Maurras (who died a Catholic), Simone Weil (who failed to), Gabriel Marcel, Stanislas Fumet, Gustave Thibon and a host of others.

"I suppose you have read Orwell's *1984*, Father? No? Well, you should. Among its themes is the manufacture of the future by the falsification of the past. This is exactly what your New Intelligentsia is doing with the Church. If you think France is still too parochial, where do you want to look? At the *Kulturkampf* in Germany? At the rise of Catholicism in Holland and the U.S.A.? At the fact that the world capital of Protestantism, Geneva, has become a predominantly Catholic city? At the history of the missions over the last hundred years? Name your subject, but produce your facts."

"No, Judith," Father Cromer replied, rather abashed by Judith's diatribe, "the trouble is not your facts but your total lack of idealism."

"So the ground has shifted. I am no longer the sentimentalist; it is you who are an idealist. I tend to agree. But have another glass of sherry and then you must go. You see, the idea of a drink can completely absorb you; the advantage of having one is that you can absorb it. Therein lies our basic difference, Father. You are a romantic who lives in his longings; I am a classic who lives in reality. At this moment of time, the reality is that George is crying, so goodbye."

Judith began to regain her strength. She no longer suffered from dizziness and occasional vomiting. She could walk to Mass herself; the church was just at the end of the drive, only a few hundred yards away. There was no need for Father to bring her Holy Communion. This did not prevent him from turning up for more punishment.

On the following Tuesday Father Cromer's theme was the manifest corruption of the Church ever since the age of Constantine. "From the moment the Church became a power it inevitably played power politics. It was a prisoner of its own wealth. For over fifteen centuries, those responsible for the Christian Faith have neglected Christ's solemn pronouncement that 'My kingdom is not of this world.' "

"Splendid, Father," Judith had replied, "but only last Friday you were damning the Church for not preaching the 'Whole Christ,' by which you seemed to mean Christian social teaching. Today you are damning her for being too involved in social affairs. But I agree that your contradiction is more apparent than real. It arises from the confusion of 'social' with 'political.' The Church is inevitably involved in social affairs because she is obliged to maintain the moral law even if it runs counter to political or penal law. On the other hand, she should steer clear of politics. If she did not, either she would establish a theocracy or she would inevitably be led to add a moral obligation to a purely penal law. Both alternatives have been tried out in history — the first by, say, Hildebrand and the second by Napoleon; neither was sufficiently successful to warrant imitation.

"For once, Father, I am not going to be horrid and I shall not jeer at you. Perhaps it is you who will jeer at me. You see, I think that the distinction between the 'social' and the 'political,' between moral law and penal law, runs very deep. The cohesion of any group of human beings, be it the family or the state, depends on its recognition of the group's basic laws. In the ideal situation these basic laws are unquestioned. They form the moral framework in which the group operates. This moral framework is the social expression of the group's religion. The members of the group are free in the measure that this moral law is sufficiently strong and universally recognized to ensure the cohesion of the group. It is only when the moral law is either too weak or not generally recognized that the group is obliged to maintain its cohesion by political or penal law. It is cohesion by coercion.

"Now it seems to me that one of the most striking contributions of Christianity to society — on a par with monogamy — is the clear recognition of this fact. It is based on Our Lord's lapidary sentence: 'Render to Caesar the things that are Caesar's, and to God, God's.' Moreover, through the institution of the Papacy, the inviolability of the state's penal law is balanced by the infallibility of the Church's moral law. It is thanks to this delicate balance that political freedom has been an offshoot of Christianity.

"Obviously, since the age of Constantine there has been constant trouble between Church and state, the one attempting to use the state to enforce the moral law, the other to use the Church to give moral force to its political law. Anyway, it is not always easy to draw the line between moral and penal, between social and political. Inevitably, a thousand errors have been made by Church and state alike.

"Given this general view, my dear Father, you can guess my reaction to the contemporary scene. We live in a society in which there is no internal cohesion: no moral standards are universally recognized and no single group within the society holds unquestioningly to its moral principles — not even Catholics, apparently. Perhaps the last vestige of the moral law is that milk bottles can still be left on the doorstep without being swiped. Very well, since the cohesion of this group called England no longer depends on the internal recognition of a moral law, the state interferes with morality under the guise of sociology. The state has added moral infallibility to its natural penal inviolability. Just meditate on that, Father: if to the state's inviolability you add the Pope's infallibility, you land up with total tyranny, with the pre-Constantinian concept of the slave-state. This is exactly what has happened behind the Iron Curtain. It is what will happen here if the process continues: we shall build concentration camps for the morally free. Already the state's interference in morality is simply prodigious. It interferes not only in borderline cases such as the 'social services,' pensions and education, employment and wages, clipping the coinage under the guise of inflation with its natural concomitant of usurious rates of interest and so on, but also with purely moral issues: marriage and divorce, contraception and abortion, homosexuality and women's rights, etc. It is quite phenomenal. No Pope ever claimed to be half as infallible as does a modern prime minister. Moreover, the latter has, as the Pope has not, the police and the law courts to enforce his decrees.

"Thus the state has ceased to be purely political in order to become social. And what of the Church, Father? She is ceasing to be social in order to become political. She no longer wants to convert; she wants to liberate. She no longer tries to deal with the infinite moral problems of individuals; she preaches the easier alternative of political revolution. Her ministers have abandoned the fag and fug of the confessional for the excitement of the hustings and the aerials of the media. You no longer seem interested in the internal cohesion of your group — the One, Holy, Catholic and Apostolic Church — in the infallible moral cohesion which alone can withstand the inviolability of the state. No, you want to swamp the Immaculate Bride in the rising flood of human pollution.

"Rightly or wrongly, that is how I see things, Father. The quarrels between Church and state since the age of Constantine seem to me admirable. By and large they have created and preserved the freedom of the subject. Even in Gallican, Orthodox and Protestant countries, the fear of the Papacy has acted as a brake on the state. You wish to take your foot off the brake. Very well: we shall hurtle into the polluted flood of tyranny. However, even in the flood of pollution there will still be an Ark of Salvation full of queer animals, two by two, who cling to freedom and the supremacy of the moral law."

"Judith," said Father Cromer at the end of this diatribe, "you are magnificent! But I don't know what it means. However, this much I will admit: we clergy have preached dogma and devotions until we are fed up with both. But we rarely preach about morality in the wide sense — what I might call the metaphysics of human acts. Anyway, I must get to the presbytery before the housekeeper's cat eats my sardines."

Thus do realities impinge on the deepest philosophical conversations.

The conversations continued. Judith and Father Cromer enjoyed them. They widened both their outlooks. Father Cromer had never imagined that there could be such a creature as an intelligent traditionalist. He discovered to his surprise that Judith was perfectly capable of defending herself, no matter how shortsighted he considered her outlook. On the other hand, Judith,

judging by the mass-media, had never imagined that a progressive
could be honest. But honest Father Cromer certainly was, no
matter how muddled she considered his arguments. How much
bitterness might have been avoided in the ensuing years if only
progressives had admitted that traditionalists were not all fools
and traditionalists that progressives were not all rogues — as did
Father Cromer and Judith. Alas! It was not to be.

On the following Friday Father Cromer waxed eloquent about
"a return to the sources, free from the mud of almost two
millenia of superstition..."

"Isn't it extraordinary, Father, how differently we view
things?" Judith asked afterwards. "You hate the broad river of
the Faith, more stupendous than the Amazon, fed by a thousand
tributaries which mingle their waters in its unity. No, you want
to find some obscure spring in the distant Andes which you claim
to be the source. But it isn't. The real source, like rain, comes
from heaven. But you will never see it as you grope about looking for sources under the protection of your umbrella. What I
will admit is that your obscure spring is likely to be so cold and
pure that nothing could live in it, not even an amoebiform
superstition.

"Yes, and concerning superstitions, they are the *fioretti* of
religion. I do not think that it would be difficult to prove the
truth of Christianity from the innocence, gaiety and moral purity
of its superstitions. Just compare them with those of ancient
Greece and Rome, let alone those of the East and darkest Africa.
Our superstitions are not mud. They are precisely *super*,
something which floats on the flood of the Faith — gay barges
with Our Lady as figurehead at the prow, a posse of saints
decorating the poop, gilt cherubs at play in the rigging and the
passengers fishing with rosary beads. The mud which chokes the
river is something heavy and dark; it sinks to the bottom. It is in-
frastition, my dear Father: great wedges of rationalism, boulders
of pride, the wreckage of doubt."

"But Judith, that is all pure poetry, metaphor," Father Cromer
objected; "there is not an argument in it."

"Of course it is. And I thank you for the compliment," Judith continued. "Until we see Absolute Truth face to face, all our truths are analogies, metaphors. That is why the deepest human thinkers, from Homer to Shakespeare and beyond, have always been poets, not philosophers. Even the blasphemies of Swinburne and Nietzsche become sublime the moment they allow their metaphors to carry them away. A metaphor always illuminates; it is some sort of reflection of the truth. It is rationalism which reduces everything to the turgid mud of our own incomprehension.

"But I wander, as women will. Let us get back to your 'sources.' The trouble, as I see it, with your 'return to the sources' is that you use the phrase to hide your intent. What you really wish to do is to jettison tradition. Back to the sources, before tradition ever existed! But this is pure archaeology. Now, archaeology is the study of what time has rejected, whereas tradition is precisely what time has preserved. You can dig up old bones, attach them with wire and jiggle them about as marionettes but, unlike a tradition, they will not be self-propelling. All you will have made is a puppet-show of skeletons.

"But why your hatred for tradition? I am pretty sure I know the answer, but I think we ought to leave it for another day."

The last of the conversations took place on Tuesday, May 21st. Judith had expected the subject to be tradition and had prepared some very formidable ammunition. Father Cromer arrived a little later than usual. He seemed hesitant and despondent. However, he brightened up after a couple of glasses of sherry. "It must have been about ten days ago, Judith," he began, "when you said that Christ's only social reform was Christian marriage. I presume consequently that in theory, at least, you approve of the marriage of the clergy." He talked about it a little in a desultory, detached sort of way.

"No, Father, I do not approve, for a variety of reasons, one of which concerns you personally. Whatever your yearnings concerning personal fulfillment, whatever your doubts about 'symbolic reality,' both you yourself and I can be certain of your good faith and basic rectitude, since you are willing daily to make the most fundamental of all human sacrifices. Celibacy is not a vow once taken, but a life lived. It is stupendous. It is because of it that I love and admire you. But there is more to it than that. It seems to me essential that the Catholic priesthood should be classless. Now, a man is not a social animal; a woman is. Be a priest the son of a railway porter, like Canon Slattery at home, or of a distinguished doctor in the I.M.S., like you, it matters not at all — and should not matter. But social status does matter to a woman, who has to rear and educate the children. You, Paul Cromer, are among the most handsome men I know; you are not a fool; you have a good social background. Women would queue up to marry you as a man. But as a priest, who do you think would marry you apart from a slut or a bitch?"

"But Judith," Father Cromer interposed, "you forget the Anglican clergy."

"No, I don't. They have precisely a social position, and it depends on whom they marry. Socially, the vicar's wife is a far more important person than her husband. Even the bachelor has a social status from the mere fact that he can marry. Moreover, a married clergy tends to become an hereditary caste — an upright and socially desirable one — but still a caste, cut off from its social unequals in a way the celibate priesthood is not. Therein, too, lies a wonderful by-product of celibacy: each generation of the laity must produce the priests for the next. Surely the most obvious manifestation of the holiness of Holy Church is that for a thousand years she has demanded such a sacrifice from her ministers — and got it. What other social group would dare demand it? The communists? Not they! No, vocations to the celibate clergy are an infallible guide to the laity's piety. I shall judge the present council by one simple statistic: the rise or fall in priestly vocations.

"But there is a side to priestly celibacy which concerns us laity. Of us the Church demands monogamy and the sanctity of the creative act. These, like celibacy, are not a vow once taken, but a life lived. You can have little notion of the discipline and sacrifice which they entail. Of course, God is not mean and gives us happiness away above our sufferings — as He does to you for your sacrifice of celibacy. Yes, but I fail to see how the Church can demand such sacrifice from the laity if she is not seen to demand yet more from her ministers. Anyway, it is ridiculous to talk about married priests before you have decided what to do with divorced ones. You are bound to get them, along with re-married ones. Moreover, you cannot fail to have noticed that the priests who advocate a married clergy are also those who preach contraception. The standards stand or fall together. There, Father: if you abolish monogamy and the sanctity of intercourse, then you can have a married clergy. But will you have Christianity? Will you have a religion of love and sacrifice — of sacrificial love on the part of God and man alike? No, you cannot empty Christianity of suffering and heroism."

"But Judith, my dear," Father Cromer interrupted, "surely this is high-flown nonsense? In actual fact, you are perfectly happily married to Edmund Rougham without all this melodrama of suffering and heroism."

"How do you know? Yes, I am wonderfully happily married to my Edmund as he is to me. We love each other body, mind and soul. But that does not preclude suffering. Dear Edmund, I think he suffers more than I."

Judith walked over to the sofa to pick up her bag. She took out a £5 note: "Here, take this and say a Mass in Thanksgiving for my Edmund."

Father Cromer had also risen. But he did not move. He looked tense. His fists were clenched. "No," he said, almost with a snarl. "I cannot possibly do that!"

"Good heavens! What's wrong? Have you got some bee in your bonnet about Mass intentions and stipends?"

"No, it's not that."

"What on earth is it?"

"I have too many stipends already."

"You can say it when you like — next year if you are as booked up as all that."

He still did not move. There was an appreciable silence. Judith felt a complete fool, standing there with a fiver in her hand. She was about to put it back into her bag when Father Cromer suddenly relaxed.

"Yes, I shall take it, Judith. And I shall say the Mass. I swear to God I shall."

He came over to her and took the money from her hand. He then folded her in his arms. Gently and slowly he kissed her on both cheeks.

Judith was so surprised that she made no resistance. She could feel his tears moistening her face.

"Thank you, Judith. You have been so kind. Thank you...I shall not be coming again as I shall have to prepare for the chancellor's visit. Goodbye! Thank you! God bless you." He left. He was still sobbing.

Judith stood for a moment in complete amazement. What could it possibly mean? Was Father Cromer in love with her? Was that why he had refused the Mass in thanksgiving for Edmund? No, it was not that: his hug and kisses had been absolutely innocent. They had been pathetic, not passionate; tender, not tense. Of that she was certain. It was a mystery. She would doubtless discover the answer after the chancellor's visit. Meanwhile, George was yelling blue murder...

XIII

DEATH AND CONVERSION

Whitsun weekend duly arrived. Judith was lucky: nobody expected her to do anything or even to appear very much. She met the chancellor and his missus at lunch on Saturday — a homely affair with no guests. The Brig and the chancellor got on fine, as oil and vinegar in a salad dressing. Perhaps neither of them had met their respective types on quite such easy terms. Obviously, the chancellor had met the noblest and richest in the land, but at functions or as critics or suitors. Apart from one of his old regimental sergeant majors, the Brig had never met anybody so unpolished yet so bright. "Blimey, Brig," said the chancellor, "how can you keep this joint going with the taxes we bung on you? You're a bloody marvel. You must take after your boy!" So that was all right.

The missus was perfectly charming. Basically she was as shy as her husband was brash, but years of political life had given her a veneer of confidence. After lunch she came up to see George. She doted on him. Poor woman, her own three children were terrible disappointments to her.

That evening there was a prodigious dinner party for the local bigwigs — social, political and union. It was the sort of mixed bag which the Brig enjoyed and handled perfectly. Judith was excused, but she joined the ladies afterwards. Later there was an unscheduled concert which she would not have missed for worlds. The distinguished gathering was entertained by the chancellor at the pianoforte, accompanying North Country songs interpreted by the missus. It was a novel experience for all. Judith loved it. It had an old-world charm which fascinated her.

It had been well-publicized that the chancellor was going to attend Sunday service in St. Gregory's Roman Catholic church. Indeed, his lordship the bishop had composed a special ecumenical form of worship for the occasion. Judith could not avoid it. It surpassed in horror her wildest nightmares. Since it would be grossly unfair to record her impressions, it would be best to quote from the local press.

Although himself a staunch Baptist, the Right Honorable the Chancellor of the Exchequer and Mrs. Barker, who have been staying with Brigadier and Mrs. Rougham at Rougham Castle, attended Divine Service at the Roman Catholic chapel of St. Gregory at Rougham on Sunday morning as an ecumenical gesture. The Service was conducted by the Reverend Paul Cromer, priest in charge of the Roman Catholic mission. The Chancellor read the Epistle, which was taken from the second chapter of the Acts of the Apostles. At the offertory Mrs. Barker gave an impressive rendering of Gounod's *Ave Maria* which was much appreciated by the large congregation. The sermon was preached by Monsignor Philip Pailey, representing the Roman Catholic bishop of Hertford. His text was: 'Outside the Church There is no Salvation,' from which, with an eloquence too rarely heard in our churches today, he showed that all men are members of the same church, 'since all are pilgrims in search of that Absolute Truth we call God.' In a fine outburst of rhetoric he exclaimed: 'For too long the Roman Church has proclaimed that she alone is in possession of the whole Truth; that Truth alone has rights; that error has none. At last we begin to realize the dignity of the human person, which transcends the accidents of right and wrong. At last we have learned — in the words of the great political thinker Gabriel Monod — 'that the essence of liberty is the liberty of error.' "

It was not really up Judith's street, nor anybody else's for that matter. Nobody dared mention it; it was unspeakable. Luckily the monsignor could not stay for lunch. But, of course, nothing could daunt the chancellor. During drinks before lunch he approached the Brig: "Didn't like your monsinger, Brig. I'm neither a theologian nor a fool myself, thank God; I've got a bit of common sense. 'The essence of liberty is the liberty of error' — poppycock. The only right that error has is to keep out of the way. That is what I am constantly telling those Tories. They won't listen. I suppose you vote for them — an error, Brig, an error: mend your ways. And who the hell is that Gabriel Moaner anyway? I suspect he's a frog. I don't like frogs — they're intellectual snobs. I prefer our class snobbery; it's more fun. Take my missus: she's a real educated, intelligent woman. Has she an ounce of intellectual snobbery? Not a bit: she married me — and good luck to her. Then, I'm a great one for maintaining that 'we're all going the same way.' I remember saying it to your Edmund. But it sounds different when another fellow says it — especially your Monsinger Pailey or Pasty or whatever he's called. If we're all going the same way, it's thumbs down, Brig, isn't it? Even if it's thumbs up, some people are going a dam' long way about it. My missus — she's an educated woman and reads books — my missus tells me that you Papists have a girl called the Little Flower (beastly name) who's found a shortcut. Well, your monsinger has found a mighty long one. I know the type well: the blighter wants a mitre." Everything about the chancellor enchanted the Brig.

Anyway, the chancellor and his missus had a grand old time and thoroughly enjoyed themselves. They departed on Monday, June 3rd, after lunch with profuse thanks and the promise to come again. They did.

Edmund drove them back to Westminster, depositing Richard at Walthamford on the way. He himself returned to the Dower House fairly early, before 7 p.m. After the excitement of the weekend he was feeling a bit lonely and did not relish the idea of supping in solemn silence, so he invited himself round to his friends the Waddingtons. After supper, Waddington insisted on listening to the 9 o'clock news. Two hours earlier, at 7:50 p.m. Italian time, Pope John XXIII had died.

It would be difficult to gauge the impact of this death on Edmund as on millions of other Catholics. The laity and lower clergy were nervous about the council but their confidence in Papa Roncalli was absolute. The laity in particular felt him to be their champion, their pope. He was gone. Presumably the council would remain. Moreover, the new pope was likely to be the nominee of the ruling clique in the council. If cardinals Lienart, Suenens, Léger, Alfrink, Döpfner, Frings and company could run without a hitch a council of three-thousand bishops, a conclave of an odd hundred cardinals would be as putty in their hands.

Edmund walked home despondent. He immediately rang up Judith. Yes, somebody had already told the Brig. Judith, of course, was not in the least upset by the Pope's death. She had always regarded him as an invention of the mass media. They would invent the new one if he played their game. Hence Edmund's and Judith's roles became reversed. Instead of Edmund's optimism bolstering Judith's misgivings, it was Judith's certainties which alleviated Edmund's depression. The net result of the conversation was that Judith felt she had better get home as soon as possible. Edmund was to fetch her and George on the following Sunday.

During the week Judith walked down to Mass on the Wednesday and Friday. On Sunday, June 9th, the whole Rougham family was present in the castle pew. Father Cromer did not preach. He merely announced that he was taking a holiday after the chancellor's visit. There would be no weekday Masses, but the dean would send a supply for the usual Masses on the following Sunday. Fair enough.

Shortly after 3 p.m., when Judith was packing George's and her own belongings in preparation for their return to Walthamford, Miss Buckett, the housekeeper at the presbytery, turned up in a great state of agitation. She demanded to see Mrs. Edmund and nobody else. She shut the door behind her and stood rigid. Great tears were rolling down her cheeks. There was nobody else in the room, as George and the nurse were next door. "He's gone," she said, "and he asked me to put this letter into your own hands." Judith took the letter from her. She read it.

Dear Judith,

I want to thank you — again and again — a thousand times!

First of all I want to thank you for taking me seriously. You were the only person to whom I could talk. I could not to a fellow priest and even less to the bishop.

You have saved my faith. It was not so much what you said but the serene conviction with which you said it. "Serene conviction" — that is what I lacked.

It started simply enough. I happen to dislike the bishop — a surly fellow and a martinet. I wrote a couple of articles which I hoped would annoy him. Doubtless he never read them. Anyway, it was innocent bishop-baiting. But I soon found myself in a clique which was not just bishop-baiting but pope-baiting and well beyond that — people to whom nothing was sacred. I was trapped.

At the other extreme, my uncle — my mother's youngest brother — was constantly badgering me to return to Bombay, where he is principal of the St. Francis Xavier Technical Institute. He could offer me the post of senior chaplain. Obviously, he knew nothing about my articles and took it for granted that I was as traditional as he. I quote from a typical letter: "The hierarchy and white priests have gone completely mad. They are foisting on us answers to problems which do not exist here. They consequently have first to create the problems. It is chaos. By and large, the Indian priests are good but gutless. It is left to us Portuguese and Goans to defend the Faith. Come, Paul…"

I was torn asunder.

The only answer seemed to be to contract out: to give up the priesthood and get married. I could do it easily enough as I am fairly well-off. Besides, I decided to marry a wealthy widow, Betty Quelch, whom the Brig knows quite well. I do not love her even remotely; but she is kindly and companionable. Moreover, she has no religion and I should not be dragging a Catholic into my sin. The wedding was fixed for Tuesday next, June 11th at Bristol, where she now lives. I chose the date so as to avoid a scandal before the chancellor's visit. I have too much respect for the Brig to do that.

It was your faith, not mine, which made me hesitate. I told Betty that I should have to think everything over after I had left Rougham and was in a calm state of mind. I consequently decided to leave Rougham today, June 9th, as arranged, but instead of getting married at Bristol on Tuesday, I should sort myself out at a pub I know in Dorset.

Then on that fatal Tuesday which I shall never forget, came the crunch. You offered me a Mass stipend. Was I to take it? Was I not? A decision had to be made taken then and there. There was no question of "sorting myself out."

I thank you. I took it. I said your Mass this morning. I shall continue to say Mass.

It is next Tuesday, June 11th, the proposed day of my marriage, that I shall fly back to Bombay. I shall do all that I can to preserve among my own people that faith which I received from my mother and has been saved by you. Please pay my deepest respects to the Brig and Mrs. Brig. What wonderful people they are: so supremely uncomplicated. And how kind to me!

And please do NOT write to me. Memories of Rougham are more likely to be tragic than agreeable. Perhaps you could just send me a Christmas card signed by Edmund and yourself.

Judith, I love you. I love you very, very dearly — but in a way of which Edmund need not be jealous.

God bless you both,
Paul Almeida

P.S.: I am reverting to my mother's maiden name.

XIV

POOR MILLI

It was on the Thursday after Judith's return from Rougham, June 13th, 1963, that Milli turned up in the late afternoon at Walthamford. It was a thing she never did. Judith used to lunch with her in central London or she and Edmund would dine in Chelsea. She was obviously upset, strange for a woman so singularly self-possessed. After nearly half a bottle of whisky she unburdened herself. She and Judith were alone. "Tubby wants me to divorce him. It's absolutely ridiculous. It's this bloody feminine possessiveness. I've told him he can sleep with Priscilla whenever he likes, but that is not good enough for her. She wants to marry him. Whatever that means.

"Tubby suggests that he marry her and then sleep with me whenever I like. But I'm not having any of that. He even hinted that, if I divorced him, he could marry Priscilla and they'd both come and live with me: Tubby and two Mrs. Bradfields, the start of an harem. He's only forty. By the time he's sixty there might be a dozen of us. Have to hire an hotel! What's your answer? Come along, Judith, advise me. Don't sit there like a gherkin. Be helpful!"

"Milli, darling, I am desperately sorry for you," said Judith with some hesitation. "But it is not terribly surprising. Tubby's a nice, fat playboy who rolls around without any sense of direction. He has no principles or morals to guide him. It must have blown up frightfully suddenly as neither of you mentioned it while I was in hospital."

"Well, I suppose it was sudden in the way that the saucepan always boils over the moment you stop looking at it."

"But if you don't really want to divorce him, I don't see why you should."

"Don't be silly, girl. If I don't divorce him he'll divorce me.

One thing: we have never hidden anything from each other. When we married, we agreed to allow each other our liberty. He must have enough evidence to sink an iceberg. Don't you think it shocking?"

"What? The evidence against you?"

"Of course not! But using it to blackmail me into divorcing him."

"Oh Milli! How can I help you? How can I advise and console and sympathise? We simply have no standards in common."

"At least you can say that Tubby's an unmitigated shit."

"But darling, I don't think so. I only think that he is very, very mistaken."

"I suppose I'm meant to take that as a compliment."

"Well, I didn't quite mean it as such, although I am sure you are worth a thousand Priscillas. What I meant was that he had a wrong view of marriage."

"I'm beginning to think that I have, too!"

"I'm sure you have, Milli. On your own lack of principles, I don't see why you should not let Tubby marry Priscilla and have him when you want to. It might save you a lot of trouble and money. I don't see what marriage means to you."

"Humph! There's something in that. But marriage does mean something. It gives one a base from which to operate. You know: like ships. They carry a flag from Liberia or somewhere, no matter at which port they happen to call. Then, there is more to it than that. Tubby has just aborted the girlfriend of a famous politician. They're bound to give him a knighthood. Priscilla wants to become Lady Bradfield. The disgusting snobbery of the lower classes!"

"Who is Priscilla, anyway?"

"A little trainee nurse at the hospital. She's very pretty, with a beautiful figure. Her breasts wobble up and down when she walks. Tubby won't get her match easily. You know, my dear, he's become frightfully gross and..."

"All I can say is that, under such circumstances, I'd divorce him even if I did not have to — as you do."

"Judith, you are a little hypocrite, aren't you? There you are, a

Roman Catholic, obliged to maintain the sanctity of marriage and you advise your darling cousin to divorce. I like that!"

"But Milli, you are not married to Tubby at all. Priscilla is merely doing to you what you did to Cynthia. It is Cynthia who is Tubby's real wife."

"Good God! I think I could sue you for that. Not married to Tubby? Of course I am! But you're not comparing me to that wet Cynthia, are you? Incidentally, I'll let you into a top-drawer secret: Cynthia was the politician's girlfriend. Don't you think it's frightfully funny?"

"No, I don't. I think it unutterably sordid and pathetic."

"You are a dear: one minute a hypocrite and the next a prude. Anyway, I suppose I have got to divorce him. It's a colossal bore."

"No, I think it good. In the eyes of God you have never been married to Tubby. You can find some upright and charming man and make a real go of marriage."

At this juncture Edmund came in. "Hello," said Milli, "Judith has just been advising me to divorce Tubby. Says I've never been married anyway. She'll be telling me I'm a virgin next. Then I'm to get tied up with somebody like you and be snug and smug like a bug in a rug. I think it's all sordid and beastly myself, but I suppose I had better follow my holy little cousin's advice, eh, Edmund?"

Well, there it was. The case was undefended. Tubby was duly divorced. Priscilla became the third Mrs., and in due course the first (but not last) Lady Bradfield.

XV

THE CONVENTIONAL CONVENT

It seemed a bit hard on Judith to have to put up with Cromer and Milli in the same week. However, neither event surprised her, and both in their very different ways were success stories.

Concerning Father Cromer, Judith had often thought that the changing attitude in the Church must put an unbearable strain on good, devout priests such as Paul Cromer — especially if they happened to be rather weak characters, such as he. Even the mightiest cathedral would collapse if all its buttresses were suddenly removed. It was scarcely surprising if the clergy did. But, weak as he was, Cromer did have principles and, consequently, a conscience.

Incidentally, Judith simply did not believe that the human conscience was some mysterious, psychological faculty all on its own. It consisted in relating one's acts to one's principles: no principles, no conscience. Cromer's religion, no matter how shaken, had given him principles and consequently a conscience. Quite unwittingly, Judith had appealed to it. The result had been marvelous. No wonder he loved her: she was a sort of mother who had given him rebirth. And Judith too loved him, precisely with the sort of tenderness a mother has. Also, he was quite right about writing: letters, inevitably trite, could only tarnish the impact of the original experience. Dear Father Cromer, she would never forget him in her prayers.

Milli, of course, was the exact opposite. She had a very forceful character but no conscience. However, quite unwittingly, of course, she was certainly doing the right thing in divorcing Tubby. Indeed, Judith was surprised the marriage had lasted as long as it had. Besides, it was invalid and Milli might be able to induce some perfectly decent man to marry her. But most important, a divorce would get Milli out of Tubby's clique. Until she became a Catholic, Judith herself had not realized how frightful that clique was: people with no principles, no consciences, no morals. They were rational, even brilliant, but mere animals. In fact they formed that world on which Pope John had wanted to open a window. Perhaps Milli could shut it out, just as Father Cromer had done. Judith prayed she would. Not only did she love Milli dearly but she was eternally grateful to her for having introduced her to Edmund and having taken her in when her father had thrown her out.

Fortunately the sheer process of living takes up most of life. These thoughts and sentiments merely flashed through Judith's mind. Most of her time was absorbed by George. Then there was Richard.

Richard had been five in March 1963. Already in the previous July Judith and Edmund had arranged for him to start school after Christmas at Waltham Convent. This was duly done. The nuns ran a minibus to pick up the children in the Walthamford area, so there was no problem of getting him there and back. Naturally enough Judith's first concern upon her return to the Dower House was to inspect the convent. Up till then she had only visited it once, and that was prior to her pregnancy with George.

Curiously enough, although she had been a Catholic for over six years, she had never had any personal contact with nuns. She was enchanted with them. They were wonderfully Irish and taught the little English boys and girls those gorgeous rebel songs. It was too sweet to hear their innocent little voices piping away about "the heel of the tyrant." The congregation was called The Daughters of St. Patrick — who seemed to have a lot of them. Their habit was most distinctive. It was black, but the very full skirt hung beautifully on fat and lean alike. The bodice and arms were close-fitting, but over them was an extremely elegant cape, elbow length. It was kept in place by a large brass and ebony crucifix hanging from the neck on the breast. The tall neck-piece was a miracle of starched and goffered linen. The head-gear was a curious square contraption which looked like nothing so much as an old-fashioned typewriter swathed in a black veil. A pair of starched blinkers and a prodigious rosary clanking from the belt completed the accoutrement. The Daughters of St. Patrick were recognizable from a mile away.

They were immensely jolly between storms of Irish paddy. Nothing was ever too much trouble. They practiced a curious kind of communism to which Judith had eventually to call a halt. One Friday afternoon Richard came back coatless from school. "You must be sure to bring it back on Monday," said Judith.

"But I can't, Mummy!"

"Don't be silly. Why can't you?"

Tears were welling in Richard's eyes: "Sister gave it to Jimmy and said you would buy me a much nicer one."

The first thing Judith noticed about nuns in those bygone days was that you could never tell their age. A beak protruding from starch provided inadequate evidence. Judith felt quite sure that the headmistress, Sister Velabra, was a woman of about forty until a parent of that age happened to mention that she had taught her mother. The combination of their agelessness and their improbable names made it awfully difficult to remember which was which. It was wiser to play safe and just call them "Sister." Judith tripped up several times, notably when she mistook the mother general, who was visiting the convent, for the old duck who pottered about weeding the garden. In fact, a not insignificant result of the habit was to give nuns the security of anonymity.

The habit also helped to make it clear that nuns were not social welfare workers, a set of do-gooders who club together for convenience's sake. Good heavens! There was not much convenience at the convent. One day Reverend Mother showed Judith with much pride four minute cubicles she had just built, with the unheard-of luxury of running water. The basins were a little bigger than a porridge bowl. Judith shuddered: if that was the new, what must the old have been like?

But the physical inconvenience was not the real point. There they were, sixteen intelligent and well-educated women, boxed up for life on top of each other, themselves with vows of virginity but intent on educating other people's children — and this for no personal recognition or reward whatsoever. It was ridiculous to talk about escapism. After six months in the convent they must have become totally disillusioned with the religious life and started to acquire fantastic illusions about the world they had left.

To leave would be escapism, not to stay. Yet there they all were. And in those days they did not pop over the wall like a set of champagne corks. It required more than discipline and high ideals. It required deep devotion, a capacity for self-abnegation, for surrender. And the surrender could not be for the sake of humankind, which might be better served if they were in the world. No, it was a surrender to God, whom they adored to the point of abnegation of their own being. Judith admired and loved them. She forgave in advance all their shortcomings, even those of Sister Cosmedine, Richard's form-mistress.

Judith saw most of Reverend Mother, an absolute poppet, whose sole concern was the welfare of the nuns, spiritual and physical. She spent most of the day praying in the chapel and keeping accounts, and most of the night sorting out the sisters' quite outrageous quarrels. She was well-versed in the great mystics and talked quite uninhibitedly about prayer and things divine.

Judith would have liked to have known the headmistress better. She was a tall woman with wonderful dark brown eyes. Her innate elegance even shone through her habit. Unfortunately, she was terribly shy, reserved and forbidding. It was the parents, however, who were frightened of her, not the children.

Then there was a young nun of whom Judith was very fond. In the middle of a perfectly normal conversation about the weather she would come out with a staggeringly disconnected remark: "Yes, it's wonderful to see the daffodils in bloom again and if only you were less intransigent, Mrs. Rougham, you would have made an excellent nun." Or, "It was very cold this morning, but that little girl over there is particularly dear to the Sacred Heart and I think it will rain this afternoon." She was a comic creature who thought on two planes at once.

In fact, the only person whom Judith disliked at the convent was the chaplain, one Father Mallon. He was getting on, but had not improved with age. To start with he was the complete hypochondriac. He brought a little bottle of pills with him onto the altar in case he got indigestion from saying Mass. He blew his nose constantly for fear that he might catch cold. He used an antiseptic talc on his fat, flabby hands. He was also a snob, both social and intellectual. Worst of all, he spoke with so refeened an accent that Judith could not help dropping her "*h*"s when she talked to him. However, at Mass one saw little more than his bald patch and heard no more than the burble of Latin.

The convent, in fact, began to play quite an important part in Judith's life. On Saturdays, when Canon Slattery said a late Mass if he did not have a wedding and Edmund started out early for Rougham, Judith drove over to the convent for Mass. She stayed for a cup of tea while she talked with Reverend Mother about things divine. It was marvelous.

One thing, however, about Reverend Mother puzzled Judith. It was her unfailing optimism concerning the council. One Saturday in October — when the second session of the council had got underway and it was not difficult to see in which direction it was going — Judith was naughty enough to tackle her on the subject.

"Tell me, Reverend Mother, you who can see so clearly that the Church needs reforming, what do you think requires reform in the Daughters of St. Patrick?"

"To be sure, we are a new congregation, only founded in 1861, so we are absolutely up-to-date. But old orders like the Benedictines, Canonesses of St. Augustine, Poor Clares, Dominicanesses, Carmelites, it is they who will have to be updated.

"Come, come, Mother! Surely you can think of something? Your headgear, for instance, seems rather fanciful."

"Oh, but if you could read the symbolism of it in our holy founder's sermons!"

"Well, your goffered neckwear. It must be a bit uncomfortable and take hours to iron."

"To be sure, it's the most comfortable neckwear in the world! If I were not a nun, I should still wear it for comfort's sake. Although, although...Thank you so much for mentioning it, Mrs. Rougham. It would never have crossed my mind. I must write it down, in case we have to throw something to the dogs, as it were. I suppose plain linen would do just as well — but it would not be as comfortable."

"What about your blinkers?"

"Quite essential! You see, we don't face each other across the choir. The holy founder wanted us to face the Blessed Sacrament. If it weren't for the blinkers, as you call them, we'd have no privacy at Mass and our devotions. Sister 'Nosey' would see exactly what her neighbours were up to. Besides, they force us to look at each other straight in the face: no shiftiness among the Daughters of St. Padrig!"

"Surely the length of your habit must be inconvenient? It practically touches the ground. Wouldn't it be more convenient if it came an inch above the ankle?"

"Really, Mrs. Rougham, how can you suggest such a thing? At the moment the sisters can wear what shoes they like as nobody sees them. And they don't have to waste time cleaning them; the habit polishes them automatically. If the habit were over the ankle they'd want expensive shoes with heels, and they'd miss morning meditation for cleaning them. And the ones with pretty ankles would want nylon stockings. And what would St. Padrig say to that? It would be the ruin of our holy congregation."

"Well, let's leave your gear. Isn't your discipline a bit meticulous and outmoded?"

"Nonsense, Mrs. Rougham! In the world you have to fall in with the whims of the people round you, your family, neighbours, workmates. That's a constantly changing discipline. Here we merely obey the rule. No, we don't even obey it; we live it. If a sister does not live it but finds the rule a discipline over and above her own life, then she has no vocation and sooner or later will leave us."

There was a look of sadness in Mother's eyes as she made the last remark. Judith felt that she was talking about a real person, not in the abstract. And she could guess whom: that youngish nun, perhaps in her thirties, Sister Pantaleone, who did not look you straight in the face and was as hard and cold as only the soft, warm-hearted Irish can be.

"But your spirituality, Mother. Don't you think that a nasty-minded reformer might suggest that you have rather too many *petites dévotions*?"

"Who has ever heard of such a thing? What you contemp-tuously call *petites dévotions* are the icing sugar on the spiritual cake. Besides, there is not one which was not recommended by our holy founder."

"Supposing the reformers said the holy founder was a fool?"

"May Jesus, his Holy Mother and St. Padrig save us from such blasphemy!"

It was wonderful. For some twenty minutes Judith questioned Reverend Mother to no purpose. Apart, as a concession, for the neckwear, all was perfect in the Congregation of the Daughters of St. Patrick. Love and loyalty were truly there.

Nevertheless, as she drove home, Judith felt depressed. The Daughters of St. Patrick were a teaching order — and a very good one at that. It took little boys up to nine, but its principal activity was to educate girls up to university level. These were the future mothers of the all-important middle classes. The reformers could scarcely be expected to keep their hands off them. Whatever Reverend Mother might say, the holy founder and his rule would certainly be relegated to the dustbin.

However, with any luck the convent would last out until September 1966, when poor little Richard would have to be banished to his boarding prep school.

XVI

OCCUPATIONAL THERAPY

After the birth of George, total continence between Edmund and Judith seemed inevitable. That it was a strain, who can doubt? But they loved each other unquestioningly. If continence was to be the expression of that love, so be it. Physically, perhaps it was harder for Edmund, but Judith felt it acutely in her mind. It was all her fault. Were it not for Richard and George, she sometimes wished to die so that Edmund could marry a stronger girl than she and lead a normal life. No, apart from the boys, that would not do. She knew that Edmund loved her — even to the point of such a sacrifice. Besides, she too loved her Edmund to the point of being willing to accept his sacrifice.

On their honeymoon Pius XII had said that "suffering is mercy." She could vaguely see what he had meant. Had she listened to the pundits neither Richard nor George would ever have existed. Neither could she have gauged the depth of Edmund's love. The marriage had entailed and was entailing some sacrifice. But what was that in comparison to its mercies? No, of course she must live! Where was her gratitude?

If Judith had one regret — but she scarcely dared let it enter her mind — it was that she did not have a little girl. She was surrounded by males: Edmund, Richard, George and brother John. She had never been close to her mother. Lucy was sweet but belonged to the Brig. She had only two girlfriends, Pamela and Milli, but she did not see them very often and neither of them was a Catholic. The only Catholic woman for whom she felt a natural affection was Mrs. Larkin, the retired postman's wife; but apart from the social gap, she was old enough to be Judith's mother. At the back of her mind Judith could not help praying: "Sometime, somehow, dear God, please give me a little girl."

Obviously their religious conviction, internal piety and external

practice all contributed to making Edmund and Judith live in continence with joy rather than just bear it with resignation. It was
much the same as Reverend Mother's nuns who, she said, lived
the rule rather than obeyed it. And they were a pious young couple. Excepting on Saturdays when Edmund drove off early to
Rougham and Judith went to the convent, they were at weekday
Mass together at Holy Cross each morning at 7:45.

It was still 1963 and 1964. That most wonderful of inventions,
the silent Low Mass, really did recharge the battered battery of
the human soul. Canon Slattery said it particularly anonymously.
His own personality never intruded in the least. He was merely
the animator of a set of vestments and manipulator of the sacred
tools. Even the parts of Mass which were said aloud did not bear
the idiosyncrasy of his intonation; they were the distant rumble
of God's thunder.

Edmund thumbed a daily missal but in fact repeated a series of
acts of contrition, thanksgiving, adoration and the like which the
Jesuits had taught him in his childhood. They were excellent
media for prayer as he knew them all by heart. They did not
distract him because he did not have to think of them. What he
did was to supply the intention with all the love of which his soul
was capable. The acts, in fact, were not a source of activity but of
recollection. Judith arrived at very much the same state of prayer,
of recollection and adoration, but without using any set form of
words at all. It was only when she felt particularly distracted that
she took out her rosary. There they were each morning, side by
side. The Rougham Crucifix looked down on them in suffering
and mercy. The baby angels caught the Precious Blood from the
Sacred Wounds in their tiny chalices. And on the altar below the
image was the Reality.

It may also have helped Judith and Edmund that during the
period 1963-1964 they were both heavily occupied. Edmund's
new job at the Treasury consisted of writing the chancellor's
speeches for him. This was both difficult and time-absorbing,
partly because the chancellor seemed to spend his life making
speeches and partly because he was bubbling over with ideas
which he could not express. Edmund had first to guess what the

idea might be and then make it comprehensible. However, in time he got inside the chancellor's mind so that the guesswork at least was considerably reduced.

Then there was the Rougham Estate. The Brig had been 42 when Edmund was born. At 76 he was hale and hearty but clearly could not go on forever. He had handed over the whole estate to Richard as soon as the baby promised to be as tough as the Roughams usually were. It was a large estate with 4,000 acres in hand and another 800 rented out. Over half the township of Rougham also belonged to it as well as a couple of villages. When the Brig had inherited it in 1923 much of the land had been mortgaged and the property, including the castle, was in wretched condition due to the 1914-1918 war and the depression which followed. After inheriting the property the Brig retired from the army to look after it and beget an heir. He married Lucy in 1925 but Edmund did not turn up until four years later. During the second war he was too old for active service but kept the local Home Guard on its toes. After forty years of continuous residence and intelligent attention, aided by inflation and the rise in both agricultural prices and land values, from a dilapidated relic of past grandeur the Rougham Estate had become an immensely valuable property. Hence Edmund spent every Saturday and sometimes Sunday there. When the Brig died, he would have to give up the Treasury to look after Rougham. His country could dispense with his services, but his land could not. An absentee landlord does more harm than a plague of rats.

Judith was not only occupied in looking after Richard and George under the exacting eye of Giacinta, but in September 1963 she felt well enough to offer once more her services as a catechist to Canon Slattery. During the year of her absence from catechism, the canon had made much progress. A new and brilliant chief education officer had been appointed for the area, who did not apply too strictly the letter of the law: provided the head teachers were willing to cooperate, Catholic children in the state schools could not only be withdrawn from Agreed Syllabus Religious Instruction, but the canon could appoint catechists to teach them their religion on the school premises. All the head teachers had agreed, although there was difficulty in arranging the timetable in one of the small primary schools. The canon himself dealt with the boys' grammar school; there were no Catholics at the girls' grammar as they were automatically transferred to the convent; a retired head teacher, one Mr. Butterworth, was coping with the boys' secondary modern; Mrs. Larkin and two retired teachers looked after the primary schools. The gap was Dame Margot Welbeloved's Secondary Modern School for Girls. The headmistress was a certain Miss Portia Sowerby. She was willing to receive a Roman Catholic catechist under the same conditions as any other member of her staff, that is to say if she survived the interview with Miss Portia Sowerby. There had been no volunteers from the parish. Would Mrs. Rougham undergo the ordeal?

Judith duly filled in a form giving her age, education and the rest. She was invited to attend an interview. Miss Sowerby sat at her desk. Judith was given a tiny straight-backed chair a good six feet the other side of the desk, so that she would have to speak up to make herself heard and Miss Sowerby could examine her from the tip of her toes to the crown of her head. The interview started.

"Mrs. Rougham, I notice that you never attended a girls' school."

"Well, I was at Rodean and Somerville, Oxford."

"Those are not girls' schools. They are academies for young ladies. What experience have you in teaching girls?"

"None, except for some dear little creatures for catechism in 1961."

"You won't find any 'dear little creatures' here."

"Why? What do you do with them?"

"Don't be impertinent. The object of Dame Margot Welbeloved's Secondary Modern School is not to produce young ladies, but hard-working, upright, civilly conscious women, good wives and loving mothers."

"I should have thought it difficult to produce the one without the other. But if you say you succeed..."

"Mrs. Rougham, is it I who am interviewing you or you me?"

"There is always an element of reciprocity in such affairs, isn't there?"

"Humph! And you propose to teach the Roman Catholic religion to girls under my care."

"Yes, if you will allow me to do so."

"Do you think it appropriate to teach sectarian religion when the whole trend is towards inter-denominational ecumenicity?"

"Most certainly. Instead of being based on respect for convictions firmly held, ecumenicity is rapidly degenerating into ambiguity, when no convictions are held at all. I am told that you are a convinced Methodist, Miss Sowerby. Will the ambiguous statements of our respective pundits change in any conceivable way what either of us really believes? Of course not!"

"You have not answered my question. I did not ask you about me but about sectarianism among my pupils."

"Well, you are here to educate hard-working, upright, civilly conscious women. In no subject do you set out deliberately to supply your pupils with ambiguous answers. Two and two make four, not 'rather less than five.' The Norman conquest was in 1066, not 'in the course of the 11th century.' An ambiguity usually contains an element of truth but is always meant to deceive. A thumping lie will contain no truth but may not be meant to deceive. It can be a sheer mistake or said thoughtlessly or even out of *joie-de-vivre*. One can believe what is false but not what is ambiguous. If one cannot believe it, neither can one teach it. To teach ambiguity in religion is to teach no religion at all. It is therefore all the more imperative, Miss Sowerby, to teach the realities and certainties of religion at the grass roots, since our pundits are preaching ambiguity."

"You are used to lecturing, I see. You realize that we have girls up to 18-plus who have long since reached puberty. In their biology and social science classes they of course receive full sexual instruction along with the knowledge of the usual means of contraception. Do you propose to contradict this teaching in order to suit the precepts of the Roman Catholic religion?"

"Of course, Miss Sowerby. That is one of the reasons why I wish to teach here."

"And do you practice what you preach?"

"Madam, you are not my Father Confessor. If I practice what I preach, so much the better. If I do not, then at least I do not preach what I practice, which is the infallible way to destroy all notion of objective morality."

"So you believe in a bit of hypocrisy?"

"Not in the least. The hypocrite is not the person who fails to practice what he preaches, but the one who does not believe what he preaches. It is the self-righteous, not sinners, who are likely to be hypocrites."

"Humph! And what experience have you in pedagogic method?"

"None, apart from two catechism classes in 1961."

"From that inadequate experience did you reach any conclusions? For instance: what do you think of audio-visual aids? Of learning by rote? Is education primarily a process of shoving in or pulling out?"

"Yes, such problems did cross my mind. Concerning the audio-visual, it seems to me that children are over-sensitive to it. By demanding of them nothing but receptivity, it damages their own creative ability and prevents the natural development of their memory. It turns them into robots. Children are already swamped by it in their homes; it should be carefully rationed, if not excluded, from schools. On the other hand, one of the essential objects of education is to train the memory. I am therefore in favour of teaching children as much by heart as they can learn. It may go through their heads but it will affect their hearts. We do not say that we learn 'by head' but precisely that we learn 'by heart.' In that connection, I found that the difference between a stupid and an intelligent child had less to do with their power of absorption than their power of expression. As for shoving in and pulling out, you cannot reap what you have not sown. After the sowing the crop must still be manured with much hard work and occasionally watered with affection. One is 'shoving in' the whole time. Even then the crop may fail, but one will probably have prevented the weeds from growing."

"So even to D-streams you intend to teach the incomprehensible mysteries of your religion: the Trinity, the Real Presence, the Immaculate Conception, grace and whatnot?"

"Of course!"

"Thank you, Mrs. Rougham. You may start when I have arranged the timetable. You will be informed. It has been a pleasure to meet you, and I look forward to our close cooperation."

So that hurdle was passed. The trouble was that Miss Sowerby was a trifle too enthusiastic and classed as a Catholic pupil any child who she felt ought to be. Judith had to dismiss a number of Belfast Protestants with Irish names. But even after reducing her classes to an honourable size, she still had to take two on Tuesdays for the 11- to 13-year-olds and two on Thursdays for the 14s and over. About two-thirds came from totally-lapsed families. Also, until she faced some of the 16- to 18-year-olds, she had never realized how brutally hard the young female could be. But on the whole she found the work infinitely rewarding.

When Judith started at Dame Margot Welbeloved's Secondary Modern School, she felt less nervous of the reaction of the girls than of the staff. How would they take to a denominational, non-professional interloper? She need not have worried: they were perfectly agreeable. Of the fifty-odd teachers, no fewer than four turned out to be crypto-Catholics, including the head of the biology department. They became less cryptic once it was realized that Miss Portia Sowerby was possibly pro-Catholic and certainly in favor of Mrs. Rougham.

The head of the biology department was the most interesting. She was under forty — about ten years older than Judith. Rebecca Elliott was her name. She was the daughter of an evangelical clergyman with a living in Bedfordshire. She had been brought up very puritanically, with an almost Manichean hatred of the flesh, but at the same time with an overwhelming emphasis on "do-gooding." When she showed signs of being intelligent, her father sent her to Cambridge to study medicine. She was to become a missionary doctor, the zenith of do-gooding in her father's eyes. She qualified all right — quite brilliantly, in fact. The trouble was that she simply could not practice. After working a couple of years in hospital she broke down: nothing but bodies, bodies, bodies — flesh, flesh, flesh — day in and day out. She could not stick it. Her puritanical background revolted.

She could not exactly explain why, but to solve the dilemma between her hatred of the flesh and being a doctor she became a Catholic. Her father promptly excommunicated her from the family. She decided to become a nun. She joined the Veronican Sisters because she knew that they ran two first-class schools in which particular attention was given to medical studies. After her probation but during her novitiate she was allowed to teach anatomy, biology and kindred subjects.

However, Catholicism seemed to have exorcised her of do-gooding and of hatred of the flesh rather too effectively. Fortunately before she took her final vows, she fell madly in love with the father of one of her pupils. He was a wealthy undertaker. Indeed, who has ever met a poor one? She left the Veronican Sisters. The undertaker installed her in a flat at Potter's End. Rebecca came to teach at Dame Margot Welbeloved's.

Judith arrived at the right psychological moment. Rebecca's atavistic revulsion against the flesh was rapidly turning against the undertaker. It required the tiniest prod from Judith for Rebecca to push him out. She then returned to the faith and practice of her religion with all the enthusiasm of her first conversion. She asked Judith to pave the way with Miss Sowerby. This Judith did with great discretion. It was not easy to explain how the most anti-religious teacher on the staff had suddenly veered toward Popery.

"Humph!" said Miss Portia Sowerby. "I knew all along, from a confidential reference, that Rebecca was some sort of ex-nun. You can tell her that pity made me appoint her but respect will make me keep her."

XVII

WITHDRAWAL

Up to this date, September 1963, the Roughams could be considered as exemplary "committed Catholics." Owing to their social position they were naturally involved in diverse national organizations. Edmund was active in charities run by the Knights of Malta. Judith was on the boards of two hospitals and was vice-chairman of the Catholic Women's Association. But apart from that, they believed implicitly the Church's dogmas and unquestioningly obeyed her moral precepts. They had founded a parish, built its church and presbytery and were even now exploring the possibility of providing a primary school — of which more anon. Moreover, Judith's commitments were still expanding: she had just undertaken religious instruction at Dame Margot's school.

It was only after December 1963 that the first symptoms of withdrawal began to manifest themselves. It was in that month that Paul VI promulgated the council's first two documents: the Decree on the Mass-media and the Constitution on the Liturgy.

The Decree on the Mass-media scarcely differed from Archbishop Stourm's *schema* of 1962. Judith thought it rubbish. It did, however, have one positive result: from its promulgation onwards it became impossible to publish any opposition views in the Catholic press. There was much talk about the People of God and democracy in religion, but it was to be a one-party system with the usual 100 percent votes in favour of the party. In the following few months both Judith and Edmund wrote vaguely-concerned letters on a variety of subjects — the liturgy, ecumenicity, family planning, etc. — to every Catholic periodical they knew. Not one was published. Later they tried to insert advertisements announcing that the Latin liturgy was available at Holy Cross, Walthamford. They were uniformly rejected although Latin was still licit at the time. The humbug of it all nauseated Judith. She cancelled her subscriptions to all Catholic periodicals. That was the first straw in the wind. The process of withdrawal had begun.

On the other hand, the Constitution on the Liturgy seemed to Judith a perfectly reasonable document. Latin and the Immemorial Mass were preserved; a few harmless changes were permitted. In January 1964 Paul VI issued a *motu proprio* fixing the parts of the Mass to be said in the vernacular: the introductory psalm, the epistle, the Gospel and the like. At Holy Cross, old Canon Slattery stuck to the Latin, however. At the convent, Father Mallon used English, but it was perfectly tolerable once a week.

In September 1964 a new instruction was issued allowing the whole of Mass in the vernacular apart from the canon. It was to come into force on the first Sunday in Advent, November 29th. Judith knew nothing about it as she had stopped taking Catholic papers in the previous June. Canon Slattery had not mentioned it from the pulpit. Reverend Mother had not thought of telling her.

On Saturday, December 5th, Judith went to Mass as usual at the convent. She could not believe her eyes or ears. The altar had been moved forward by four or five feet. The tabernacle had been shifted and placed in a corner to the left on a tall, rickety Victorian stand with spindly legs such as convents seem to collect. It had previously supported an aspidistra. There was no crucifix. In its place stood a microphone. It looked like a serpent coming up from the bowels of the earth and rearing its ugly head to hiss at the priest.

Father Mallon tripped in. Judith had always avoided looking at him. But there he was, exactly where the Blessed Sacrament had been. To Judith's eyes the sight was unpleasant: the carefully pomaded hair, the protruding eyes with their condescending stare, the large sniffing nose, the precise little mouth with its deprecatory twist, the podgy hands.

It is common experience that the less pleasant a personality the more its possessor wishes to impose it. Father Mallon was no exception. All his life he must have been waiting for the new liturgy. In the name of God everybody would have to take a good look at him. All his movements had become significant, whether he waved his silk bandanna about before he blew his nose or made genteel movements with his little finger as he poured the wine into the chalice. It was all didactic, teaching common people how they should behave. That was bad enough, but the sound was infinitely worse. Judith could close her eyes, but she could not close her ears. The microphone seemed to add to the refeenement of his voice. Then, Father Mallon had a nervous sniff. It had not mattered in the old Mass as you could not see the twitch of nose and lip. Now, not only could the twitch be seen but the sniff came over the microphone high, clear, insistent; it compelled attention. He blew his nose, too, in a high tenor which made the microphone crackle. And the refeened voice over all!

After Mass Judith went to have her usual cup of tea with Reverend Mother.

"Good heavens, Reverend Mother," she exclaimed, "has Father Mallon gone crazy?"

"Didn't you know, my dear? Since Sunday last that is how Mass is to be said."

"What! A special decree from the council that all Catholics must look at Father Mallon?"

"That is more or less it, my dear. Of course, Father Mallon is a very clever and well-informed priest. There is nothing about turning the altar round, and the canon should be said in Latin. But Father knows an expert in Rome who says that is what is coming, so he might as well do it now. His lordship the bishop is enthusiastic."

"Well, it's ghastly," said Judith.

"Father says it is just how Mass was celebrated in the catacombs."

"It isn't. There were no microphones there. It might be tolerable if Father did a couple of turns: turned off the microphone and turned his back."

"It would help. But anyway, I cannot imagine John of the Cross saying Mass that way or St. Teresa answering up. A divine drama at which we were permitted to assist has become a musical comedy in which we are the actors. We shall be able to hear what is said all right, but we can never hear what's done: the Father uttering the Word made Flesh and the Word returning to the Father as the sacrifice for our redemption."

"Yes, Reverend Mother, and even on the human side all recollection has become impossible."

"Too true, my dear. The microphone cannot carry our adoration and gratitude, the emptying of our being in front of the only Real Presence there is.

"Cannot you do anything about it, Mother?"

"Nothing. I shall adore as I always have. But there will be an added note of gratitude: Jesus has allowed my heart to be broken at Mass just as His was pierced on the Cross." And Reverend Mother said this perfectly calmly, without any emotion. It was in Judith's eyes that the tears welled up.

Fortunately, in Judith, as in most people, compassion was an even stronger sentiment than passion. Her own dismay and anger at Father Mallon's performance was far outweighed by her sympathy for Reverend Mother's broken heart.

As she drove home, Judith could not help feeling how tragic it was that the priest had lost his anonymity. Of old, his personality and mannerisms simply had not mattered. In future they would matter enormously. It was all right for her, Judith, because she could drive round and pick her own priest. In which connection, thank God for old Slattery! But not so Reverend Mother; her daily Mass was indissolubly tied to enduring Father Mallon's idiosyncrasies.

But it was not only the priest who had lost his anonymity, so had the congregation. The faithful were meant to be up and doing, to participate, to express their personalities and be conscious of the community around them. Of old, the Mass provided almost the only time and place in all the world where one could get away from oneself, get lost. The expressions "lost in prayer," "lost in wonder," "lost in adoration" and the like are perfectly accurate. Of old, distractions had been the problem. Now, distraction was organized and continuous. The problem had become how to get lost.

It was not only the loss of personal anonymity which worried

Judith but that of the congregation as an entity. How vividly she remembered her first Mass at St. Aloysius's over seven years ago: the boisterous family with the kids with sticky sweets; the rosaries and *The Garden of the Soul*; its utter theocentricity focused on the Real Presence. It did not matter what the congregation did or who composed it. It would not have mattered had there been none at all. The congregation was as anonymous as Father McEnery. Its astonishing unity did not spring from human activity but from human surrender.

But the anonymity of the congregation had vanished completely. If Judith could complain of Father Mallon's idiosyncrasies, he must feel even more justified in complaining about his congregation. Nuns, parents, children, strays, were they playing their part properly? Luckily, he was facing them to make sure they did. But who was that fellow who did not follow the gym? Why could not people speak up? Was that woman shouting on purpose? Who the hell was bashing a rosary against the bench? And so on. Judith began to feel sorry for Father Mallon. Yes, poor Father Mallon; it was not really his fault. Anyway, she would put up with him for Reverend Mother's sake. She would turn up as usual on Saturday.

She did, on December 12th. The Mass seemed even more ghastly, now that she knew exactly what to expect. When it was over, she gathered up her belongings and went to the parlour for her cup of tea. She opened the door. Reverend Mother was not there. It was the headmistress, Sister Velabra.

"Do come in, Mrs. Rougham. Let me pour you a cup of tea. Sister Jane has asked me to explain certain things to you. Last week she felt unable to do it and this week she has had to go to the provincial chapter."

"And who is Sister Jane?"

"Reverend Mother. That is one of the things she has asked me to explain."

Judith sat down nonplussed and grateful for the alibi of the cup of tea. Sister Velabra remained standing, rigid and imperious. She continued: "Sister Jane asked me particularly to show you these photographs."

Judith picked them up. They represented a rather pretty young woman, presumably some welfare officer from the County Council. She was dressed in a fairly tight-fitting black coat and skirt. The skirt came to about two inches below the knee. She had on a white V-necked blouse with the collar folded over the jacket at the back. She wore a sort of veil — about the size of a man's handkerchief. It was pinned to the back of her head so that her ears were showing, as was her hair in the front.

"Yes, Sister, and what about her?"

"Sister Jane said that you might remember her spirited defense of our old habit. Well, that is the one due to be worn by all Daughters of St. Patrick as from New Year's Day."

"You're not joking, Sister?"

"Of course I'm not," said Sister Velabra, who was still standing, rigid and imperious.

"You don't mean to say that you are going to go about like that, Sister?"

"Of course I'm not. I shall wear this habit until it falls to pieces."

"But I suppose most of the nuns will?"

"The older ones, yes. The younger ones are already asking parents of the appropriate size to provide them with civilian clothes."

"You don't mean to say that they are all going to jump over the wall?"

"Not exactly, Mrs. Rougham. The fact is that there is no longer any wall to jump over."

"Sister, Sister, it is unbelievable!"

"Perfectly unbelievable, Mrs. Rougham. The Daughters of St. Patrick are the guinea pigs of the renewal. We have the honour to be the first congregation of women to be brought up to date."

"But what of Reverend Mother?"

"She has been summoned to the provincial chapter to hand in her resignation. The title and office of reverend mother have been abolished. So, incidentally, have our names in religion; that is why I call her Sister Jane. In her stead we shall have an elected sister superior."

"But won't the nuns re-elect her?"

"They cannot. She has been sent to a convent in Cornwall."

"Will they elect you?"

"They could not if they wanted to. I have been appointed to take a class of mentally-handicapped children in Jarrow. Besides, his lordship the bishop has indicated that the sisters should elect a member of their own community who is under forty years of age but over ten in religion."

"That restricts the field very drastically."

"In this community, it restricts it to one: Sister Gertrude, whom you may remember as Sister Pantaleone."

"That's the one who never looks you in the eyes?"

"Exactly."

There was silence.

Eventually Judith broke it. "Would you be so kind as to get me a piece of paper and an envelope, Sister?"

"You will find all you need in that little desk over there."

This is what Judith wrote:

Dear Sister Superior,

This is to inform you that I shall be removing my son, Richard, from your school at the end of this term. As I have not given you a full term's notice, I enclose a check for next term's fees. I remain deeply grateful for what the nuns — and particularly Reverend Mother and the Headmistress — have done for my little boy and have meant to me.

She handed it, open, to Sister Velabra. "Yes, Sister, and I am grateful. And I do admire you. And I love you dearly," she said as she rushed out of the room with tears in her eyes.

Sister Velabra remained standing, rigid and imperious. But there were tears in her eyes, too.

Withdrawal had indeed got underway.

In January, Edmund and Judith drove down to Cornwall to visit Reverend Mother. She looked frightfully old in her "renewed" getup. One could see her spindly legs, her scraggy neck, her rather large ears and the thin wisps of her dull grey hair. But she was still her old, gay self.

"I'm the scullery maid and do all the washing-up. It's wonderful! The best job I've had. Until now, I have always been a teacher or a reverend mother. I could never see the result of my work. It was terribly disheartening. But now, they bring me a pile of filthy plates; I go through a sort of baptismal liturgy and they all come up smiling and immaculate. And, as a bonus, I get my hands warm. It's marvelous! No wonder St. Teresa said that 'God strolls among the pots and pumpkins.' "

Yes, she was gay and sweet. But she could not hide the tragedy lurking in her eyes. Dear, dear Reverend Mother. She died in the February.

XVIII

VICTIMS OF RENEWAL

In the previous chapter the mass-media and the vernacular Mass have been combined because their respective decrees were promulgated at the same time, in December 1963. *The Constitution on the Liturgy,* however, did not affect Judith until a whole year later, in December 1964. In the meantime things had not stood still.

The diocesan schools commission had been in the habit of issuing syllabi for the guidance of teachers in Catholic schools. Canon Slattery had given Judith copies covering a four-year course at a senior school. She found them extremely helpful. Indeed, without them she would not have known where to start. In April 1964, Mr. Butterworth, who took catechism at the boys' secondary modern, delivered a bundle of catechetical literature at the Dower House. It was supposed to contain a new syllabus for senior schools. Judith read it all carefully. She found it devoid of catechetical content; pure propaganda in favour of the new activist outlook; pedagogically unsound. It was too bulky to file anywhere, so she lit bonfires with it. Perhaps unwisely, she mentioned the fact to Mr. Butterworth. Towards the end of June a Monsignor Philip Pailey called. He was the diocesan director of catechetics. He wanted to know how the new syllabus was faring at Dame Margot's. Judith explained that she had thought it unsuitable for her children and that she, anyway, was unable to use it. "I cannot teach questions without providing answers."

Msgr. Pailey was a large, handsome man in his mid-forties, with dark curly hair. He was obviously used to sweeping everything before him. The conversation was short, to the point and disagreeable. He issued his verdict: "Very well, Mrs. Rougham, unless you use the approved diocesan syllabus you cannot claim to teach the Catholic religion in this diocese. It is with the greatest regret that I shall have to inform the head-mistress of Dame Margot Welbeloved's school and the chief education officer that you are not a licensed person to instruct in the Catholic Faith."

"You realize that you will find it difficult to replace me," said Judith.

"I am aware of that, but, in the interest of the children as well as of the Faith, it is better that they should grow up in an atmosphere of liberty, openness and personal commitment than in one of fear, compulsion and superstition."

Judith could not help laughing: "You really have a gift for rhetoric, Monsignor! Yes, I should be grateful if you would explain my dismissal to the headmistress and chief education officer, as you suggest. I shall finish the term and then the girls can be as free as you like from the fear of the Lord and the beginning of wisdom."

Naturally things did not work out quite as Msgr. Pailey imagined. Judith did not tell Miss Sowerby. She let Msgr. Pailey do so. When Miss Sowerby received his letter she exploded. Some miserable little clergyman interfering with her staff! Judith had to calm her down.

"At all events, the skunk won't get his way," she said and called for Rebecca Elliott. When Rebecca arrived, Miss Sowerby commanded her to read the letter.

"Now, Miss Elliott, I want you to continue Mrs. Rougham's work. From next term onwards you will take four special biology classes for Roman Catholics. Mrs. Rougham will show you how to do it. I shall fix your timetable accordingly and arrange with the chief education officer to adjust your salary to meet this added responsibility."

Judith had a wonderful send-off from Dame Margot's. Miss Portia Sowerby was positively affectionate. Thanks to her and to Rebecca Elliott Dame Margot Welbeloved's Secondary Modern School for Girls remains to this day a hotbed of Catholic resistance.

Poor Canon Slattery was heartbroken. Apart from Mrs. Rougham, two other catechists had been dismissed over his head, one of whom was Mrs. Larkin. His carefully-erected catechetical structure had been reduced to ruins. However, Judith made him promise not to tell Edmund. Neither did she tell Edmund herself. This was for two reasons. She knew that it would upset him more than it did her because at that time he still trusted the clergy. Besides, hot news always hurts more than a cold *fait accompli*. Then, Edmund was sure to raise trouble. He would get the Brig to intervene with the bishop, the chancellor, with the cardinal and even the prime minister with the Vatican! He would defend his wife to the last ditch. Anyway, there would be one hell of a row. If as a result of Edmund's efforts she were reinstated, her position would nonetheless remain untenable. If she were not, much harm would have been done to no purpose. Besides, Judith was not interested in being reinstated by external pressure. What she wanted was that ecclesiastical authority of its own free will should continue to teach the faith and formularies which it existed to safeguard.

As a matter of fact, Edmund only learned about the Pailey affair in mid-September; it was then too late to do anything. He wanted to get in touch urgently with Judith on a Tuesday morning when he thought she would be teaching at Dame Margot's. He rang up the school to ask that Mrs. Rougham should ring him back as soon as she had finished her classes. The secretary put him through to Miss Sowerby. That lady was in a position to inform Edmund of the situation far more forcefully than Judith could have done herself. She even got Pailey's letter from the file and read it to him. The effect on Edmund was profound. It undermined, if it did not quite destroy, Edmund's confidence in the clergy.

Msgr. Pailey's visit in June, Edmund's discovery thereof in September and Father Mallon's Mass in December inevitably led to repercussions. The first of these has already been mentioned: Richard's removal from the convent. It is highly doubtful if Judith would have taken so drastic a step on the sole ground of the dismissal of Reverend Mother and the appointment of Sister Pantaleone. Father Mallon's Mass and Msgr. Pailey's syllabus were just as important. Judith could foresee that the convent would become an up-to-date ghetto of "liberty, openness and personal commitment." Under no circumstances would she allow her little boy to be brought up in a religion different from his parents'. In January 1965 she sent him to a perfectly decent Anglican school where he could be withdrawn from religious instruction, which Judith would provide at home. Poor old Canon Slattery was horrified but there was nothing he could do about it. As Judith said, "It is not so much we who are withdrawing from the ecclesial community — as they call it in their jargon — as it is the ecclesial community which is rejecting us. I can assure you, my dear Canon, that personal pique over Msgr. Pailey's action does not enter into the matter. The fact is that a new idea of the Church is gradually emerging. Under the old ecclesiology I could think of myself as being a reasonably good Catholic. I must now reconcile myself to being a bad one. But it is not I who have changed."

Then there was the problem of the projected primary school. It was in view of this project that the chief education officer had allowed the canon to arrange for catechism in the state schools: Slattery obviously had to round up the R.C. children before he could open his school.

It will be remembered that the parish hall had not been built when Canon Slattery had been appointed to Holy Cross in February 1961. He soon discovered that Walthamford was a hotbed of Popery. What was wanted was not a hall but a primary school. The ministry would agree provided he built for 150 places, that is, if he could guarantee an intake of over twenty children a year. By diligent rooting round in 1962 and 1963, the canon got the necessary forms filled in by the prospective parents to show an intake of over thirty children a year. This implied a school of 220 places. What was left of the church site — the space for the hall, the presbytery garden and the car park — was not big enough for a school of that size. The ministry did not insist on playing-fields but it did insist on adequate playgrounds. Even if the school were built on two floors, 1.8 acres was still the minimum size for the site. Where was it to be found within reasonable distance of the church?

The answer was obvious. Although the Dower House was only twenty yards from the road, it stood in a corner of 5.5 acres of land. Would the Roughams surrender two acres and transfer their generous offer to build the parish hall to building the promoters' share of the new school?

When in March 1963, with great delicacy and diffidence, dear Canon Slattery first proposed it, Edmund was enthusiastic. Yes, there were about two acres of flat land to the north of the house. Access to the road could be supplied along the property's northern boundary with about 60 feet of frontage. It was no use building churches if you failed to educate the children to worship in them. He was absolutely delighted. It would crown Judith's work in establishing Walthamford parish. Canon Slattery, with a song in his heart, continued to collect baptismal certificates and signed parents' intention forms. He notified the chief education officer of the proposal. He was most cooperative and promised to navigate the proposal through the ministry and local education authority once it was officially lodged by the diocesan authorities. The then-secretary of the diocesan schools commission, Msgr. Pailey's predecessor, was also very helpful in supplying forms and advice as to how to proceed. Yes, but that was early in 1963.

It was on Thursday, January 21st, 1965, that the canon invited himself to dinner at the Dower House "to talk about the school."

He arrived fairly early as he wanted to have the discussion before rather than after dinner. Judith was putting George to bed and Giacinta was cooking the meal.

"Well, Mr. Rougham, I handed over the complete dossier to Mr. Mount (the chief education officer) on Thursday. We have only to survey the land, get building permission and the bishop's formal approval, then we're off..."

"My dear Canon," said Edmund when he thought the moment opportune, "I suppose I should have raised the matter with you sooner, but the truth is that my doubts have only crystalized in the last few weeks and now you have forestalled me. It seems to me that the idea of a school will have to be dropped."

The poor canon nearly dropped, too.

"You see," Edmund continued, "a school isn't merely a question of land and bricks and mortar. There have to be children, a teaching staff and subjects to be taught."

"But I've got the children," gasped poor Slattery.

"I rather doubt it. As you know full well, over the last eighteen months inside and outside the council the bishops and pundits have been discussing contraception. Bishop vies with bishop in propagating pornography until the Pope has had to intervene. That was only three months ago, if my memory serves me correctly. But the porn still continues. We are assured on all sides that a papal bull will eventually have to swallow the pill. Contraception has already established itself, they say, as a 'probable opinion.' Now, one of the great weaknesses in moral theology, as I see it, is 'probabilism.' It amounts to this: what somebody manages to justify is permitted; there is a probable opinion in its favour. Then there is a little jump and one finds that what is permitted has become obligatory. Until now contraception has been condemned. Crowds of bishops now justify it; it is permitted; it will soon be obligatory. Anyway, Catholics will surge towards contraception with all the enthusiasm of neophytes. The last published for infant baptisms are those for 1963, when there were over 136,000. Ten years hence I doubt if there will be much over 100,000. Your 220-place school will be lucky to have 150 pupils. Even this is optimistic. As you know, my wife and I have removed Richard from the convent. The urge for Catholic parents to bring up their children in Catholic schools is on the wane. You think you have got the children, my dear Canon, but they will run through your fingers like sand.

"Then you will have to find staff. Before the council this presented no problem. Of course Catholic teachers taught in Catholic schools! In future the most dedicated and convinced Catholics will avoid Catholic schools because they will not be allowed to teach the religion in which they believe and which they love. They will emigrate to non-Catholic schools in which they are not obliged to teach religion. If we open a school at Walthamford, my dear Canon, we shall acquire a staff of about 60 percent Catholics of sorts and the rest non-Catholics.

"As for the religion which will be taught in our school, it will be the syllabus followed by Mr. Butterworth and enforced by Msgr. Pailey. Is it worthwhile to build a school for Paileyism?"

There was a long pause. Edmund felt desperately sorry for Slattery. He looked shriveled, grey, sick.

"So the school is out," he said at last. "The labour and hope of three years are all wiped out — just like that."

There was silence. Edmund simply did not know what to say. It was the canon who broke it.

"You are wrong, Edmund. Probabilism does not work as simply as you imagine. Anyway, the hot air of a few bishops is not going to deform the consciences of the laity. You are maligning them. Of course every Catholic will send his children to a Catholic school. It is in the blood. We, clergy and laity, have fought for them ever since emancipation. It has been a hard struggle, as I know from my personal experience. And at last we have won the battle. With the new government grants it is no longer even a burden to build them. It is not now, when the hierarchy has won, that it is going to cave in. I shall be frank with you, Edmund: it is the way in which Msgr. Pailey treated your wife which has warped your judgment."

"I agree that Pailey has a lot to do with it," Edmund replied, "but it is not his personal treatment of Judith which I find sinister. It is the utter ruthlessness with which he imposes a brand new religious outlook — and that on defenseless children. It is a totalitarian technique. As for the hierarchy surrendering when it has won the battle, you have hit the nail on the head. That is precisely what it is doing all along the line, be it in ecumenism, in the relations of Church and state, in morals and even in dogma — at least in its formulation. On all fronts the Church has triumphed; on all fronts she is now abdicating. I see no reason why the schools should be an exception — on the contrary.

"You are doubtless right," Edmund continued, "that I oversimplify probabilism, but I am not trying to express the system as would a professor of morals but as the humble laity understand it. We are brought up to give blind obedience to our bishops. If a bishop makes a statement which is not forthwith and firmly condemned by the Holy See, then it is clear that the bishop's statement

can licitly be held by a Catholic. That is what probabilism means
to the laity.

"Also, I am not maligning the Catholic laity. The number of
children per Catholic marriage is significantly greater than the national average — as, incidentally, is the number of illegitimates. I
have not got the statistics to hand but I have seen them for the
decade 1951-1961. It works out at about 2.8 children per Catholic
marriage as against a national average of 2.2 — which includes
the Catholics. Who can tell what heroism it has required to produce so wide a gap? To turn round and tell these heroic people
that they were a set of fools can lead only to revolt or despair.
Moreover, if you remove heroism and sacrifice from our religion,
there is nothing left. No, Canon: you are unfair when you ascribe
my pessimism to the treatment of my wife."

Slattery had somewhat regained his composure: "Very well,
I'll take your word for it. But what am I to do?"

Edmund pondered for a moment. "I think you ought to write to
the bishop along these lines. I'll make a draft for you. Of course you
can alter it as you please." Edmund was used to drafting letters for
the chancellor; he had it done in a couple of minutes.

My Lord,
    Yesterday I called on Mr. Rougham to tell him that I had given
the complete dossier on our proposed Primary School to the Chief
Education Officer. All that was now required was Your
Lordship's formal proposal and the transfer of the two acres of
land which Mr. Rougham had so generously offered.

    To my immense surprise he raised a number of objections. He
now appears to be unwilling to let us have the site.

    It is surely not unlikely that the reason for Mr. Rougham's *volte-
face* is the rather high-handed dismissal of his wife from teaching
catechism at the Girls' Secondary Modern school.

    It is obviously too late to reinstate Mrs. Rougham. It strikes
me, however, that if Your Lordship wrote a personal letter to Mr.
Rougham saying how much you regretted the incident; that you
sincerely hoped he would still let us have the school site; and — if I
dare suggest such a thing, My Lord — that the new religious
syllabus would not be obligatory but would depend on the judgment of the School Managers, of whom he and his wife would be

two — then, I have reason to believe, Mr. Rougham would still be willing to let us have the land.

I need not remind you, My Lord, that, quite apart from money, the whole school project depends on Mr. Rougham's decision as there is no other reasonable site available.

Edmund handed the draft to Slattery. "That is the sort of letter which I should write. It throws the ball into the bishop's court. The position may be clearer when we get his reply."

"Thank you, Edmund; thank you so much. I'll send it off tomorrow. But please ask Mrs. Rougham to excuse me: I don't feel well enough to stay for dinner." He left disconsolate.

On the following Thursday morning Slattery rang up to say that he had received an answer to his letter. Could he come round to dinner that evening? But he would dine first and discuss the matter afterwards, "In case I get no dinner at all, like last week." Yes, both Judith and Edmund would be at home.

The poor canon looked very haggard but was his usual charming self. After dinner he handed the letter to Edmund. It was not from the bishop but from Msgr. Pailey. It was dated January 26th, 1965, and read:

Dear Canon Slattery,

His Lordship has asked me to thank you for your letter of the 23rd instant.

He has also instructed me to tell you that he is unwilling to accept the site on the terms which you suggest:

1) The new catechetical syllabus is obligatory throughout the diocese. Any exception would of its nature be divisive.

2) His Lordship must preserve his liberty as to the appointment of school managers. These he will choose from among the parents of the pupils. Under such circumstances Mr. and Mrs. Rougham are clearly ineligible.

As a matter of fact His Lordship is not displeased to have this excuse to drop the proposed school at Walthamford. It is against diocesan policy to open small, one-form-entry schools. Not only are they too vulnerable to fluctuation in numbers and too small to provide adequate secular education, but they inevitably perpetuate the ghetto psychology of a small Catholic community. Besides, having already given church and presbytery, if the Roughams also give the school it will make the Church appear to be the flunky of the rich instead of the ally of the underprivileged.

I write the above, my dear Canon, by way of consolation for what must be a bitter disappointment to you. The fact is that Mr. Rougham's action is a blessing in disguise.

The absence of a Catholic school implies the continuation of your system of catechesis in the state schools. In this connection I have been in contact with your excellent Mr. Butterworth. He has seen the Headmistress of the Girls' Secondary School, who has kindly made arrangements for the head of the biology department to give courses on the facts of life to the Catholic girls. She is the daughter of the well-known Evangelical preacher, the Reverend Simeon Elliott. As for the two Primary Schools, Mr. Butterworth has arranged for them to join with the Anglicans. This is indeed most fortunate as the curate at St. Olaf's is none other than the Reverend Hugh Pyne-Pugh, the author of "From Christ to Marx" and "First Steps in Christian Socialism." Have you read them, Canon? They are quite remarkable and have had no little influence on His Lordship's recent catechetical syllabus.

His Lordship sends you his very special blessing.

> Yours devotedly in Jesus and Mary,
> Philip Pailey

Edmund read the letter aloud for Judith's benefit. Both had difficulty in refraining from laughing outright for fear of hurting Slattery's feelings. "What do you think of it?" he asked.

"Well, it is very much what I had expected," said Edmund, "except that it is so naively expressed. I have not come across the argument from 'divisiveness' before. It obviously has a great future in front of it. It will justify the most ruthless suppression of other people's rights. Last Thursday I felt an absolute cad, my dear Canon, but this evening I feel that I have saved both of us from endless trouble and disappointment."

Anyway, Judith and Edmund managed to cheer the canon up before he left.

*   *   *   *   *

Yes, Edmund's original optimism, which had survived the death of John XXIII, had given way to complete pessimism by the end of the third session of the council in November 1964. He was a cradle Catholic and Jesuit-educated to boot. He was inured to ecclesiastical discipline. He was like the centurion in Matthew VIII: "I too know what it is to obey authority; I have soldiers under me, and I say, 'go,' to one man, and he goes, or, 'come,' to another, and he comes." That was all very well so long as the officers themselves did not question the system. But that was precisely what the bishops were doing during the third session from September 15th to November 21st. The haggling over their own collegiality, over the sources of revelation, over the nature of the Church, was upon analysis no more than questioning authority: that of the Church, of the Pope, of divine revelation. If the centurion did not obey, there was no reason why the soldier should. Like any other chain, the chain of command is no stronger than its weakest link.

But what most astonished and depressed Edmund was what he called episcopal porn: the constant harping on sex. Marriage was all the rage, with married deacons and hopefully married priests. But there was much doubt as to what marriage was. The more vociferous bishops were quite sure that it had nothing to do with the procreation of children but was "the expression of conjugal love." And it was made quite clear what that meant: contraception would not merely be allowed but would be virtuous if it helped to preserve "conjugal love." Edmund wondered if pederastic and lesbian marriages would be encouraged. Homosexuals showed lots of conjugal love and did not even require the pill. Indeed, they were helping to curb the population explosion. That was all bad enough, but what depressed Edmund most was not what Cardinals Léger and Suenens might say on the subject but that the propaganda in favour of episcopal porn appeared to be orchestrated by an Englishman, a gentleman and a Jesuit: one Archbishop Thomas Roberts, retired archbishop of Bombay, whose Mass he had served many times as a boy at Beaumont. Later he had often met him socially. That was perhaps his trouble: he was too social.

Then there was the specific trouble of the pill. Edmund could well understand onanism and direct contraception in the act of intercourse. After all, everyone sinned in different ways and more or less. There was only one human being who was Immaculate. That was fair enough. But the pill was quite a different matter. It was a perpetual state of sin in view of a possible future act. It was totally cold-blooded without the excuse of passion and temptation. What it did to the body heaven alone knows, but it must certainly destroy the soul.

Edmund was rather friendly with the local chemist. He was not a Catholic but his wife was. Edmund asked him one day about contraceptives.

"Good heavens! The place is chock-ablock with them. Umpteen varieties for either sex and umpteen brands of each variety. It's big business. Then it goes by fashion. One month it's one sort for a man, the next it's another for the woman. At the moment it's the pill...What does it do? Well, it injects the hormones into the woman which signal to her body that she is already pregnant, so she stops ovulating. Often enough her body is so deceived that she starts lactating. You'll see few flat-chested girls about our days. Never have women had such powerful breasts and never have they been less used for their natural function. Mad!...Well, it's too early to say what physical and mental harm it does, but it's pretty obvious that you cannot go on deceiving your body year in, year out, without its taking its revenge. Then, as there is no control, anybody takes them. A couple of months ago a woman came in and took a month's supply. She was back again a week later because her kiddies had found them and eaten them as sweeties...I believe at the start the hormones were taken from some South American animal. Now they are synthetic — a petrochemical product I think. We could probably muck along without petrol but not without the pill."

Edmund's certainties were falling away from under his feet. He had imagined himself as standing on a tiny little projection of the Petrine Rock. Not at all; he was paddling about in quicksand. It is true that in October 1964 Pope Paul, presumably as shocked as Edmund by episcopal porn, had reserved the whole question of contraception to a special commission set up by himself. This may have saved Edmund's faith — but only just. Firstly, the bishops, headed by Roberts, continued to screech their porn in the media since they could no longer do so in St. Peter's. Secondly, what was the use of a special commission if the problem was perfectly clear? Edmund was well-acquainted with special commissions at the Treasury; their object was to lend respectability to a lie.

Edmund had no doubts on the subject. His whole married life with Judith was based on the immorality of artificial contraception. That "everybody" used it did not make it right, no more than lying is right because everybody lies. Edmund simply could not understand the itch people have to justify themselves in their own eyes — and that by external authority. Even extreme Protestants, to whom Rome was the Scarlet Woman, would enjoy an added feeling of coziness if Pope or council sprinkled holy water on the pill. If Edmund knew what was right and wrong without a special commission, how came it that the Pope did not? Anyway, until the commission reported and the Pope pronounced, would there not be doubt in a million minds? The Church existed to solve doubts. Had she the right to raise them?

Edmund well remembered how he had laughed at Judith two years previously. She had said that one should decide in advance when to dig one's toes in. She had given by way of examples: "The licitness of artificial contraception; the recognition of Protestant orders; the jettisoning of the immemorial Mass." At the time they seemed pure fantasy. It was also true that none of them had come to pass as yet. But each of them had become possible. It was no laughing matter.

More dire thoughts revolved in Edmund's mind. At Beaumont he had been made to read Bossuet's *Histoire des Variations*. Its main thesis was still perfectly clear to him and he thought it unanswerable. A religion which changes in a basic point of faith or morals must be a false religion. The truth is the same for all people, in all places, at all times. A religion which changes either was wrong before the change or wrong after it. In either case such a religion is open to error. It can deceive and, indeed, has done so. It has lost its credibility. Now, supposing that in such an universal and basic practice as intercourse the Church changes its morality, then it is clear that the Church has taught in the past or will be teaching in the future what is false. The "gates of hell" have prevailed against her. Not only is she a false religion, but Christ is a false prophet. And if Christ is a false prophet — there is no God. And if there is no God...

One must abstain from picking holes in Edmund's logic. One might satisfy oneself but not Edmund. These were the sort of thoughts which kept cropping up in his mind from October 1964 onwards. He managed to dismiss them. He led a normal life. He clung like mad to the Mass, although he felt sure that it would be taken away from him. But they could not take his crucifix away. Twice a day, at Mass in the morning and before going home in the evening, he visited Holy Cross. The Cross was the reality, be it in its image or in the Real Presence. Pope, bishops and council were insignificant figures in a dream world. They might frighten him, like a nightmare, but basically they were unreal. He was already reassured by the time he got home. He kissed his Judith and his children in complete happiness.

But next day the thoughts returned.

XIX

FIRST HOLY COMMUNION

Judith, being a woman and a convert, was far less depressed than Edmund. She had fallen in love with the Catholic Faith as Father McEnery had revealed it to her. That was that. If Pope or council tried to rob her of it, then they were a set of slimy rogues. Unfortunately, the laity were completely defenseless. She had no arms with which to fight them back. But at least nothing would induce her to obey them. Neither was it only on her own account. How dared they fiddle about with the religion of her children? The slimy rogues talked about "divisiveness" but before they had finished they would divide every family in the Church.

Judith was aware of Edmund's problems but, while showing all the sympathy she could, she dismissed them as male abstractions, divorced from reality. The reality had nothing to do with the council: it was Richard's First Holy Communion.

Richard was not a particularly brilliant child but, like his father, was serious and conscientious. If Judith forgot to say grace, he would remind her of the black spot on her soul. He felt a grave responsibility for his parents' religious behaviour. In part, doubtless, to educate them, he took hours over his night prayers, which he ended with an enormous Sign of the Cross: "In the Name of the Father and of the Son and of the Holy Goats, Amen."

The canon very wisely believed in separating First Confession from First Holy Communion. "If the two sacraments are dealt with together the emotional strain is too great," he said. "Besides, they require the opposite attitudes in the child. In confession he must be active by confessing his sins, expressing his sorrow and saying his penance. In Holy Communion he must be recessive to receive his Redeemer."

Since Judith had difficulty herself with confession, she got Mrs.

Larkin to prepare Richard. He made his first Confession on Ash Wednesday, March 3rd, 1965. If Judith hated going, her little boy simply loved it. He toddled off every Saturday with the regularity of clockwork. Grownups may think that children cannot sin; children think otherwise.

On the Sunday after Corpus Christi, June 20th, Richard made his First Holy Communion along with the other non-convent children. It was no different from any other but it is perhaps worth remembering how solemn it used to be. The little girls were dressed as brides. The little boys for once looked clean, with hair brushed, teeth brushed, nails brushed, shoes brushed, wearing white shirts, red ties and blue shorts. They were marshalled to their places with their hands joined and looking frightfully smug. In due course they knelt motionless at the altar rails, their little hands under the cloth which hung from them, a golden plate held under their chins. Slattery looked immeasurably ancient in comparison. He made a tiny Sign of the Cross with the host before he placed the Word of God onto the tongue of a child. Judith's little fellow was as solemn as the occasion. She wept for joy.

Breakfast followed under a marquee in the presbytery garden. The children were still trying to behave and be nice, not grabbing the jelly nor punching or pinching their neighbours. The parents stood round as proud as punch and also trying to be nice.

After a few hours respite, at 3 p.m., it started up again with the Corpus Christi procession.

This by now had become an immemorial tradition, dating back to the foundation of the parish in 1961. Once more everyone gathered in the marquee, cleared of tables, benches and buns but with an altar at one end. The procession got underway, marshalled by the Knights of St. Columba. It was led by the men of the Guild of the Blessed Sacrament, Edmund bearing the cross and young Mr. Larkin (the retired postman's son) the banner. The First Holy Communicants followed, the boys in front, then the girls throwing rose petals in front of the Blessed Sacrament. Behind the Blessed Sacrament came the choir, the football club, the Catholic Women's League, Children of Mary, Legion of

Mary and all the rest. Perhaps about five-hundred people all told.

The first altar was in the garden of the Dower House. Then it moved south. At the main road the police stopped all traffic for it to cross. There was no hooting from the cars. And so to the next altar in the cinema car-park, hired for the occasion. After that it moved northwest through rather a slummy district to the area behind the fried-fish shop. Finally it took a slightly devious direction, re-crossing the main road at the Ploughman's Arms and so back to Holy Cross. In the meantime the Rosary and litanies were recited, punctuated by splendid Catholic hymns which any lapsed Catholic would recognize, to the accompaniment of the local band. At Holy Cross the last Benediction was given and everybody went home, thoroughly exhausted. Both children and parents were still trying to be nice, although by this time success did not always crown their efforts.

To be honest Edmund hated it. It was frightfully blush-making. But he did it each year as a member of the Blessed Sacrament Guild. So did Judith, as she belonged to the Catholic Women's League. But Judith loved it. It was pathetic and absurd, like all attempts of man to honour God. How can a void pretend to give honour to the Absolute without looking ridiculous?

There was no difficulty getting Richard off to sleep that night. Neither was there in getting him to school next morning. It was Judith who had to stay in bed with a temperature of 104 degrees, a swollen abdomen and dizziness. The doctor came round and gave her lots of pills. He called again in the evening to report to Edmund.

Edmund had made a personal friend of Doctor McAuley. From time to time he invited him down to shoot at the castle. He was a Belfast Orangeman by extraction but a thoroughly good fellow and a painstaking medico. "You know, Edmund, the trouble with your wife is that she is a bag of nerves without a safety margin. Everything works but only just. She is like a bridge with a ten-ton limit. If a ten-ton lorry passes over, it holds up. If a sparrow lands on the lorry in transit, the bridge caves in. No safety margin. You can see it with her babies. I am told that she had

great difficulty in carrying Richard and I know the trouble she had
with the last one. She can keep one person going, herself, but not
two. At the moment she has an internal infection which an ordinary person might scarcely notice. It knocks her flat. Why? It is
the physical manifestation of over-excitement; the nervous strain
has been too much for her body. I know Richard made his First
Holy Communion yesterday and that means a lot to a woman like
Judith. Of course I can get her all right with sulfonomides but that
merely removes the symptoms. What she needs is her nervous
energy building up. We quacks cannot do that. We can give pep
to the nervous system, but we cannot build it up. The factors involved are too complex. Anyway, what she needs is a complete
change. If you belonged to the working classes I should advise
Blackpool or Southend. I am not sure what would be your wife's
equivalent. Probably not Capri or Monte Carlo. What about
Venice, Tuscany or Seville? Somewhere where she can expand. At
the moment her nervous system is contracted."

"It is easy for you doctors to prescribe such remedies," said Edmund, "but they are not so easily arranged. Should I and the
children go with her or should she go alone? When and for how
long?"

"You should go. She probably does not see enough of you.
You are always at the Treasury or the castle and you are not
frightfully interesting when you are asleep. But the children, no.
She worries far too much about them when they are under her
feet. It will be a change to worry about them when they are a
thousand miles away. It does not matter when, as long as she can
look forward to it within the next six months. As for how long,
I suppose that the Treasury only allows you about a month. Try
and make it six weeks."

Such was McAuley's advice. He was quite right on a couple of
points. Judith did not have Edmund very much to herself. He
was only at the Dower House of an evening but they entertained
or were entertained rather a lot. He was always at the castle on
Saturdays and sometimes on Sundays. All holidays, short or long,
were spent at the castle. Judith loved it because she loved the
place, the Brig and Lucy but it was in no sense a holiday for her.

Curiously enough, although they had been married for over eight years, Edmund and Judith had scarcely had continuous personal contact since their honeymoon. McAuley, being the old-fashioned family doctor, had sensed this.

Judith's temperature dropped on the fourth day. She was up and about on the sixth. That Saturday evening — Edmund had not gone to the castle — he mentioned in an off-hand way the possibility of a continental holiday. Judith jumped for joy: "Darling, what a splendid idea! A sort of second honeymoon. How wonderful of you to think of it!" Edmund did not mention that the idea was McAuley's.

It so happened that ten days later, on July 8th, Ronnie Stanningfield came to stay at the Dower House for a couple of nights. It was he who had sold the Rougham Crucifix out of his aunt's estate. Although he and Edmund were both nephews of the late Lady Stanningfield, he was twenty years older than Edmund on account of the Brig's late marriage. In fact Ronnie became a grandfather shortly before George was born. As has been said, he was in the diplomatic service and had been Minister to the Vatican since April 1962. He often came over to England and he and Edmund would meet in London. It was the first time, however, that he had invited himself to the Dower House, as he was usually encumbered with his family. This time he was all alone. His wife was clucking around her first grandchild in Italy.

On the morning after Ronnie's arrival Edmund showed him over Holy Cross. He was duly impressed. "By Jove! That's a splendid crucifix you've got over the altar."

"Yes, that was the one in Aunt Eleanor's private chapel which you flogged for a fiver."

"Good heavens! You're not pulling my leg? Yes, I remember it. It can't have been in Aunt Eleanor's inventory of Rougham property. I was in South America at the time and arranged for everything to be sold that wasn't in the inventory. You got the rest, I hope?"

"Dear me, yes! Your solicitors must have a receipt for it. But the crucifix was not in the inventory for the simple reason that Aunt Eleanor had calmly swiped it."

"How on earth did you get it back?"

Edmund told him the strange story of how it had returned to the family along with his wife.

That evening, while Judith was bathing George and the two men were having drinks, Edmund mentioned that Judith was pretty run-down and needed a complete change. Did Ronnie have any bright suggestions for somewhere in Tuscany or Umbria?"

"I've got exactly what you want. I have rented a villa for Susan (the elder daughter, responsible for the grandchild) up to October 11th. Servants provided. That is where she is now. It is beyond Porto Santo Stefano, at the tip of the Argentario Peninsula. Susan has got to get back to England on September 16th. You can have it for the rest of the time. Jane (Viscountess Stanningfield) will return to England with Susan and stay here throughout October. Early in October you can come to the legation and Judith will entertain for me. I shall be proud to show off my Popish connections."

So the holiday was settled. Judith was thrilled with the idea. Apart from the joy it would give her, it would ease an insignificant tension in the family: Lady Milden was desperately jealous of Lucy Rougham. She was never asked to do anything or to be useful. Very well, Mary Milden could live in the Dower House and watch Giacinta look after Richard and George. If that was not useful, what was?

Edmund and Judith would leave Walthamford on Monday, September 13th, drive slowly through the glories that were France and arrive at the Argentario on Sunday, the 19th. They would stay with Ronnie at the legation from Thursday, October 7th, to Wednesday, the 13th, so as to return home on Saturday, the 16th. But Judith put her foot down about entertaining bishops. That would spoil everything.

XX

DEATH AND BLESSING

Poor Canon Slattery never really recovered from his disappointment over the school. His complexion turned from white to grey and his clothes hung even more dejectedly around him. Perhaps his only recreation was to dine at the Dower House on Thursday evenings — provided there were no other guests. From being sociable and affectionate by nature he had become a bit of a misanthropist. His conversation had been interesting and entertaining, enlivened by impish but innocent wit. This had all vanished and on Thursday evenings Edmund and Judith had to listen to a gentle, continuous moan. This is more or less how it ran.

"Yes, I am turned seventy-three and in a few months time I shall have been ordained for half-a-century. How I used to look forward to my jubilee! Fifty years in the Lord's vineyard and with nothing with which to reproach myself except for mistakes of human error in judgment and for the desperate intransigence of youth. I once refused the last sacraments to a dying man because he was excommunicated for having attempted marriage in a Protestant church. By the time I had thought it over and gone back to give them to him, he was dead. It has been on my conscience ever since. I can still see his face. He was under thirty and a handsome young fellow from South Wales with beautiful golden hair. Ever since I have made a special memento for him at Mass. Yes, I reproach myself for that, but I had only been a curate for a few months. I still had to learn that there is only one law by which to govern our actions: of a dozen alternatives, do that which is least likely to cause remorse. The human soul, Mr. Rougham, can heal everything except remorse. That is what purgatory is: God in his mercy cauterizing the remorse in the soul. . . .

"Yes, I was so looking forward to my jubilee. Fifty years of priesthood. And God gives priests great happiness, you know.

There would have been a High Mass in the beautiful church you have built for us, Mrs. Rougham, with the bishop enthroned and the chapter around me. I always got on pretty well with my fellow-priests. We manage to be childish in one respect: even if we are desperately jealous, we rarely bear malice...But now I hope I shall not live to see it. It would not be a High Mass but one of those new concelebrations with the bishop acting as Punch and we as a bunch of Judies. Somehow it is a fake. When one is concelebrating with Jesus, what is the point of concelebrating with a few more clowns like oneself? And the unbearable heartiness of it all when at least some of us are heartbroken. No, I hope I don't live to see it...

"You know, it is hard at my time of life to see all my work undone, my hopes shattered, my loves derided. You were right, Mr. Rougham, not to let me build that school. It would not have been my crowning achievement but my crowning disappointment. I have built three schools in my time. I visited one of them last month. The spirit has gone. At ten the children do not know their prayers and catechism. There is no school Mass or school confessions. Ah! Mrs. Rougham, the confessions of children are quite wonderful. Even if they tell fibs in the confessional, it is somehow beautifully transparent. The tragedy is less that children no longer confess than that priests no longer hear them. The priests could learn so much...

"That, I suppose, is where I am most at variance with the new outlook. The new people despise the common faithful. They hate poverty and talk of nothing but social justice; they hate stupidity because 'we now know'; they hate piety because it is uncritical; they hate childishness and only tolerate 'adult Christians' — and so on. Well, I love my parishioners and love them as they are: poor, stupid, uncritical and childish. It is thanks to them that I have absorbed a little of the discipline of poverty; that I have learnt how little I know; that I prefer piety to criticism and faith to rationalism. Yes, Mrs. Rougham, I feel deeply indebted to my parishioners. God has given me so much through them. It is not for my own sake that I refuse the new outlook. It is for theirs. I simply do not accept the implication that they have been wrong merely because they have been poor, stupid, uncritical, childish. It is my unshakable belief that these are precisely the reasons why they are right. Rather than criticize them even by implication I should prefer to die...

"No, I hope I shall not live to see my jubilee."

Such is a fair sample of the canon's moan. There were variations. For instance, in April 1965, after publication of *Inter Oecumenici* in the previous September, the bishop threatened either to send Slattery a curate or retire him to an old priests' home if he failed to say two of the three Sunday Masses in the vernacular. Edmund made arrangements for him to go as private chaplain to the castle. However, nothing came of the threat. But it made the canon all the more determined to die.

He did. He said his three Sunday Masses as usual September 5th. He took to his bed on Monday, was anointed on Tuesday morning and died on Tuesday night.

The Requiem was at 12 noon on Saturday, September 11th. It was exactly what Slattery had foreseen for his jubilee. The bishop concelebrated with a host of clergy. In view of the large number of non-Catholics who, as a matter of fact, were not present, his lordship dispensed himself from the liturgical regulations laid down by the Pope's *motu proprio* and the recent *Inter Oecumenici*: the whole Mass, including the consecration, was said aloud and in the vernacular. It was further adorned with a few *ex tempore* prayers and interspersed with non-Catholic hymns blared over the microphone by Mr. Butterworth and friends. Needless to say, the panegyric was preached by Msgr. Pailey. Its theme was Slattery's unswerving loyalty to the bishop and total dedication to the spirit of Vatican II. Among the many examples, two were particularly familiar to the people of Walthamford: how he had dismissed those catechists who felt unable to follow the diocesan syllabus; how he had sacrificed his plan for a parochial school the moment he knew it to be contrary to diocesan policy and, consequently, to the best interests of the children.

Judith was grateful to Pailey for the panegyric. It took her mind off the ceremony. Who on earth was Pailey trying to deceive? He must know that it would not deceive the parishioners. Neither could it deceive the bishop or clergy. He must be trying to deceive God. Yes, that was it: he was giving an idealized portrait of Slattery, as he would be in heaven, once the flames of purgatory had purified him of the dross of traditionalism.

Edmund and Judith slipped out of the church immediately Mass was ended. They did not wait for the absolutions, nor did they attend the committal. They were frightened of being button-holed by Pailey or the bishop. They felt uncertain of being able to control their tempers. Poor old Slattery! No insult had been spared him.

At the crack of dawn on Monday they set off on their second honeymoon.

*   *   *   *   *

It would be idle to describe their trip to the Argentario. Suffice it to say that the villa was quite magnificent. It was perched on an overhanging cliff. From the dining room terrace they could throw their olive stones into the sea 400 feet below them. And the sea was dotted with islands: Giannutri, Giglio, Montecristo, Pianosa and Elba over to the north. Judith felt that Napoleon must have been a bit of an idiot: fancy wanting to be Emperor of the French when he could have been Duke of Elba!

Edmund could see that McAuley had been quite right. In spite of exhausting visits to the great Lazian villas, Etruscan necropoli and trips to Lucca and Siena, she was putting on weight. She was eating pasta and seafoods by the bucketful. He was not doing too badly himself. Too soon it was October 7th and they were due in Rome.

Ronnie was delighted to see them. "I am so sorry I was unable to visit you at the Argentario but this beastly council leads me a dog's life. You enjoyed it? That's good! It really is a beautiful place...Incidentally, I have arranged a papal audience for you. Thanks to the council, they are rather difficult to obtain. It's for Tuesday 12th, the day before you leave. The only trouble is that for security reasons — the Vatican is mad keen on security these days — you have to go and collect your *biglietto* yourselves on Saturday morning. You go to the main entrance on the right side of Bernini's Colonnade, present my card and ask to see Msgr. Tarquinio Testastorta. He's a decent fellow and speaks perfect English. I told him you are my first cousin, heir to one of our stateliest homes and enlarged on the antiquity and importance of the Rougham family. As a matter of fact, he had heard of it. He's a walking encyclopedia."

Edmund and Judith were thrilled. They would see Pope Paul VI on their second honeymoon as they had Pius XII on their first.

On Saturday morning they duly appeared in Msgr. Testastorta's office. He rose from his desk and came towards them with both hands extended: "What an honour to meet the heir of the great Ruffamo family! I wrote my thesis for my degree in diplomacy on the foreign policy of Innocento XI Odescalchi, in which the Cardinale Ruffamo played so important a part. And what an able diplomat is your cousin Lord Stanningfield! He showed me a photograph of your *castello* in England. It is truly magnificent.

"Now, on Tuesday you are to have an audience with His Holiness. No, you need not come in evening dress; just a dark suit for the gentlemen and long sleeves and skirts below the knees for ladies. Ah! So you had an audience with Pius XII. We have simplified and humanized things a lot since then. And in what language would you like the audience to be conducted? His Holiness's English is not very fluent but I could act as interpreter. Ah! You both speak French. That is good. His Holiness speaks French perfectly."

Judith did not mention that she spoke Italian as well because Edmund did not.

Testastorta continued. "Is there any subject which you wish to bring particularly to His Holiness's attention? Do you wish to express the feelings of English Catholics on any particular problem facing the Holy Father and the council?"

Neither of them was prepared for this question. Judith was the first off the mark. "Yes, I wish to appeal to His Holiness for the retention in England of the immemorial Latin Mass in the name of our martyrs and, in the particular instance, of the Blessed Gregory Rougham. You see, in England we Catholics are a minority and it is in no small measure the traditional Latin Mass which gives that minority its cohesion."

"Exactly, Mrs. Rougham," said the monsignor. "I understand you perfectly. You feel that the council's objective in creating the necessary atmosphere for ecumenicity would best be fostered by preserving the Catholic minority's rite and rights."

"No, Monsignor," said Judith, "I was not thinking of ecumenicity and our separated brethren. You see, I am a convert and am consequently in a position to feel, quite disinterestedly, that even cradle Catholics have rights."

"Ah! You are a convert, Mrs. Ruffamo. How wonderful! Of course it is so difficult for you to see that what you have rejected has rights as well."

"Don't talk nonsense, Monsignor. Of course Protestants have rights, but it does not prevent them from being wrong."

It may be remembered from her first meeting with Miss Portia Sowerby that Judith was not the easiest person in the world to interview.

"You are a reincarnation of Santa Caterina, Mrs. Ruffamo. And you, Don Edmundo, is there anything you wish to bring to the Holy Father's special attention?"

Edmund had had time to collect his thoughts. "Yes, in the first place I should like to appeal for the canonization of the English Martyrs and in particular for that of Blessed Gregory Rougham."

"I feel sure the Holy Father would welcome such an appeal — especially if you reminded him that in the final analysis they died for liberty of conscience."

"But they didn't!"

The monsignor just shrugged his shoulders.

Edmund continued. "Then, for the last two years we have constantly heard the Church's laws on contraception derided by eminent ecclesiastics. I should like to express my gratitude to the Holy Father for having excluded the subject from the council's deliberations. However, I fail to see why he should set up a special commission to study the matter. I, as a married man, must make my decision tonight. I cannot set up a special commission of aunts and uncles to decide what I am going to do here and now. We all know what the Church has always taught. Even a moment's hesitation makes it appear that the Church can be in error."

"Thank you so much," said Testastorta, "for expressing so clearly the problems which you wish to bring to the Holy Father's attention. They are of great importance. I just make a note so that the Holy Father may be prepared to answer you. Yes, in French. Here is your *biglietto*. Be sure that you are in the vestibule by 10:30 a.m. in case His Holiness is on the early side. I shall see you on Tuesday as I shall be accompanying His Holiness during the audiences. It has been a great honour to meet you, Mr. and Mrs. Ruffamo, and I hope that when I next come to England I shall be able to see the great *castello*."

So that was all in order. Edmund and Judith had less free time in Rome than they had expected. There was so much they wanted to see again but too little time to see it. Try as she would, Judith could not recapture the emotions of her honeymoon. She no longer felt that Rome belonged to her and she to it, that it was the expression of her faith. Something had changed. Its monuments were no longer throbbing with joy and life. They formed the sad — almost to the point of being painful — mausoleum to Rome's departed glory.

Tuesday soon arrived. Judith and Edmund were duly in the vestibule by 10:30 a.m. His Holiness was not on the early side. It was well past eleven when they were shown into a large antechamber. It was not the one in which they had seen Pius XII. Although not dissimilar it was considerably bigger. It had two doors opposite each other at the far end of the room from the windows. It was not going to be a private audience after all but a semi-private one. Three other groups besides the Roughams were ushered in as well. Three Italian priests were placed halfway along the wall immediately to the left of the door by which all had entered. A couple of American women were placed between the windows. Two aged and one young Far Easterners, Indo-Chinese perhaps, were opposite the Italian priests. The Roughams were placed opposite the Americans and between the two doors. They waited another half-hour before the Pope entered by the door to the Roughams' left, accompanied by

Msgr. Testastorta and a security man dressed as a flunky. Testastorta guided the Pope straight to the Italian priests. The Roughams therefore knew that they would be last on the list.

Judith understood Italian perfectly well but she could not quite hear. It was clear that the priests had come to thank the Holy Father for some benefit received by their congregation. They presented him with a beautifully bound book and a little statue carved in amber which Judith would have liked to have seen at close quarters. Testastorta took the gifts. The conversation between priests and Pope was animated and pleasant. Although she could not distinguish the words, the Pope's tone of voice was very affable, as of a man who wished to please. The interview might have dragged on for quite a long time had Testastorta not put an end to it. Judith felt that she had judged Paul VI too harshly on the strength of his photographs.

His Holiness then moved on to the American ladies. They were both good-looking women of about forty but too well-groomed — mechanically, impersonally. Judith had no difficulty in understanding. One of the ladies spoke fluent Italian at the top of her voice. They represented CWAC. They had brought a petition signed by a quarter of a million free American Catholic women begging the Holy Father to bless their association and urging him to make sure that this wonderful, world-renewing council did not close without passing pastoral legislation in line with its objective. Judith could not hear the Pope say a word. It was Testastorta who was affable and encouraging. This interview too might have lasted longer but this time it was Pope Paul who put a sudden end to it. Later, on the way out, Judith learned that CWAC stood for Catholic Women's Association for Contraception.

His Holiness then moved on to the Far Easterners. One of the two old men did the talking, the other nodding assent. The young man was the interpreter. Judith was deeply struck by both of the old gentlemen. Refinement and dignity must still exist in the East although difficult to locate in the West. Unfortunately, she could not hear. The translator spoke very quickly in a soft as well as a low-pitched voice. It was clear that things were not going too well. She could hear odd words of Paul VI: trust, obedience, peace. The nodder started to cry. The nodder fell on his knees and gesticulated with his wonderfully neat oriental hands. The translator gave up. Testastorta pulled at the Pope's elbow. The orientals knelt as he gave them his blessing but the nodder was up like a bullet and said in broken French: "Take this! At least take this!" He produced a document. It was too late; the Pope and Testastorta had already turned to the Roughams. But the flunky took the document.

The Pope and the monsignor came forward to about halfway between the easterners and the Roughams. They stopped and Judith could hear Testastorta say to the Pope: "They are of no interest — *sono degli integristi inglesi* — they are English traditionalists." The Pope took another step forward but Testastorta was too quick for him. He left the Pope and came straight at Edmund: "The Holy Father is behind schedule, but I shall see to it that he is made acquainted with your observations. Please kneel for the papal blessing." They obeyed. He waved to the Pope to give his blessing. He obeyed. Pope, monsignor and flunky disappeared through the door to the Roughams' right.

So that was that.

It was 12:30 before Judith and Edmund emerged from the Vatican. They found a congenial *trattoria* for lunch. Judith told Edmund what she had understood of the conversations, ending up with: "They are of no interest — just English traditionalists." Edmund was obviously deeply upset. Something had snapped in his makeup.

Judith did not react in the same way at all. The audience — or lack of it — did not worry her. What puzzled her was Pope Paul's eyes. She had seen from photographs that he had weak hands and no lips, but she had thought that his eyes looked human enough. Although quite humourless, she imagined that they craved for understanding, even affection. She had seen his eyes very clearly when he had turned from the easterners to Edmund and herself. Indeed, while Testastorta had spoken to Edmund, the Pope's eyes and hers had met. For an appreciable time, for something like twenty seconds, they had stared at each other.

No, there was no affection there nor craving for it. Those large brown eyes hypnotized her. Less expressive only than the hands, eyes can radiate so much: joy or sorrow, openness or cunning; generosity or meanness — the whole gamut of human attitudes. What was it exactly that the Pope's eyes radiated? That was the wrong word: they expressed something but radiated nothing. Somehow they were negative. It was not suffering they expressed nor sorrow. Melancholy was nearer the mark but the term was too poetic and too weak. They were wells of loneliness dropping into an abyss of sadness, a sort of primeval sadness before the first day dawned. Neither did they evoke pity and compassion. To Judith they seemed terrifying. She dared not mention her reaction to Edmund. He was bad enough as it was.

They saw Ronnie that evening. He merely burst into laughter. "It's all my fault, entirely my fault! You see, one gets so used to Roman ways that one forgets to warn people. I ought to have primed you to tell Testastorta that you had come to Rome on purpose to inform the Holy Father of the enthusiastic reception among English Catholics of the decrees on the mass media, the reform of the liturgy and above all *Lumen Gentium.* You would then have had a pucka private audience in which you could have said what you liked. My dear, innocent cousins, what a bloomer! Thank God I'm not a Papist or I should have had to resign my post as being tarred with the *integriste* brush. As a respectable Protestant I am fortunately above suspicion..."

To Judith's dismay, Ronnie's jollity merely augmented Edmund's gloom. Luckily on the following morning at the crack of dawn the Roughams set out for home.

XXI

THE LOSS OF THE CROSS

Judith and Edmund arrived home rather later than they had expected on the evening of Saturday, October 16th. It was nearly 11 p.m. The traffic had held them up and, in making a short cut, Edmund had lost his way. But they had rung up from both Dover and some unknown place in the vicinity of Romford. Only George was in bed. Lady Milden, Giacinta and Richard were all there to greet them. There was much kissing and chatter along with the distribution of presents before Giacinta took Richard upstairs.

It must be remembered that, although Judith wrote a little letter to Richard each evening, Judith had had no news from home. Richard had sent one postcard to prove that he was still alive. Lady Milden swore that she had written twice but the Italian post had clearly decided against delivery. Giacinta was illiterate anyway. In fact the impact of coming home was unimpaired by correspondence. Judith was overjoyed. She was also in better health than she had been since before her pregnancy with Richard eight years previously.

Edmund and Judith decided to have a lie-in on the Sunday morning. Giacinta would take Richard to the eight o'clock Mass and they would go to the eleven o'clock. Giacinta said something about the new priest being *orribile* and "every zing is cambiato excepta zee ora of zee Missa." They paid no attention.

At exactly eleven o'clock Edmund and Judith entered Holy Cross. It was unrecognizable. The rather nice oak benches had gone. They were replaced by aluminum chairs with brightly coloured plastic seats and backs. The confessionals had disappeared. So had the two side altars with the pictures by Piola. There were no altar rails. The High Altar had vanished along with the reredos with the Rougham Crucifix.

In the middle of the church was a trestle table with a white oil-cloth covering on which stood a microphone. The chairs surrounded the trestle table except on the sanctuary side, where a wide passage was left containing two cheap-jack lecterns surmounted by more microphones. The ex-sanctuary, which was raised, contained Mr. and Mrs. Butterworth, more microphones and some odd bodies who turned out to form the choir. The Blessed Sacrament was nowhere apparent.

Edmund and Judith were stunned. They stood gaping in the doorway. Mrs. Larkin saw them and came up: "My poor darlings," she said with the intimacy of shared suffering, "your Italian lady told me that you were expected back last night. There are a couple of seats beside me."

There is no need to describe the ceremony. Although this was in October 1965 and consequently before the disastrous reform of May 1967 and the New Ordo of 1969, it was possibly even more grim than what Catholics have since got used to. Doubtless the priest, whose name turned out to be Thomas Todson, still said the old Preface and Canon in Latin, but the silence was drowned by Mr. and Mrs. Butterworth and friends over the microphones. Anyway, Edmund and Judith were not in a frame of mind to pay sympathetic attention. Luckily they did not attempt to go to Holy Communion. Although it was still illicit for communicants to receive the Sacrament standing up, Father Todson insisted on his parishioners doing just that.

After the ceremony, instead of going into the sacristy to make his thanksgiving, Father Todson made a dash for the main door, the two side ones being locked, while Mr. and Mrs. Butterworth and friends sang the last hymn, which had replaced the Last Gospel. This rather annoyed Edmund. He would have liked to have seen the priest in the privacy of the sacristy. However, if the fellow wanted things in public, in public they would be. He took Judith's arm: "Come along. We'll have it out with this little twerp straight away." Mrs. Larkin remained in her place, thumbing hard at her rosary.

Only about a third of the congregation had got out when the exit was blocked by Father Todson and Mr. and Mrs. Rougham.

"My name is Rougham and this is my wife. It so happens that we are the donors of this church and presbytery. I want to know..."

"So it shows that you could well afford it," interrupted the good father.

"And I want to know what has become of the High Altar with its reredos and crucifix, the side altars with their pictures and the confessionals."

"I thought you said you had given them," the father replied. "They consequently have nothing to do with you."

"We had given them for a purpose and that purpose has clearly been defeated."

There was a murmur of "Hear, hear! Mr. Rougham" and the like from the audience still blocked in the porch.

"Your gift has been spent according to your intention," said the father, "which I generously presume to have been for the welfare of the Church and not for your personal gratification."

"Quite right!" said Mr. and Mrs. Butterworth and friends, who by this time had pushed their way through the throng.

"Curiously enough," said Edmund, "I have not accused you of misappropriation, although I could. I have merely asked you what you have done with them."

"I have sold them," said the father.

"That I gathered from your previous answer," said Edmund. "What I want to know is whether any of our gifts remain unsold and to whom you have sold the rest."

There was much "Fair enough," and "That's right, Mr. Rougham" from the audience — except of course from the Butterworth elite.

"Well, you can take back what you like from the presbytery and sacristy," said the good father. "I should hate to feel beholden to any bloody capitalist. You either owe it in justice or you don't. As for the High Altar and other examples of bourgeois culture you mention, I flogged them to a dealer and have forgotten his name. You can console yourself in the knowledge that the parish is still in credit after paying for what was needed to make this place suitable for the liturgy decreed by the council."

Edmund would have liked to hit the fellow firmly on the jaw but refrained: firstly Todson was much smaller than he and, secondly, he was a priest. Instead, Edmund put his hands on his shoulders and shook him: "Wake up, little man! And try to be civil and talk sense."

He cannot have shaken Todson very violently for the simple reason that he was encumbered by his walking-stick in his right hand and his Daily Missal in the left. However, either from shock or fear, little Todson collapsed. He did not actually faint but lay prone on the ground. Now, it is not easy to continue a conversation with a person at foot-level, so Edmund took Judith's arm and retired from the scene while Mr. and Mrs. Butterworth and friends carried the prostrate priest into the presbytery.

The interview had been eminently unsatisfactory since Edmund still did not know to whom the Rougham Crucifix had been sold. When they got back to the Dower House, Judith thought she would have a try. She immediately rang up the presbytery as Father was probably in no condition to answer the phone. Priests may come and priests may go, but not always the housekeepers. It was still Mrs. Cusson as in the days of Canon Slattery.

Judith first inquired after the father. Yes, he had quite recovered from his little shakeup. And by the way, did Mrs. Cusson remember to whom the High Altar and the rest had been sold? Indeed yes: Mrs. Cusson had given cups of tea to the men. They had had such a time in moving the altar. She had noticed the name on the van: Charles Brack, Antique Dealer, Church Street, Kensington. "But Father is not like the dear canon at all, Mrs. Rougham. He has such strange ways and invites such funny people. Not like the canon at all..."

They found "Brack, Charles B." in the telephone book all right. Being Sunday, there was no answer. They tried a "Brack, Mrs. C. B." but there was no answer either. Edmund rang up again as soon as he got to the Treasury on Monday morning. Yes, Mr. Brack had bought a load of stuff from a father at Waltham-ford some three weeks ago. He had already sold some but was transforming the rest to secular use.

"Those confessionals will make wonderful display cabinets, worth at least fifteen-hundred each." The crucifix had gone last week. He would keep open that afternoon until Mr. Rougham called and would not sell anything else from Walthamford.

There was a pile of work at the Treasury, including a draft speech for the chancellor. When Edmund finally got to Church Street, Mr. Brack was still there. "It is awfully kind of you to keep open for me. I have a personal interest in the objects from Walthamford as I happen to have given most of them to the church."

"And the reverend sold them behind your back?"

"Exactly."

"That's a new one on me. You don't kill the goose but sell the golden egg for coppers to guarantee that he won't lay another."

"Yes, I fear you have got it right. That is what I was: a goose with starry eyes."

"Sorry! I wasn't thinking of it that way round. No offense meant."

The crucifix? It was a splendid piece all right, worth a couple of thousand or more. But difficult to sell; it might be hanging round the place for a couple of years, so he had only given the father £800 for it. He looked up his records. It was exactly a week ago that a foreign gentleman had come in. He was quite excited over the crucifix.

"I quoted him £1,250 for a quick sale. That was cheap. He took one of the two side altars as well, which I'd turned into a console. He got that expensive."

"I suppose you have his name, Mr. Brack?"

"Let me see. No, no name."

"But he must have spent some three-thousand pounds in your shop. Surely he gave you a cheque?"

"No. Look for yourself in my book: 'paid cash.' You see, he was a foreign gentleman and perhaps had no English account."

Edmund understood perfectly. Cheques left traces for the tax people; cash did not. Mr. Brack preferred cash payments.

"It was on the Monday he came in but on the Tuesday — see the date: October 12th — he came back with the cash and a

builder's van. I did not look at the number plate. The van driver
helped me to pack it all in. Apart from your crucifix, took a lot of
oddments, including bits of furniture which had not come from
your reverend."

Anyway, Edmund bought back at a very reasonable price the
High Altar, the Jacobean reredos and the two Piolas. The remains
of the Rougham property, such as the second side altar, the two
confessionals and the candelabra, he left as being of considerably
more value to Mr. Brack than to himself. He also bought
whatever the Waddington's had given. It seemed to him that
some of it was missing, notably a magnificent Sicilian chalice,
but he was too upset at the loss of his crucifix to bother Mr.
Brack about it. He rang up the Brig there and then to send down
a lorry the following day to collect the stuff. The Waddingtons'
property was to be left at Walthamford. The rest was to go to the
castle.

"Here is a cheque for £1,000 on account and I'll bring you the
rest in cash at lunch time tomorrow, when the lorry should be
here. Is that all right?" he asked Brack.

"Thanks! Yes, that will do fine." Mr. Brack hesitated for a moment and then continued. "I take it, Mister, that you are a
Catholic. Perhaps you can explain something to me. You see, I'm a
Jew and don't understand. I've always had a good line in religious
art: I like it myself. Well, up to about three years ago Catholic
fathers were among my best customers. Prices ran high. You could
not buy a decent ivory crucifix for love nor money. Well, I've got
drawers full of 'em. I give between £20 and £30 for them to take
'em off the market. You see that magnificent Louis XV sideboard
over there? Well, it isn't a sideboard; it's an altar. I sold it to a
reverend about ten years ago for £500 when that was a lot of
money. Six months ago the same reverend came back and begged
me to give him £200 for it. I did. I've mucked it up a bit to make it
a sideboard and shall sell it for £3,000. What puzzles me is that in
most cases it's the same father. Take your reverend at Walthamford. Why do you think he contacted me to get rid of the stuff in
his church? Because a few years ago he bought that off me."

"That" was an embroidery of Our Lady after a Sassoferrato in the Louvre. It was not Edmund's taste but the workmanship was astonishing. Mr. Brack continued:

"When he sold the church stuff, he threw that in with it and asked me to give him a good price for it. 'Look here, Reverend,' I said, 'I can't. Nobody wants Madonnas now, not even you reverends. As a special favour I'll give you a tenner for it, but I'll probably have to chuck it in with the lot.' That's your father at Walthamford. They used to buy expensively and now they chuck it out. Later they'll be blaming the bloody Jews for making money out of them."

"My dear Mr. Brack, it is as much a mystery to me as it is to you. All I can say is that the Catholic clergy is suffering from collective lunacy. Incidentally, I shall buy the embroidery of the Madonna as well."

"No you won't. I'll give it to you as permanent evidence of the collective lunacy."

That was all very fine and large — as well as a lot of money. However, there was no trace of the one thing Edmund wanted: the Rougham Crucifix. During the next few weeks he had advertisements with a picture to catch the eye inserted in all the art magazines and antique trade papers. They drew no reply.

Edmund had taken note of the day on which Brack had sold the crucifix. It was Tuesday, October 12th, the day on which he and Judith had been received in audience by Pope Paul VI.

XXII

PARADISE LOST

Edmund was a cradle Catholic. He had never questioned his religion. To do so would be graver sin than dirty thoughts. This had enormous advantages. He had automatic certitudes. His obedience to the Church was not lip service but soul service. Judith loved him for it: in his way he was as innocent as her Richard. It is true that before he went to Rome Edmund's faith had already been tottering. It was not because he questioned it but because the bishops did. It was like vertigo: those who suffer from it feel it just as acutely at seeing another person on the edge of a cliff as they would if they stood there themselves. However, his hope in the Church and his love of it remained fairly intact. He placed his hope in the Sovereign Pontiff and his love in the piety of the humble clergy.

In the same week both were shattered. He had seen the Pope with his own eyes. His hope had vanished in that audience. He had returned to his parish to witness its destruction. The disappearance of the crucifix was the symbol of his vanished charity. The impact of these events on Edmund is beyond description.

They had an immediate physical effect. It will be remembered that every morning except Saturday Edmund and Judith walked to Mass hand-in-hand like children. On Monday Judith got up as usual. When she got downstairs Edmund was still dawdling over his breakfast.

"Aren't you coming?" she asked.

"No, I cannot stand it," was the reply. "The crucifix is no longer there and I fail to see why I should adore a microphone. I shall go straight to the Treasury." For the first time at Holy Cross Judith went to Mass alone. It hurt her.

It was the same on Sunday. "No, dear, you go and pray for me. I loved my religion too much to watch a clown make a farce of it."

"But Edmund, the Mass is still the Mass even if said by a clown."

"Yes, and it will still be the Mass whether I am there or not."

"Besides, Todson may be a fool, but that does not necessarily make him a clown."

"He sold the embroidery of his heavenly mother for £10. I have hung it up in my study to remind me. I would not give a penny for his conscience."

There was nothing doing. Judith went with George in the pram. Giacinta was taking Richard later.

That same Sunday evening after dinner Judith tackled Edmund directly: had he really given up the practice of his religion?

"Yes."

"But surely the behaviour of the Pope and the disappearance of the crucifix do not alter it?"

"Doubtless not — at least not the content of the religion. But they do alter its manifestation. I suppose that somehow, somewhere, I still have the Faith; I don't know. But to practice one's religion is to manifest it. That, under the present circumstances, I refuse to do.

"Do you remember my saying to you a couple of years ago that we looked at religion in different ways? You, as a convert, looked at it from the inside as a set of truths woven into a wonderful unity. Cut one strand and the unity would be irremediably destroyed. You were consequently prepared to fight the visible authority to preserve the integrity of the Faith — the content of the religion.

"I, as a cradle Catholic, have always looked at my religion from the outside, as a visible, hierarchical institution. I remember saying that what we must preserve at all costs was the authority of the visible church. Do you remember that? Ah! Judith, my love, where is that visible, hierarchical authority now? I have seen the Pope. I know my bishop. I have witnessed what my parish priest is capable of doing.

"You said that we must decide then and there when we should dig our toes in — if the Mass were jettisoned, Protestant ministries recognized, contraception condoned. You were probably right and they may all come about. But I do not need those criteria. To my way of thinking the credibility of the clergy from Pope to Todson has collapsed.

"Perhaps I have not lost the Faith. As I said, I don't know. What I do know is that I hate the visible, hierarchical church because she has deceived me by undermining her own authority. It was finally in her authority that I believed. Doubtless my religion was too 'clerical.' At least I have been cured of that. I hate the clergy to the core of my being."

There was a long pause. Judith felt it wiser to say nothing. Eventually Edmund continued in a much more peaceful tone:

"Yes, Judith, my religion was a wonderful dream. I am grateful to have had it and shall not forget it. It represented to me all that was pure, beautiful, noble, glorious, self-sacrificing. But a dream it was. I have woken up to discover that I am looking at a heap of dung."

Edmund paused again. Judith felt too sad to speak. He continued: "I know for certain that I had the dream. I also know that in some way, a way I fail to understand, the dream must be true because it was too beautiful to be a lie. But it has vanished, as dreams do, and no longer has contact with reality. No, that is not quite true. It still has one contact with reality. It is certainly irrational — but then, man is everything except a rational animal. It is irrational, but my dream still strikes reality at one point. That point is you, Judith. You must promise me never to give up practicing, no matter how distasteful it may be to you; and you must promise to stick by me no matter what a cur I may be. You are the only part of my dream which is still clothed in flesh and blood."

There was more silence. Edmund stood up: "It is utterly illogical but such is the fact. I cannot go to Mass; it would be the ultimate in hypocrisy. I should never forgive you if you did not; you would have wiped out the only surviving evidence of my dream. Good night, Judith, my love and my life."

In its way, life was even more difficult for Judith than it was for Edmund. He had lapsed, so that was that. Judith had not. Every morning she went alone to Holy Microphone. She even went there on Saturdays as she preferred Todson's vulgarity to Mallon's refeenement at the convent. Anyway, it was not too bad on a weekday. Only about fifteen people turned up, all died-in-the-wool traditionalists. A deputation composed of the Larkins, Waddingtons and Judith convinced Father Todson that the microphones were quite unnecessary on weekdays and that, with so few people, there was no point in having Communion standing. Todson attempted to have Mass sitting down round the breakfast table in the presbytery. The excuse, of course, was that he suffered from lumbago. This was miraculously cured when nobody turned up. Like many converts, Judith had found the Rosary a particularly difficult Catholic devotion. It was, however, indispensable on Sundays; it could deaden even the microphones and the Butterworth choir. Perhaps Father Todson was a secret agent for the Rosary Crusade.

All that was disagreeable enough but was fairly superficial. The real trouble lay deeper. Up till now the Dower House had contained a wonderfully united family. The cause and focal point of this unity had been its religion. The marriage had been due to it, as also the existence of Richard and George. The years of continence and the attempt at the "safe period" would have been impossible without a religious motive. Above all, their reciprocal trust and esteem was grounded in their common religion. Richard, too, had so far grown up with the undivided example of his parents. That was all wonderful and gave rise to the undefinable sentiment called happiness.

Thanks to the council — and Judith had not the slightest doubt where to lay the blame — all that had vanished. The Dower House contained a divided family. Religion was no longer the cause of unity but of dissent. And this must be happening in hundreds of thousands of families throughout the world. Doubtless each family had different problems but all had been held together by the internal, intrinsic grip of their religion. As Judith meditated on these things she could foresee that Catholic decrees of nullity would soon be as common as non-Catholic divorces. That brought her to a halt. Would she and Edmund get divorced? It was unthinkable! No, since the council, nothing was unthinkable. Anyway, for the sake of an illusory ecumenism — or so it was said — the council had shattered the only true unity in the world, that of the Catholic Faith. And along with that unity all lesser, dependent unities had been cracked if not broken asunder.

Edmund had ceased to practice on Monday, October 18th, 1965. Things jogged along much as usual until after Christmas. Christmas itself was something of a trial. Edmund did not go to Mass. This made the ensuing festivities a hollow sham. But it gave Judith the opportunity to talk to her in-laws about Edmund. They could see the fact for themselves. There was nothing much they could do about it except advise patience and prudence and give Judith their moral support. The Brig was wonderfully consoling: "Do you know, Judith, without any dam' council to worry about, I lapsed for about eighteen months? It was years back, in Poonah. It wasn't over girls, either. I had plenty of them but I never took 'em seriously. A girl only becomes serious when you marry her. It was polo. There was a bleeding padre, a real Jansenist, who would not change the times of Masses. So polo it was. But, Judith, God's divine providence always has the last word. God's divine providence — that's what you've got to remember, my dear. Well, I bust both of my legs: not one but two; my left leg and my right leg. After that it was all Mass and no polo. It will be the same with Edmund. The less you do about it the better — apart from wearing your knees out. God's divine providence, that's the real stuff. When you least expect it — and nothing to do with you — he'll be licking the altar like a lapdog. No, that's the wrong metaphor, but you know what I mean. And once more he will be the faithful hound sniffing round his wife and children. Leave it to God's divine providence and wear your knees out, Judith." Judith loved the Brig.

The first actual row with Edmund was over Richard's education. At birth he had been put down for Beaumont, where the Roughams had been educated ever since it was founded. In September 1966 he would go to St. John's, Beaumont's preparatory school, and so work his way through as Edmund himself and the Brig had done. Incidentally, in 1958 the Brig had subscribed £10,000 for the enlargement and modernization of the

school. In July 1965 Edmund received a circular that Beaumont
was to be closed in favor of Stonyhurst, but St. John's would continue. Quite apart from the wasted £10,000 of his father's, this
upset Edmund considerably: he had loved his school. Of course,
with Jesuits jumping over the wall at two a minute and no vocations, you could not expect them to keep open two major public
schools. It was just another victim of the renewal. So in July it
was decided that Richard should go to St. John's in September
1966 and thence proceed to Stonyhurst.

Yes, but that was before the audience with the Pope and the
return to Holy Cross. One evening at the end of January 1966,
Judith mentioned by chance that it was about time Edmund went
over to St. John's to make final arrangements about Richard's ad-
mission in September. Edmund flared up: "Never shall a son of
mine be subjected to such hypocrites and robbers..." No, the boy
would be much better off at the Anglican school where he was.
Then at fourteen he could be sent to a decent public school. He
was not in favour of Eton, partly because it had become the "tech
school" for the stock exchange, but principally because it had an
official Catholic chaplaincy. No, he would prefer a decent,
honest, agnostic school like Stowe.

It was all frightfully difficult and some unpleasant things were
said. The situation was odd: it was the marriage convert who was
insisting on the Catholic education of the child against her cradle
husband. Moreover, Judith's brother, John, had been educated at
Stowe.

With time and patience Judith won. In September Richard
was to go to St. John's. After that, one would see: Stonyhurst or
Stowe. Edmund drove over to Stowe, interviewed the head-
master and put Richard's name down. He did not go to St. John's
or Beaumont. The conflict left a scar. Edmund became touchy
and disagreeable.

Early in March things got worse. In spite of total continence,
Judith and Edmund still slept in the main bedroom, although in
different beds. Up to their return from Italy one of Judith's main
pleasures in life was chatting away with Edmund after the day
was over from the comfort of the bed. Often they did not put

their lights out until the early hours of the morning. She tried to keep it up after Edmund had lapsed, but it was somehow artificial. The lights were switched off progressively earlier.

Well, in early March Edmund moved into one of the spare rooms. The excuse was that it made continence easier. Judith knew that to be rubbish. It pained her. At about the same time Edmund stopped coming home from the castle on Saturday nights. The excuse was that he would not be giving a bad example to Richard by obviously missing Mass on Sunday mornings. This Judith also knew to be rubbish. Actually, the Brig had told her that instead of being useful Edmund had become a positive pest at the castle. He quarreled with the tenants, was sharp with the farmhands, impolite to the neighbours. There was nothing the Brig could do about it. Edmund had become so incredibly touchy that the most remote criticism merely made him walk out of the room.

It is true that Edmund had always been extremely conscientious over his work. If he and Judith were not entertaining, he often brought files home and after dinner did two, three and sometimes four hours of work in the quiet of his study. Judith had objected to more than two because it deprived her of the chat in bed. That was all changed. Instead of bringing files home he completed them at the Treasury. Even if there were guests, he sometimes rang up to apologize for his absence. Fairly often he did not get back to Dower House until the early hours of the morning:

There was one detail in the new curriculum of life which hurt Judith particularly: they never kissed. It seems absurd. What is a kiss anyway? But the fact is that it did not happen.

There were a thousand other details — ticking off Richard, being negligent of George and thoughtless with Giacinta. The trouble was that they all came so gradually that there was never a precise moment when Judith felt that she could make a stand. By the time the symptom was evident in Edmund, it was too late to apply a remedy. So the symptoms just accrued and of remedy there was none.

Judith could see this quite clearly. With hindsight there were at least a half-dozen points at which she could and should have put her foot down. But in practice it is not easy to put your foot down on something that has not happened. By the time it has, it is too late. Anyway, Edmund was as stubborn as a mule. In September at the start of the term she did her utmost to make him take Richard over to St. John's. After all, it was the child's first boarding school. "No! It is you who insist on sending him there, so you can take him. I shall not put my foot in the place. I accepted unquestioningly from the Jesuits an outlook on life which they now deny. It is enough that I entrust my child to them — for your sake. To smile and make pleasant conversation with that set of rogues is beyond the capacity of my hypocrisy."

"But Edmund, you are being grossly unfair. You yourself still visit Father Martin."

Edmund did not answer straight away. When he did it was in a gentler voice. "Poor Father Martin, the most refined thinker the society has produced this century. They leave him alone if he keeps his mouth shut but jeer at him if he dares to open it. Dear Father Martin, his suppression is even more callous than that of Beaumont. I have not seen him since we returned from Rome."

Judith thought that Edmund's eyes looked moist. There was still hope. There was still some softness in his makeup. "That was nearly a year ago. I think you ought to call on him. He must be getting pretty old."

"Perhaps I shall — sometime."

Once Richard was at school the alienation became almost complete. It was not only Edmund who had drifted away from Judith, but Judith also found herself doing the same from him. Without Edmund or Richard she felt lonely. At first she invited herself round to Milli's. The trouble was that Milli was so difficult to get hold of. Ever since she had divorced Tubby she had thrown herself with equal passion into her work and gadding around. She was never at home. Then Milli upset Judith. It was in October, a month after Richard had gone to St. John's. They were lunching together in a restaurant near Milli's hospital. Judith confided to Milli her troubles with Edmund. As she stuffed spaghetti into her mouth, Milli said in her usual matter-of-fact way: "He's got a girl. Ever seen his secretary at the Treasury?"

Now this had never crossed Judith's mind. Once it was said, however, it was perfectly obvious. Judith was stunned. No, it could not be true. It was Milli herself who was totally immoral and took it for granted that everybody was as promiscuous as herself. At any rate, Judith knew Edmund's secretary perfectly well. She was the backbone and terror of the Treasury: an older and more formidable version of Miss Portia Sowerby. Milli was incapable of understanding what loss of faith could mean because she had none. She reduced everything to what she understood: sex.

Clearly the idea rankled in Judith's mind. She managed finally to reject it, but along with the idea she rejected Milli. She still admired her and was very fond of her, but to see her revived the memory of her accusation against Edmund. It was the same situation which had arisen years before and unbeknown to Judith between her father and herself.

There remained Pamela, brother John and Mother. The Brig was no use because Edmund went to the castle for weekends, when Judith felt particularly lonely. Pamela was very useful for lunch on Saturdays. She lived quite near, just the other side of Epping. She was now a Mrs. Mainwaring, having married one of the directors of Christie's, where she still had a part-time job. She had married much later than Judith and her first-born was a little girl six months younger than George. What fun if they married! Judith did not confide her troubles to her but Pamela realized that all was not well between Judith and Edmund because he never turned up and his name was never mentioned. However, she was far too discreet to pry into Judith's business.

Brother John could always be relied on, but Judith did not like to impose on her sister-in-law. She already had three children to look after without her landing up with George. There remained Lady Milden, Judith's rather neglected mother. She suddenly realized that Mother was growing old and lonely. She needed company. Judith provided it. She slipped into the habit of spending Saturday night and Sunday in Hampstead. Judith and Edmund rarely saw each other.

It was all immeasurably sad. A marriage of untold happiness

and sacrifice had been created by Catholicism and destroyed by the council. However, the Brig was undoubtedly right: Judith must wear her knees out and be prepared to grasp the intervention of Divine Providence, irrespective of what form it took.

XXIII

PARADISE REGAINED

Judith would never forget the date. It was Sunday, January 8th, 1967. She had spent Saturday night at her mother's along with George. Richard had not gone back to school but she had left him with Giacinta. He would be far happier at home playing with his toys and mucking about in the garden than "being a good boy" at his granny's. Lady Milden had a knack for making children feel miserable. As Judith was absent, Edmund had spent the weekend at the Dower House. This was not an unusual discourtesy. Judith returned fairly early on Sunday evening, before 6 p.m. When she got into the hall, she could hear thumps interspersed with shrieks of merriment coming from the drawing-room. She peeped in. It was Edmund and Richard wrestling on the floor. Judith was dumbfounded. Edmund cried out between two buffetings from Richard: "Hello, Judith! Let me know when you have put George to bed; I'll come up and listen to his prayers." He did, too, and knelt down.

Richard dined with his parents, so nothing important was said. Edmund, however, was perfectly charming. He inquired after Lady Milden. He thanked Giacinta for something or other. He was gay and considerate. Most astonishing of all, he said grace. When Richard disappeared, instead of disappearing himself into his study, he poured out two glasses of port, as of old, and carried them into the drawing-room. As of old, they sat down in the arm chairs either side of the fire.

"Judith," he said, "I am feeling a bit feverish and shall go to bed as soon as I have finished my port. By the way, do you mind if I sleep in your bedroom? I am frightened of being sick.

"I want to tell you something. Milli has been here this afternoon. It is entirely my fault and I do not blame your cousin in the least. I have quarreled with her irremediably and have forbidden her to set foot again over this threshold."

"But Edmund, darling, what's wrong with you? You have become so quarrelsome. You quarrel with me, Giacinta, Richard — even with the Brig and Lucy who, heaven alone knows, are easy enough. And now it's Milli. Surely we cannot all be always wrong. What's the matter with you?"

"Yes, Judith, there is a lot the matter with me. You don't mind me sleeping in your bedroom tonight?"

"Of course not, Edmund! But what is all this about?"

"I shall tell you everything in the morning. I promise. But I want to have one night of happiness. I'll go and change the bed-clothes. No, don't come up; I shall do it myself."

He came over to Judith, who was sitting in a low armchair. He knelt beside her and kissed her tenderly and lingeringly: "Good night, Judith, my life and only love. Yes, I swear to that: my only love. I have tried to live without you and my religion; I cannot."

Judith could hear him dashing up the stairs, taking them two at a time. He certainly did not feel sick, so that was not the reason why he wanted to sleep in his old bed. Equally certainly he was immensely happy.

Judith poured herself out another glass of port. What on earth was he going to tell her tomorrow morning? It must be something to do with Milli. But it did not surprise her that he had quarreled with her. He had always disliked her: "Your cousin is a brain without a heart and a body without a soul," was his dictum. But why was he so affectionate and what had he meant by wanting one night of happiness?

Suddenly the truth flashed across her mind. It was perfectly obvious. How could she be so blind! A couple of months ago, it was Milli who had suggested that Edmund was involved with a girl. Yes, she had known that all right because it was she. The bitch!

For a couple of minutes Judith was consumed with rage. Had either of them been to hand she would willingly have committed murder. She even started out of her chair to go upstairs and have it out with Edmund, but by the time she had got to the door her rage had subsided. She sank back into her chair. Rage had given way to self-pity: that of all the people in the world the two she most loved (apart from her children) should deceive her! Why should Milli pick on Edmund? Any man was the same to her. But how could Edmund manage it? Did he hate her, Judith, more than he despised Milli? Had they done it deliberately to spite her?

But at last the "self" fell away from the pity. Pity remained alone. Poor Milli had no Tubby. Poor Edmund had scarcely had a wife since his honeymoon. It was not their fault. Milli was just made like that. As for Edmund, he had not married to become a monk. At least in part it was her fault. Judith had always despised people who justified themselves by blaming others. Fair enough. Why should God not put her sincerity to the test? Was she going to blame Edmund morally, when she was perhaps physically responsible?

Like most women, Judith thought men frightfully clever but unbelievably weak in character: they were overgrown children. Her darling Edmund was no exception. He must have been like putty in Milli's powerful embrace. And in fact he had confessed — in the rather roundabout way in which children normally do. Dear, darling Edmund, of course he was forgiven. Indeed, he had much to forgive her.

Milli was different. She was a harder pill to swallow. She was not a manchild but a woman — and consequently knew what she was doing. She must have felt very sure of her ground when she told Judith over her spaghetti that Edmund had a girlfriend. Yet in fact she had failed: that very afternoon Edmund had turned her out of the house. Poor, dear Edmund, it must have required a lot of courage: Milli was not an easy customer. But at this point, Judith's pity even reached down to Milli. She had failed. And so, with a great gulp, even Milli was forgiven: she was just made that way.

However, there were some people whom Judith would not forgive. She knew perfectly well who had turned Edmund's certainties into doubt; by whom his moral standards had been questioned; who had substituted permissiveness for sacrifice, convenience for good, the religion of man for the religion of God. She could place the blame fairly and squarely on the council. She did.

By now it was one o'clock in the morning. Judith fell on her knees and took the rosary out of her bag. She clutched the little crucifix. "Thank you, Jesus, for giving back to me my Edmund. I shall be a wife to him, secure in your Divine Providence. I confess that I have been selfish all along. Selfish in our continence. Even selfish over George; it was I who wanted him. This time I shall not be selfish. I should like a little girl; but you need not give her — or you can take her. And I thank you for turning even our selfishness and sins into such happiness. And I thank you even more for making your ways incomprehensible to us. I should despise them if I understood them. So thank you. Forgive me. Bless my Edmund...and poor Milli."

It was nearly two in the morning when Judith went to bed. There lay Edmund, sleeping like a baby. She dared not kiss him for fear of waking him. She kissed the bed-post instead.

Judith lay awake for most of the night. However, she dozed off in the morning and when she woke up at a quarter to eight Edmund had already left the room. She slipped on a dressing gown and went downstairs.

Edmund had finished his breakfast and was smoking a cigarette. He stood up as Judith entered: "Sit down, my love. I shall tell you everything, as I promised."

Judith flung herself into his arms. "Edmund, my Edmund! You told it all to me last night. I know it was Milli. But it is finished — over and done with. It would only hurt us both to tell me the details."

Edmund said nothing. He was trying to keep back tears of gratitude. For a moment they stood embracing each other. Then Judith noticed a missal on the table. "You are not going to Mass, Edmund?" she asked.

"Yes, my dear. My two loves are inseparable: you and my religion. I have re-found them both. I have tried to live without them, but I cannot."

"But darling, I'm not dressed; I cannot come with you."

"No, my dear. Anyway, I cannot face Todson and what was once Holy Cross. I shall stop off at Edmonton on my way to the office. You see, I must ask forgiveness of God as well as from you. I must be off if I am to be there in a quarter of an hour."

When Edmund had gone, Judith wept for joy. Perhaps she had never felt so happy in her life. Years ago, Edmund had given her the experience of innocence; now he had given her the experience of forgiving — and it was the more sublime of the two.

*   *   *   *   *

Judith was, of course, quite right concerning Edmund and Milli. In moments of depression they had consoled each other. No, that is not exact: Milli never needed consoling; it was Edmund who did. Judith probably never realized how much. She lived in a closed circle of friends and relatives. Within the limits of her domestic obligations she led her own life as she pleased.

Not so Edmund. He had to face the world. He bore a famous recusant name, so everybody knew he was a Catholic. He was the only Catholic of his grade at the Treasury. He was the chancellor's pet and, aside from writing his speeches, acted more or less as his liaison officer with other ministries. He lived in fact among non-Catholics who were not of his choosing.

It will be remembered, moreover, that during the pontificate of John XXIII and the first two sessions of the council Edmund had been positively optimistic. The old sectarian shrieks of "No Popery" had been turned into veneration of the Pope and admiration for the council. Now, it was precisely that — the very cause of his optimism — which had become the principal cause of his depression, along with Archbishop Roberts and episcopal porn. Every day he had to put up with well-intentioned compliments. "That's a wonderful pope you've got. Seen this article? He says we're all Christians together, be we Jews or Muslims. That's what I've always believed." "By Jove, Rougham, you've got a bright boy in that Cardinal Suenens. He says we marry to have intercourse, nothing to do with bloody brats. Didn't know you Papists were so broad-minded." "Hello, Rougham! You're a Papist, aren't you? Congratulations! Your church has shed the blinkers. I married my daughter to one of yours last Saturday. No dam' nonsense about promises and so on. The vicar did it splendidly in the village church with your chap in attendance. Just right. That's Christian charity for you." "Went to one of your services the other day. A bit Low Church for my taste, but at least one knows what it's about." "Have you read what your pope said yesterday (December 7th, 1965)? 'The religion of God made man has met the religion of man made God...There is no opposition...We, more than anyone, favour the promotion of man.' That's what free-thinkers and humanists have said all along. Shake hands, Rougham, old boy!" "Good show, Edmund! I suppose that now you Catholics have become Protestants, we shall have to become R.C.'s to preserve our independence." And so on and on, day in, day out. It was a cross which the laity but not the clergy had to endure. Can there be a more painful predicament than to have to accept as a compliment what in all the world one most hates? Such was the situation in which the council placed millions of Catholics all over the world. Edmund stuck it until the audience with Paul VI and the disappearance of the crucifix. That was the end.

Edmund did not strictly get depressed; he was permanently depressed. He consoled himself with Milli. At first there was nothing regular about it but, like all human actions, it tended to become a habit. Curiously enough, Edmund did not really feel unfaithful to Judith for the simple reason that he despised Milli, almost hated her. That was why he could use her. Milli's attitude was different. It was this difference in attitude which led to the rupture on Sunday, January 8th, 1967. Milli knew that Judith was visiting her mother and that Edmund was not going to the castle. She would consequently find him alone at Walthamford. She overlooked Richard. This in itself annoyed Edmund. He did not mind going to Chelsea but he objected to the presence of Milli in his own home.

She arrived before lunch. After lunch Edmund played with Richard on the drawing-room floor. Milli was sitting very upright in a Louis XVI armchair. Richard had not enjoyed so much paternal attention for a long time. Seeing that Richard was the centre of attention, Milli called him over to her and sat him on her lap. Richard was an affectionate child and was well used to Aunty Milli. She kissed and hugged and petted him in a way which revolted Edmund.

"Let the child go," he said.

"Why should I?" asked Milli. "After all, he has got to get used to me about the place." Then to Richard: "Kiss me, Richard; I want you to think of me as another Mummy."

"Get out!" said Edmund tensely. "Get out! How dare you place yourself on a par with my wife? Richard, come away from that woman and go into the kitchen. Jump to it, boy!...Get out, you bitch! And don't darken my door again."

Milli did not move and said not a word. At last she stood up. "Yes, I suppose I shall have to go for Judith's sake. But of all the men I have ever had, you are the only one I have ever loved." She went.

He paced up and down for a good half-hour. That a creature like Milli should dare ask Richard to call her "another Mummy"! All his love of Judith welled up in his heart. It acted like a blood transfusion. His whole being came to life. He remembered saying to Judith some eighteen months ago that his religion had become a dream and its only contact with reality lay in her. Yes, but life with Milli had been a nightmare. He would return to the reality of Judith. Perhaps she could revive the dream. At least it had been beautiful. The moment that he invoked the dream it reinfused itself into his soul. His faith bubbled up in him again with the irresistible strength of omnipotence.

He collapsed in a big armchair, his heart, mind and soul completely at rest. He had tea in the kitchen with Richard and Giacinta. He then played with Richard on the floor of the drawing-room since he too had re-found his innocence. That is how Judith had found him.

XXIV

CROSS PURPOSES

The extraordinary thing about life, if one examines it at all closely, is that it is composed of innumerable coincidences. A thousand disconnected incidents all fall together in time and space, fit perfectly into each other like the pieces of a puzzle and form the pattern of our lives. We use the term "coincidence," however, for our surprise when we happen to notice a particular case in this normal process.

It was on January 13th, the Friday after paradise regained, that Pamela rang Judith up. "You remember telling me that your priest had sold the Rougham Crucifix? Well, I've found it."

Apparently a Frenchman by the odd name of Dileut had died recently at Chalfont. His son had asked Christie's to sell some of his effects, notably a very fine crucifix. Pamela was sent over to have a look at what was there.

"It was a new little bungalow — not very promising. There was some nice French furniture, Napoleon III, but nothing outstanding. The son, Jacques Dileut, then opened a door into a tiny little oratory or chapel. There was a fine console in lieu of an altar and above it your crucifix...No, there is no possible doubt. I got Dileut to get it down. On the back is branded the Rougham crest over the initials 'R.R.' and the date 1520. All the stuff in the chapel was first class. I told Dileut that Christie's would certainly accept for sale most of the stuff in the chapel, but I knew of a private collector who would probably give a better price for the crucifix — especially if one takes commission and tax into account. You know what I mean: you could pay cash...Yes, I gave Dileut a valuation. I don't see how you can offer less than £2,000 for the crucifix alone or £3,000 for the total contents of the chapel. Dileut would prefer the latter and you would get a better bargain...Well, it's up to you, my dear. Only if you want it you will have to move fairly quickly — before I give a report to Christie's...Got a pencil? Here's the address of the bungalow at Chalfont...This is Dileut's telephone number and address in Bayswater...His office number is..."

Judith got on to Monsieur Dileut straight away. Yes, the lady from Christie's had suggested a private sale: £2,000 for the crucifix alone or £3,000 for the contents of the chapel; but it must be in cash. Could Judith view it next Tuesday at 3 p.m.? So it was arranged. Judith was walking on air. She clapped her hands for joy. She would be able to give back to Edmund her original wedding present precisely when the marriage had been renewed. She would not tell Edmund. It must be a surprise.

It was a bit steep to have to pay a couple of thousand for what she had originally only given £55. Yes, that was a bit of a bore. She had nothing like £2,000 in her banking account. She would have to borrow the money from Edmund without telling him what it was for. No, that was no use. Brother John might lend it to her but he would have to be told why. However, he was the soul of discretion. She rang up and told him her story. "Yes, Judith, I'll get Edmund to pay me back later. Come to lunch at 1 p.m. on Tuesday and we shall drive over to Chalfont together. I shall have the cash on me and a bit more in case anything takes my fancy."

So all was in order. When Edmund returned that evening, he found his wife flushed and beautiful and gay as she had been when they were courting.

At 3 p.m. on Tuesday Judith and John arrived at the bungalow at Chalfont. Monsieur Dileut showed them straight into the chapel. "Yes, that's it!" Judith exclaimed. "And the altar is one of the side-altars a bit cut about. The chalice is Waddington's, as are the vestments, the cruets and the missal. It's all ours or the Waddingtons', every stick of it. Isn't it wonderful, John? We'll have to take the lot."

Monsieur Dileut was a trifle non-plussed. Were these people claiming that it was stolen property?

"Excuse me, Madam, but what do you mean by saying that it is all yours or the Waddingtons'?"

Judith explained how the crucifix had been in the Rougham family for over four-hundred years. How her husband had built the church at Walthamford and given it to be placed over the High Altar. How he and the Waddingtons had furnished the church down to the minutest details. How the priest had sold the lot while she and her husband were abroad. "That is my story, Monsieur Dileut. Now you can tell me how you have come into possession of the Rougham Crucifix."

"My story is stranger than yours, Mrs. Rougham, and will take longer to tell." Dileut hesitated. "Perhaps I should not tell it at all."

"Do; please do, Monsieur Dileut."

"Yes, perhaps I should, as it forms part of the story of your husband's crucifix. But if you repeat the tale I trust you to reveal neither my father's nor my name. Come and sit down. I shall make a cup of tea and tell you in comfort."

This is Monsieur Dileut's story:

My father and mother were both French. So am I, although I was born in London. My elder sister was born in Paris but I scarcely remember her. She died quite young of leukemia. My younger brother was born in London like me but was killed in the war, fighting for the Free French.

My father was the London agent for a Parisian manufacturer of costume jewelry. It did not make him rich but we lacked for nothing. We had our own freehold house in Islington. In those days it was not fashionable. I took over my father's business about fifteen years ago.

Father was a practicing Catholic. It was he who taught us our catechism and took us to Mass each Sunday. We thought that he was, perhaps, a bit scrupulous or Jansenistic as he never went to Communion. However, he always went on retreat with the Jesuits during the first week in Lent, when we presumed that he made his Easter Duties. He was fairly strict but immensely gentle. I do not remember my father ever being angry.

Mother was very different. She was a good mother to us and I don't want to say anything against her. But she was bitterly anti-Catholic and anti-clerical. Poor dear, she was a bitter woman altogether. She subscribed to several anti-clerical French rags. She used to cut out any particularly scandalous tit-bits and put them on Father's plate for breakfast. He always read them carefully, thanked Mother for keeping him informed and stuck them in an album. I have found it. It's that thick album on the bottom shelf over there.

Mother died in October 1964 without seeing a priest. She was buried civilly as she had wished. Father immediately sold the house. I was married, of course, and was already living in my present house in Bayswater. Father simply vanished. Once he sent me a postcard from Paris but with no address. That was all. A year later, in November 1965, he sent me a charming letter to say that he had built himself this bungalow at Chalfont and hoped that I, wife and children would call on him on Christmas afternoon as he could not give us a meal.

We turned up. You may have noticed that this bungalow has a surprisingly large hall for so small a house. Well, he received us in the hall. There were presents for all of us and a wonderful spread of French pastries. He was his usual gentle, courteous self. But he would not allow us into the rest of the house. To save us the trouble of trying the doors, he pointed out that they were locked! It was the same when we came at Easter and All Saints — *la Toussaint* is a big feast in France. In fact I never saw the inside of this bungalow until after my father's death. While we were there for the *Toussaint* he invited us back for Christmas. He said that he hoped to have something very important to tell us.

However, three weeks later, on November 23rd, the police rang up. It was fairly early in the morning as I had not yet gone to the office. The milkman had reported that the milk had not been collected at the bungalow for a couple of days and there was no answer to the bell. The police had forced the door and had found my father dead. They would like me to see the body as they had found it before they did anything else. I shot out to Chalfont straight away, fortunately without Mary, my wife. I called at the police station. A very amiable sergeant accompanied me. For the first time I penetrated the bungalow beyond the hall. The sergeant unlocked that little door over there and switched on the lights. As you probably noticed, the room has no window. It was a tiny chapel. Crouched over a *prie dieu* in front of the altar, fully vested in chasuble and the rest, was a priest. It was the corpse of my father.

You can imagine my sentiments better than I can describe them.

I shall not bore you with details except to say that he had finished Mass when he died. The veil was on the chalice, the corporal was in the burse, the cruets were empty and the candles had been blown out. He must have felt too weak to unvest, have gone straight to the *prie dieu* and died.

Later I found on his desk a thick envelope addressed to me. The top page was a very affectionate letter postdated the Christmas which never came. The rest was a precis of his life. It was doubtless what he had referred to on All Saints' Day. The precis is not without interest.

My father was born in 1883 and was therefore eighty-three when he died. His real name was du Teil, of which Dileut is an anagram. His family was traditional and very devout. From earliest childhood he, like his parents, took it for granted that he would become a priest.

Already at St. Sulpice — his seminary — his piety had veered toward activism. He says that he was not strictly a "modernist" but was deeply affected by the works of Laberthonnière. He kept this to himself so as not to be expelled.

He was ordained just before his twenty-fourth birthday at Pentecost, 1907. The decree *Lamentabili* against modernism was issued in July that same year. A little later the works of his hero, Laberthonnière, were placed on the Index.

With the fervour of a young man he wrote articles attacking the whole policy of Pius X in Naudet's *Justice Sociale* and Dabry's *La Vie Catholique*. Both were condemned in the following year, 1908.

He then joined up with Marc Sagnier and *Le Sillon*. By this time he thought of himself as a "christian Socialist" rather than a "socialist Christian."

When *Le Sillon* was condemned in 1910 he took to writing under diverse pseudonyms virulent attacks against Pius X in the non-Catholic press. Some of these were eventually pinned down to him. Upon his refusal to retract he was defrocked and excommunicated in 1913.

He lived by his pen until he was called up for the war. Incidentally, all those reviews in that book-case over there contain his articles. The rest of the books must form the most complete collection of modernist and Sillonist literature in private hands. It had been stored in Paris. Doubtless we had not been allowed in the bungalow in case we saw it.

He married mother, civilly of course, in 1916. She was an ex-Trappistine nun. They had met at a sort of club for defrocked priests in Paris, *rue des Ecoles*. My sister was born the next year.

By the end of war and after a year at Verdun, Loisy, Laberthonnière, Dabry, even Marc Sagnier all seemed very far away. He was also helped by his sergeant, who was a distinguished Jesuit. He regained the piety of his childhood. But he was excommunicated and had a wife and daughter.

On demobilization he found that he could not live in Paris. Thanks to a cousin he got his job in London. I was born there in 1920 and my brother in 1923.

When mother died father set about rehabilitating himself as a priest. It took endless time. Paris, his diocese of origin, passed the buck to Aylesbury, his diocese of domicile, and *vice versa*. I have found all the correspondence. I shall not bore you with details. Suffice it to say that the delay was not caused by difficulties over his excommunication and marriage. It was caused by father's own obstinacy. Indeed, he was as stubborn as he was gentle.

He had been excommunicated under two principal headings: firstly for maintaining modernist propositions; secondly for using the vernacular and innovating in the rite of Mass. Father refused to accept the lifting of excommunication unless he abjured its causes: he insisted that he take the anti-modernist oath at the hands of the bishop and that he celebrate Mass according to the rite in use prior to his excommunication.

As you can imagine, there was much pooh-poohing. The anti-modernist oath had been abolished and the immemorial Mass was undergoing monthly changes. Finally, however, in view of father's age, the bishop of Aylesbury had the courtesy to give in. He came to Chalfont and administered the oath in front of two witnesses on Wednesday, November 16th.

Knowing my father as I do, I am certain that he would have prepared himself scrupulously for his second "First Mass." He would not have presumed to jump to the altar, but waited for the Lord's Day. (Besides, only one host was missing from a box of fifty.) The Mass after which he died must have been the first he had said for fifty-three years. God rest his soul!

You can tell your husband, Mrs. Rougham, that his cross has not been idle. If your parish priest turned it out, an apostate priest took it in. It was in front of your crucifix that my father said his final Mass. In God's providence it has fulfilled its purpose here. You can take it back.

Judith and John drove off with the total contents of the chapel except for the *prie dieu*.

"By Jove! That was a rum story," said John. "Fancy discovering at the age of forty-five that your father was an R.C. priest and your mother a nun. Of course I did not understand who all those people were but I got the gist of it. Nice chap, Dileut; I must buy some jewelry off him for Joan."

"Yes, it was a strange tale all right," Judith replied. "Poor Father du Teil, excommunicated under Pius X for being a modernist and fiddling about with the Mass; almost excommunicated under Paul VI for not being a modernist and failing to fiddle about with the Mass. I must meditate on it. But I do not want to at the moment; I feel too happy.

"John, I've had an idea. I want the crucifix to be a surprise to Edmund, but it won't be much of one if he finds us unloading the van. I want to do things properly. You drop me off at the Dower House — with any luck I shall get there before Edmund — but take the stuff back to Hampstead. Can you and Joan dine with us on Thursday? Very well, send the stuff up on Thursday morning so that it arrives at about ten. It's awfully short notice but I shall try to get hold of the Mainwarings and Waddingtons for dinner." She explained her idea.

Judith did get back to the Dower House before Edmund. She even had time to ring up Pamela and the Waddingtons. Both couples could come on Thursday. When Edmund came in she merely told him that she had arranged a little party for close friends. He was delighted.

"It's some time since I have seen any of them. Besides it will show them that all is well at the Dower House." And he kissed Judith.

The stuff was duly delivered on Thursday morning. Apart from the crucifix, the rest of the Rougham property was hidden in a garden shed. One of old Larkin's sons came to secure the crucifix to the wall over the chimney piece in the drawing-room.

The beautiful picture of the Baptist by Schedone which had previously hung there was hidden in the pantry. The crucifix was covered in white satin as it had been on the wedding day, with a cord hanging down to unveil it. The Waddington properties — chalice, vestments and the rest — were arranged on a long table and covered with a great damask tablecloth.

When Edmund got home he found the doors to the drawing-room locked. He was told that there was going to be a surprise. He presumed that it would be an agreeable one or there would not be so much fuss about it. By the time he had changed, John and Joan had already arrived. He thought John looked a bit more smug than usual. Dinner was a great success. Everybody shared in the happiness of seeing Edmund and Judith reunited.

After dinner, instead of the ladies retiring, John said: "Now we all move into the drawing-room." He took a key from his pocket and unlocked the door. "Henry and Anne (the Waddingtons), you sit in those two chairs behind the sofa and look as solemn as you would in church. Edmund and Judith, you stand in front of the sofa in case you fall over. Arthur (Mainwaring), you go to the other side of Edmund as though you were best man. Pamela here, as bridesmaid. Joan, come and buttress me." He then repeated as far as memory allowed and the changed circumstances permitted, his speech at the wedding.

"Edmund, in the odd thousand years that your family has an historic existence, think of the contributions it has received from outside. I need only mention your dear mother Lucy, who is a poppet if ever there was one. Well, the Mildens have given you Judith who, I am confident, has not let the side down. Today, Edmund, your wife stands beside you. She has given you two brand-new Roughams who never existed before, Richard and George. They are the guarantee of the future of your illustrious line. But your wife has not only contributed these new and living beings to your family. She has also something very old to return to you, something which has always been yours and which represents your living faith." John pulled the cord. The satin covering fell off.

"Good God! It's the Rougham Crucifix," was all that Edmund could say.

After that the unveiling of the table with the Waddingtons' lost property was rather an anti-climax. However, interest was revived, although a solemn note was given to the occasion, when John insisted that Judith tell the strange story of Monsieur X.

XXV

A RETURN

It was a wonderfully happy time at the Dower House after the return of the crucifix. Richard was doing well at St. John's and Edmund had agreed to send him to Stonyhurst. George had started at the nursery class in the Anglican school since the convent, under the tender care of Father Mallon and Sister Pantaleone-Gertrude, had become quite impossible.

The immediate cause of the happiness was that Edmund had lost his bitterness the moment he had re-found his religion. Rather than the opium of the people, religion is an effective form of bicarbonate of soda: it reduces acidity. Having regained his certainties, Edmund could take a detached view of the council. Its fruits seemed unripe and sour, but he was not. They made life slightly more difficult, but that was a good thing: like most Catholics, he had taken his religion too much for granted. It had been handed to him on a plate. All he had to do was to swallow it. But one could not expect that any more. It was the age of self-service, of do-it-yourself. Gone were the days when you could expect the clergy to dish up your religion for you.

Edmund realized that he had thought of his religion far too much as an institution. The institution was there to guard and guarantee the religion, but the religion itself was away above the institution. Its image was his crucifix, so mysteriously returned to him. Yes, with the little angels collecting the redeeming Blood which we frail humans would have to drink to the dregs. That was his religion all right. The council had been a lot of hot air escaping from under episcopal mitres — which looked like tea-cozies anyway. Once he had regained his certainties Edmund could laugh. His bitterness vanished.

He and Judith also came to a *modus vivendi* with the Church. On weekdays they went to Holy Cross (or Holy Microphone as

Edmund insisted on calling it) because it was tolerable. On Sundays, when it was intolerable at Holy Cross, they went to Potters End, where Mass was still said with a modicum of reverence. Edmund even made peace with Father Todson. He grew almost to like the little fellow, he was so amusingly cocky and bumptious.

To crown their joy Judith became pregnant again shortly before Christmas. This time she felt perfectly well. Although she had carried George successfully, both with him as with Richard she had felt sick and miserable almost from the moment of conception. Dr. McAuley was most encouraging: "You see, with both your previous births you have had some form of toxaemia, either before or after delivery. But medically there is absolutely no reason why it should recur. The trouble with you, as I have told your husband, is that you have no reserve of energy. So one has to be careful. Let me see: you are expecting around September 20th. You will have to go into hospital early in August — say Monday 5th. I'll book you in. This is so that the pundits can decide what to do: leave you alone, induce the baby a bit early or perform a caesarean. Incidentally, I see no point in calling in a pundit from Harley Street; your case is quite straightforward. Also, Hertford Hospital is perfectly all right. The gynaecologist there is as good as you'll get. As a matter of fact you have met him a couple of times when you have dined with us. He is the dark, curly-haired little Welshman — Edwards — with the enormous blonde wife." Yes, Judith remembered him. He was obviously as clever as a box of tricks.

"In the meantime," McAuley continued, "you have nothing to worry about. But you must take regular exercise, by which I mean ordinary walking, at a good pace with arms swinging and low-heeled shoes: a short mile in the morning and a long one in the afternoon. You can also do the exercises in this pamphlet. Never kneel, not even in church — a most unnatural position — and stand still as little as possible. In fact, either put your feet up or keep them moving."

It was exactly the opposite treatment to Tubby's: the minimum of medicine and the maximum of drill. McAuley had qualified just before the outbreak of war and his first experience of doctoring had been in the army. Hence was derived his trust in drill to keep up the morale of his patients as it did of the troops — same thing.

Anyway, everything went splendidly. Judith was as perky as a sparrow. She did her drill with the precision of a guardsman. This led to a comic misapprehension. Since she was not allowed to kneel, Judith took Holy Communion standing. Father Todson thought at last his efforts had been crowned with success. He knew that the Roughams went elsewhere on Sundays, so it could not be the result of one of his brilliant homilies. There was only one explanation: grace. It almost made Father Todson believe in miracles.

*   *   *   *   *

Towards the end of May — we are now in 1968 — a large poster went up in the porch of Holy Cross to say that on Sunday, June 23rd, there would be a special appeal for the Indian missions. It would be made by Father Philip McEnery, S.J., provincial of the Jesuits in the Bombay Presidency.

Philip McEnery; yes, he was the splendid, cadaverous priest who twelve years previously, almost to the day, had received Judith into the Church. Wasn't it marvelous! She still possessed her notes on his instructions and had read them so often that she almost knew them by heart. She had not kept in touch with him because he obviously had other things to do. She was only one among dozens of converts and he could not be expected to remain in contact with them all. But this was different: it was he who was arriving on her doorstep. It was providential. She looked forward with deep emotion to meeting again the priest from whom she had received the Faith.

She explained to Father Todson that she very much wanted to entertain Father McEnery and asked for his address. She wrote to him that very afternoon.

Dear Father McEnery,

I wonder if you remember me? You received me into the Church twelve years ago, on June 28th, 1956. My name was Judith Milden. It was my last term at Somerville. We have not met since.

I have married a cradle Catholic, Edmund Rougham. It is his father who lives at Rougham Castle. We live at the above address at Walthamford, where you will be making an appeal on June 23rd.

Will you give Edmund and myself the pleasure of staying the nights of Saturday and Sunday at the Dower House or, if you are booked elsewhere, lunch or dine with us on Sunday — whatever is the least inconvenient to you?

You can have no idea how much I look forward to meeting you again. It is you who gave me what I most prize in life: my faith.

As gratefully as sincerely yours,

A week later Judith received the following reply:

Dear Mrs. Rougham,

For once the advertisements are correct: Milden sticks. Yes, I remember Judith Milden: a thin strip of a girl and a frightfully elegant blue-stocking. I also recollect that the motive for your conversion was the purchase of a crucifix. My instructions consisted largely in listening to details about it — cherubs with little cups and what-not. I look forward to seeing it.

Thank you for your kind invitation. I cannot stay the night as I shall be arriving from Enfield on Sunday morning with a busload of catechists and children and we shall have to return that afternoon. Lunch is laid on for them at the Taj Mahal restaurant but I can easily escape. I shall consequently lunch with you at 1 p.m., but must be away by 2:30.

I much look forward to meeting your husband, seeing you and inspecting your crucifix.

God bless you,

Judith was so excited that she could scarcely wait for June 23rd. So he had remembered the crucifix! After the unveiling ceremony it had been removed from the drawing-room to the bedroom. On Saturday it was brought back to the drawing-room and placed on an easel for Father to inspect it. So that she and Edmund could have him all to themselves, Judith invited nobody to meet him.

On the Sunday morning, Giacinta went to the 9:30 Mass. Edmund, Judith, Richard and George all went at 11. Some charming little Indian children, all brightly dressed up, received people in the porch and conducted them to their seats. Fortunately the Roughams were not the first to arrive and were placed far to the right of the eucharistic table, just beside the south door. The church had been decorated with Indian paper swags and banners and with lots of little lanterns. Judith approved: it gave life to the otherwise empty building. She had something of a shock, however, when she looked at what had been the sanctuary. On a high pedestal, exactly where the reredos with the crucifix had been, was a life-size statue of Vishnu. The god was lying down full-length and, although his head was uncomfortably perched on his left hand, he was smiling and asleep.

Edmund had seen it too. "Ought we to go?" he asked, pointing to the statue.

"It must be to illustrate the horrors of paganism," Judith replied without any conviction.

At 11 o'clock sharp plaintive yodeling in oriental quarter-tones could be heard. Through the main door the procession entered. It was led by the charming Indian children carrying more banners, more lanterns and burning joss-sticks and fuming bowls of incense. Then came some beautiful young women, so graceful in their flowing saris, followed by some turbaned men in gaily-coloured plus-fours and finally Father McEnery in bright green silk pyjamas.

Having incensed the table and Vishnu and the yodeling having stopped, Father McEnery announced: "These lovely little Indian children were all of them abandoned in infancy. This was not due to parental callousness but to total destitution. The missions do their best to look after them. They have just sung the Introductory Psalm, which is taken from the Rig-Veda of 1,000 B.C. A catechist, Miss Gutarjee, will read the lesson, taken from the Upanishad of the Yajur-Veda. The children will sing another *raga* and I shall read the Gospel of Our Lord."

Yes, it was the same Father McEnery. He had the same hair, nose and voice. But he looked much younger. Instead of being cadaverous he had grown quite fat. There was not a wrinkle in his chubby face. Of old, his nose protruded beyond his stomach; now it was the reverse. He was the same person but not the same personality.

The sermon was certainly very ably delivered. It was of the sort which deeply impresses those who do not listen. Edmund and

Judith did. Its opening gambit was the iniquity of the British Raj.

Now, there are few things which the English enjoy more than beating their own breasts. In a cold, damp climate, it helps to keep one warm. The message was that whatever the congregation gave should not be considered charity: it was a minute token payment for what we owed in justice to these wonderful Indians whom we had been ruthlessly exploiting for three-hundred years and more. Stirring stuff!

Having laid his foundation, Father McEnery proceeded to missionary activity. "We first sent out missionaries and, when everybody's eyes were shut tight in prayer, we hoisted the Union Jack." But was it Christianity we gave them? Was it love and understanding etc.? No! It was the religion of capitalism and cricket. Cricket has produced a few elite players whom we can watch on television. Capitalism has produced the defenseless, starving masses. At last the missionaries had realized that they had as much to learn as to teach.

"The Church is a learning community, and the process never ends." There followed some splendid rhetoric on ecumenicity. It wound up with: "Behind this altar is a statue of Vishnu, the Incarnation of India. He lies there smiling in expectation of the redemption of his people. But it is not only their redemption in the next world for which he is waiting, but also their redemption in this."

The third and last part of his sermon dealt with financial technicalities: how many children you could nourish for how long for £10; deeds of covenant and the like.

As soon as the sermon ended the charming children went round the congregation two by two: one carried a basket in which to put money; the other had a box of hosts, and you put one into his basket if you were going to Holy Communion. Edmund whispered firmly: "I forbid anyone to put anything into either basket." Judith knew that he had written out a substantial cheque for the Indian missions; she could hear him crumpling it up in his pocket.

The charming children assembled at the back of the church for the offertory procession. They advanced as the lovely young women yodeled another *raga*, this time accompanied by little drums and weird wind instruments played by the men in brightly-coloured plus-fours. The baskets containing hosts were placed on the eucharistic table, the baskets with money in front of Vishnu. The charming children regrouped themselves round the table and, led by the lovely young women and to the music provided by the gentlemen in plus-fours, slowly danced round it, oriental fashion, with much finger motion, arm-twiddling and belly-wabbling.

Edmund was at the end of his tether. "I've had enough. Judith, take Richard's hand. When I say 'go,' go — through the south door." He took George into his arms. "Ready? — go!" Nobody saw them go: all eyes were riveted on the belly-wabbling.

When they were outside, "Puff!" said Edmund. "It would have been a jolly good show at a pantomime; not a hitch in the performance. To think that the Mass has been reduced to that!"

"Yes, Edmund darling, but it is perhaps worse for me. I am sure I told you of my first Mass at St. Aloysius's. The utter theocentricity of it all: the priest with his little mate laying on the fountain of eternal life; the people grovelling on the floor in front of the Divine Presence; the children who stopped sucking sticky sweets. Well, it was the same priest then as today. Edmund, I'm heart-broken."

"Yes, darling; I well understand. But our purgatory is still not over. We have to have him for lunch."

When they got home, it was Richard, who was both scrupulous and intelligent, who was the principal trouble. "Daddy, we haven't been to Mass...We have big black spots on our souls...It's your fault, Daddy...Why was Jesus asleep instead of on the cross?...Who was the funny fat priest who did not know how to say Mass?...Why were those girls waggling their bottoms?...Why did they put brown shoe-polish on their face?...Why did they dress up for a pantomime?...Why was the priest wearing pyjamas?...Why?...Why?...Why?..."

"Now run along to the kitchen," said Edmund, "and ask Giacinta."

"Why, don't you know?"

"Yes, but Giacinta will be able to give you a cream bun." And Edmund locked himself into his study.

Judith collapsed into an armchair in the drawing-room. What she had imagined was going to be one of the happiest reunions in her life was going to be one of the most difficult. She could not even plan the conversation. It seemed that nothing, absolutely nothing, remained in common between herself and the man who had moulded her spiritual outlook and thereby dominated all the actions of her subsequent life.

The crucifix was there on the easel in front of her. "Dear God, yes I realize what it was you revealed, what no human could conceive: your humility. You even humbled yourself beyond death on the cross when you descended into hell. The humility of God and the pride of men — that is what life is really about...Help me to be humble. I am so sharp, so harsh...Help me to be kind and patient with the priest who received me into your church."

By the time Edmund came out of his study Judith had regained her composure. "Edmund dear, we must try to be kind and understanding with poor Father McEnery. It may be a bit of a penance but it can only last ninety minutes."

"Very well, my dear, but it is you who will have to ooze kindness. I shall do my best to keep out of the way."

Father arrived promptly at 1 o'clock. Judith stood as he entered. He stopped at the door and had a good look at her. "Yes, that is Judith Milden all right. You have not changed a bit. And still the same elegant young woman."

This last remark was in fact quite true. Although six months pregnant, Judith was carrying very lightly and her beautifully-cut clothes completely disguised her condition.

"That is very kind of you, Father. But you look a great deal younger. The responsibility of being provincial has made you put on weight; it suits you. And let me introduce my husband, Edmund Rougham, to Father Philip McEnery." Curiously enough, they had never met. Father had taught at Beaumont before Edmund's time. They talked of the acquaintances they had in common.

"And now I must introduce you to my crucifix," said Judith as she brought him over to the easel.

"By Jove! It is a magnificent piece," Father remarked. "And do you know its history?"

"Yes, and that is what I want to tell you." As they drank their sherry Judith told him the story. How the crucifix had belonged to the Roughams since 1520. How Ronnie Stanningfield had sold it and Judith bought it. How it was part cause of her conversion and of her marriage to Edmund, which brought it back into the family. How Pius XII had blessed it. How they had given it to Holy Cross. How Paul VI had failed to bless it on the very day that it was sold. How Edmund had stopped practicing after it had disappeared. How it had turned up again the week after Edmund had regained his faith. Finally, the strange story of Monsieur X. "So here it is, home again."

"Yours and Monsieur X's are the only stories we know about it," Father remarked. "I wonder how many others it could tell? It has certainly protected you Roughams all down the centuries of persecution, since you are still here. And what an astonishing interview with Pius XII! What was it he said? 'Suffering is mercy and those little cups of mercy will have to be drunk to the dregs in suffering.' Is that right? I must jot it down."

They were still talking about the crucifix when they went in to lunch. "Where was it in the church?" Father asked. Judith explained that the whole church had been gutted and the altar moved forward. "Our crucifix was over the High Altar, exactly where you placed the statue of Vishnu."

Edmund butted in: "Yes, Father, and it came as a bit of a shock to see the second deity of the Brahmin triad in the place of the Second Person of the Holy Trinity."

Judith felt anxious for the peace and altered the tack: "It must have been awfully difficult to transport a great big statue like that and hoist it up there."

"No, perfectly easy," said Father; "it's plastic and only weighs a few pounds. Wonderful stuff, plastic. The original is at Benares, but it's a very convincing reproduction."

"And entirely out of place," said Edmund.

"I am not all that sure, Mr. Rougham," Father continued. "When one is attempting to deal with India, one must know what one is really dealing with. One must get under the Indian skin. That means understanding and respecting his religion, i.e., his fundamental motives of action. I am not criticizing the old missionaries — they did heroic work — but they were trying to impose Christianity as something external coming from outside, instead of something emerging from Indian culture itself and completing it. Instead of 'converting' one should attempt to 'converge' India to Christianity. It is putting into practice that remarkable document of Vatican II, *Lumen Gentium*."

"I suppose you would call it the ecumenic instead of the dogmatic approach," said Edmund.

"That is exactly it."

Judith felt very upset. "But Father, what you have been saying does represent a total change of attitude from what you told me during instructions. You said such wonderful things about Christianity introducing the notion of truth into religion; about the Crucifixion being proof of the truth of Christianity; about truth being exclusive and universal and so on. Also, you spoke so movingly of the Mass that you yourself were moved. You said that in comparison with the Mass the creation was a bauble. It was the supreme manifestation of God's omnipotence, turning the evidence of the ultimate in crime into the salvation of the criminals. But we did not get that impression from the ceremony which you performed scarcely two hours ago. Do you still believe what you told me in instructions?"

"Of course I do, Judith — although experience may have taught me to express those truths rather differently."

"But of necessity a different expression carries a different meaning. 'I love cats' and 'I hate cats' do not mean quite the same, even if you argue that both carry the basic significance that 'I have an emotional reaction to cats.' But I do not want to argue. What I should sincerely love to know is what were the experiences which have made you express yourself so differently?"

Father McEnery was obviously delighted to avoid an argument and willingly turned to his motives for changing the expression of his convictions. Illumination had come from the council documents, notably *Lumen Gentium* and *Gaudium et Spes*.

However, he would never have been able to grasp their full significance had he not been faced with the problem of India. One of the first things which had struck him upon his arrival in Bombay was the political-racial-religious *apartheid* of the Portuguese community. It was clearly disastrous.

This immediately rang a bell in the minds of both Edmund and Judith. "You haven't by any chance come across a priest by the name of Almeida?" Edmund asked.

"Scores of them! There is at least one bishop and a couple of dozen priests who answer to that name."

"Ours is Paul Almeida," said Judith, "and he is or was chaplain at the St. Francis Xavier Technical Institute."

"That one! Incidentally, he's an illegitimate. Almeida was his mother's name. His father must have been a Dravidian, an 'untouchable,' because he's as black as your boot."

"You're quite wrong," Edmund explained. "His real name is Cromer. His late father was a distinguished member of the I.M.S., who ended up as director of medical services for the Bombay Presidency. He was a childless widower who married an Almeida fairly late in life. She gave him three children, of whom Father Paul is one. For some time he was parish priest of Rougham. That is how we come to know him. Indeed, he married us. But when he returned to India at the instigation of his uncle, Professor Manuel Almeida, he decided fairly naturally to adopt his mother's name." Edmund was delighted to put Father McEnery in his place.

And Judith added: "I have good reason for admiring Father Paul. Please remember me very kindly to him when you return to India."

"Well, that is most interesting," said Father McEnery. "His English father perhaps explains his unusual ability to organize things. Unfortunately he uses it in the wrong direction. He is, in fact, the leader of the opposition."

"The opposition to what?" asked Edmund.

"To renewal in any shape or form — even to the decrees of the council. For instance, he has organized a whole network of Latin Masses throughout the archdiocese and beyond on the grounds that English and Portuguese are imperial languages which can do nothing but harm and the native languages and dialects, apart from the fact that none of them is universal, have pagan associations."

"What exactly is wrong with that?" Edmund asked.

"It's pure sophistry. Besides, it's divisive, anti-participational and above all, anti-ecumenical."

"But is it untrue, Father?" Judith dared to ask in spite of her good resolution.

"It is not untrue on the parochial level. But that is precisely what I have against your Father Almeida or Cromer. He seems incapable of seeing things in the wider context of India as a whole or of understanding the social implications of Christianity." To Judith's surprise, Father McEnery enlarged on this theme in very much the same way that Father Paul had done five years previously at Rougham. There was, however, one noticeable difference: Father McEnery was constantly throwing in political asides. "Representative democracy is useless in India; what is needed is functional democracy — like the soviets" — "We merely provided a super-caste, ourselves, the English; communism is the only practical way of ridding India of the caste system" — "Communist ruthlessness would do far less harm than western permissiveness" — "I realize that communism is anti-religious in the sense that the only dogma permitted is communism itself, but it is not anti-spiritual; Indian spirituality would survive because it has no dogmas" etc...

By the time coffee was reached McEnery had reverted to Father Paul. "Thanks to your friend, I cannot get a single Portuguese to sit on any commission or committee dealing with all-India problems. He is parochial all along the line. And he even seems to have the present archbishop, Cardinal Gracias, completely under his thumb. What a change from dear, good Archbishop Roberts!"

Archbishop Roberts, it will be remembered, was Edmund's pet aversion, and more than any other had been responsible for his lapsing. All Edmund said, however, was: "Surely it is conceivable that a Portuguese Indian, such as Cardinal Gracias, may understand India better than an English Jesuit such as Archbishop Roberts. And it is just possible that Paul Almeida knows it quite as well as you do.

Judith was exultant. Her darling Edmund had said just the sort of thing which she would have liked to have said herself.

The criticism made Father McEnery explode. "Don't talk nonsense, Mr. Rougham. As anyone can see — and as Archbishop Roberts never failed to point out — the basic problem in India is over-population. And what does your friend do about it? He goes around preaching against every possible solution. As a matter of fact, there is only one: to sterilize all women after their second child."

"I see," said Edmund. "You want a political instead of a moral solution: communism instead of Christianity."

Judith had put her elbows on the table and rested her head in her hands, covering her eyes. She spoke slowly and softly: "You should not have said that Father. I am expecting my third baby in three months' time. Edmund, will you show Father out? It is already half-past two."

Judith did not move, did not answer Father's profuse apologies and goodbye, still sat with her hands over her eyes. Edmund drove Father McEnery to the restaurant to join his party. When he returned, Judith was exactly as he had left her.

"Dear, darling Edmund," she said as at last she looked up, "I feel sick and giddy. You will have to help me upstairs. I want to go to bed and cry."

He lifted her up. She was as light as when he had lifted her over the threshold of Rougham Castle on her wedding day. She was shivering and obviously running a temperature.

He got her to bed. "I'll go and ring up McAuley."

"No, don't leave me. And hold my hand. Wasn't it wonderful to hear about dear Father Cromer?"

She slept for over an hour. Edmund rang up the doctor; it was Mrs. McAuley who answered, as her husband was playing his Sunday afternoon round of golf. "No, don't try to get hold of him. There does not appear to be anything urgent. But in view of Judith's past history, I think your husband ought to have a look at her. Yes, 5 p.m. would suit admirably."

When Judith woke she was much better; she no longer felt giddy and sick. She even asked Edmund to make her a cup of tea.

"I cannot say how happy I am to hear about Father Paul. Who

would have imagined that he had the guts to stick up against the ecclesiastical establishment — and against a man as formidable as McEnery? I felt sick because I had been thinking about Father McEnery — and I felt better as soon as I began thinking about Father Paul...But how can one explain Father McE.? You have read my notes on his instructions. How can a man who held such convictions swivel round and maintain the opposite? I simply do not understand it. I am quite sure that he was in good faith when he instructed me. Is he now? And that incredible Mass with Vishnu and the dancing children! Can you explain it?"

"Yes, Judith, I think I can," Edmund replied. "You see, Father McE. and myself have much in common. We are both cradle Catholics who have taken the certainties of our religion for granted. Moreover, he is a Jesuit priest and I am Jesuit-educated. The Jesuit system tried to rationalize these certainties in an attempt to drive them home. This, I think, was fair enough as far as it went, but I rather doubt if it went the whole way. It tended to reduce certainty to its intellectual formulation. In your notes I seem to remember that McEnery equated 'believe-belove.' It is true, but I do not think that it is typically Jesuit. The emphasis tended to be that 'to believe equals to act'. Our actions, consequently, became very closely linked to our certainties.

"That is perhaps why you, as a convert, can have little idea of the impact it made on people like McEnery and myself to have all our certainties questioned — and questioned, if not exactly *by* the Church, at least *in* the Church. The moment they were even allowed to be questioned, they ceased to be certain. And this all along the line: it was certainty itself which had become doubtful. There could no longer be certainty between truth and error, between good and bad. And our actions, so closely wedded to our beliefs, lost all sense of direction. There was no longer any purpose in anything; nothing seemed worthwhile.

"I express myself badly, but do you follow me? Anyway, you have experienced the result. I lapsed. As you must realize, Milli was not the cause of my lapsing, but its expression. 'To lapse' really means 'to slip,' but McEnery and myself, like many others, cannot slip without falling. I fell very low — and as far as I was concerned, the lower the better. Can you understand that? I slept with Milli precisely because I hated her.

"Now, I rather imagine that poor Father McEnery is in very much the same position as I was. He has lapsed and consequently fallen. He is not in bad faith for the simple reason that he has lost it. How low he will fall, none can say. Unlike many priests, he has not yet found a Milli — but he may. At the moment he seems to have fallen for communism. That does not surprise me. Having lost his certainty in the sublime, he is looking for it in the infernal. Does that all make sense?"

"I think I follow the gist of your argument," said Judith with some hesitation. "In practice it means that, instead of being horrified by McEnery, I should pity him."

"Yes — or at least be patient, as you were with me."

"But you managed to recover your certainty in the sublime. Do you think McEnery ever will?"

"It is always possible. And, by Divine Providence, it will probably come about in some quite unexpected, almost trivial way. For instance, in my case it really had nothing to do with me. It was Milli who said exactly the wrong thing — perhaps the only wrong thing she could have said."

"You have never told me the details of that."

"I shall tell you whenever you ask me. But to return to McEnery, you may well have saved his faith this afternoon."

"Good heavens! How that?"

"I am not inventing it. It struck me forceably at that very moment. It was a totally unforeseen remark — like everything providential; and you said it in a way which gave it immense weight: 'You should not have said that, Father. I am expecting my third baby in three months' time.' That is the sort of peg on which eternity hangs. God always produces vast scenarios in order to hide the minute details with which he works. Incidentally, I suppose you realize that Giacinta had left the doors to the drawing-room open, so from where he was sitting, McEnery could see the crucifix protruding above your head. When you leaned forward with your head in your hands, it must have looked as though the crucifix was speaking. Anyway, the event certainly impressed him. When I drove him back, he never said a word, except to ask me to drop him in the car park instead of at the restaurant. I got out to open the door of the bus for him. Vishnu was lying smiling on the back seat. McEnery turned him round to face the cushions. Who was that fellow in the Old Testament who was lifted by his hair to Babylon just to supply lunch to Daniel in the lions' pit? Habacuc, was it? Well, perhaps McEnery has been lifted all the way from Bombay to Walthamford just to hear that one remark, made by one of his converts, under those precise circumstances...There goes the bell. It's Dr. McAuley. I thought he had better have a look at you, as I ought to drive over to St. John's with Richard."

McAuley was very reassuring. "There is no trace whatsoever of toxaemia. It is her heart which is fluffing and beating irregularly: pure nerves. She tells me that she was terribly distressed. I am glad to have seen her in this condition, so as to warn Edwards at Hertford Hospital; the neurologist ought to know. I shall call tomorrow at midday, but by then she will be as right as rain. In the meantime you need have no anxiety. The crisis passed a couple of hours ago. Of course you can take Richard back to school: Judith will probably be asleep anyway...You know, Edmund, your wife is perhaps the most remarkable woman I have met; but one has to pay for being *extra* ordinary."

XXVI

THE DREGS OF THE CHALICE

After June 23rd, Dr. McAuley insisted that Judith should not get up before 7:30 a.m. She should then do her exercises. They were not exhausting, but time-consuming. As weekday Mass was also at 7:30 this meant that she could not get to it. However, on Wednesdays Father Todson had a frightful Children's Eucharist at 9:15. This one she could manage physically and, thanks to the Rosary, spiritually.

It was exactly a month after Father McEnery's visit, on Wednesday, July 24th, that Father Todson edged up to her after the Eucharist to ask when he could call round. There was something he wished to discuss with her. "What about this afternoon between five and six?" Judith asked. So it was arranged. Only after she got home did she realize that it was rather inconvenient. Giacinta was out on Wednesday afternoons and evenings visiting her sons. But it did not much matter. Todson would not stay long. She could bathe George after he had gone. Richard was on holiday but was staying with a school friend.

As has been said, Judith got on quite well with Father Todson. She thought him a perfectly decent little fellow, only unbelievably stupid. Father Todson thought otherwise. After billions of years of evolution, at long last Tommy Todson had turned up, the final product of the process. Actually, Judith was much younger than he and therefore newer and still more brilliant. But that did not work because she was only a marriage convert and had not a clue. Besides, her whole outlook was warped by bourgeois culture. That was something which riled Father Todson. He simply could not conceive that people were in good faith who pretended to prefer natural flowers to plastic ones. He had himself listened to items of music by Mozart and Haydn; from his own experience he knew that it was a lot of gut-scraping. Then all that fuss about the

Rougham Crucifix — a hideous job; a decent cross in plywood was far more effective. But what made him hate bourgeois culture was not the fact that it was obviously valueless, but that it supplied its possessors with an impenetrable veneer of superiority. Luckily, not many people in the parish had it. The Waddingtons were the worst. Edmund Rougham was pretty awful. There might, however, be a chink in Mrs. Rougham's bourgeois armor. He did not for a moment deny her piety. Also, she never got cross with him but laughed in a rather pleasant way. Finally — and even a priest notices such things — she was a very beautiful young woman, and unbelievably elegant, although of late she had let the standard down. This, he was told, was because she was expecting a baby.

Anyway, he turned up at the Dower House shortly after 5 p.m. on Wednesday, July 24th, 1968. He was dressed as usual like an unsuccessful commercial traveler who had spent a holiday in France. He carefully placed his precious *béret* on the chest in the hall. He spent quite a time beating about the bush and Judith had to ask him to what she owed the pleasure of his visit. Finally he came to the point.

"Actually, Mrs. Rougham, I have called round to ask you a favour. The Church is going through a very critical period and the Holy Father needs all the prayers and guidance the People of God can give him. I have started, as the council requires, a few study groups in the parish which have not been unfruitful. But their scope has been rather theoretic and there has been a lack of real dialogue owing to the absence of what I should like to call 'Mature Christians.' I cannot help feeling that educated Catholics like yourself and Mr. Rougham owe it to your less fortunate brethren to share in dialogue their experiences and their outlook."

Judith, of course, had heard about the diverse parochial, inter-parochial and ecumenical discussion groups going on in the parish but had already refused to join any of them. She was an elected member of the so-called Parish Council but only turned up when Mrs. Larkin ordered her to do so. At these meetings she was quite useful in preserving peace and decorum and protecting

Father Todson from vicious attacks by the tobacconist. So what on earth did Father want now?

"Mrs. Rougham," he continued, "it is a problem of the utmost urgency not only to the People of God but to the people of the world. As I have already had occasion to remark, I am not particularly impressed by what I call 'the bourgeois outlook,' but here is a matter which the educated classes have faced fearlessly and left the less educated in ignorance and superstition."

At this point Judith luckily got a premonition as to what Father had in mind. She was sitting with her feet up on the sofa. She drew the cushions around her to help her "sit tight." She was determined to remain calm.

Father continued: "Of course, I am able to deal with the girls at the convent thanks to the cooperation of Father Mallon, and Mr. Butterworth is a tower of strength at the senior boys' school. But this is quite inadequate. What we desperately need is a parish discussion group on family planning, responsible parenthood and contraception."

Judith clenched her fists until her nails dug into her skin: at all costs she must not explode. Her silence encouraged Father Todson.

"You see," he went on, "you have only two children, Richard, born in 1958 and George, born in 1963. I understand that you are expecting another now in 1968. That is precisely five years between each child. But look at old Mrs. Larkin. She has had eleven children. Only four of them are married but already she has twelve grandchildren. It's impossible! I have asked her and other ladies with unplanned families to receive instruction, but they refuse to do so unless you preside. It is a moral obligation, Mrs. Rougham, for you to help me."

Judith's mind started reeling. It had nothing to do with Edmund and herself. It was the image of the convent girls and of Mr. Butterworth which started things off; she felt dizzy but still had control. It was the mention of Mrs. Larkin which somehow turned the dizziness into a nightmare.

"Get out, you scum!" she screamed. She jumped off the sofa and rushed to the fireplace to pick up the poker. As he opened the door into the hall, it just missed his head and came thump on his shoulder. She moved a bit slowly as the world was turning round her. He was out of the house. However, from behind the protection of the front door he claimed his *béret*. Judith got it and chucked it out like a disc. It went soaring into the air and landed somewhere in the rhododendrons. She slammed the door.

It was about twenty minutes later, after 6 p.m., that Edmund drove through the gates of the Dower House. The first object to strike his gaze was Father Todson's rather vacant face sticking out of the bushes. Nothing that Todson did could surprise Edmund.

"May I assist you in any way?" he asked with concerned urbanity.

"Well, yes; I am looking for my *béret*."

"And what makes you suppose that it is growing in my garden?"

"It's your wife who chucked it there. I seem to have upset her over something. I can't imagine why; I only asked her to preside over a meeting."

"Ah! That explains everything. Never ask pregnant women to preside over meetings. They are already presiding over a more important one."

Father Todson and Edmund scoured the bushes. The *béret* was eventually located on the branch of a birch tree. Father Todson tried climbing it to no avail. They threw stones at it, but it paid not the slightest attention. Eventually Edmund tied a hoe to the end of a rake and down it came. Father Todson disappeared, duly coiffed in his *béret*. Edmund put the car away.

Edmund put the key into the latch of the front door. It would not open. It stuck at about six inches. He rang the bell. There was no answer. He pushed the door hard but it would not budge. He was frightened. He went back to the shed and got the rake so as to push away whatever was blocking the door. It was something heavy. He managed to get in. It was Judith.

Edmund did what he could. He did not dare lift her, but he managed to slip a mattress under her and pull her away from the door. He got a pair of large scissors from the kitchen and cut the clothes off her. He covered her with a sheet. She was jerking frightfully. At one moment he thought her conscious, at the next, not. He rang up McAuley. He was not back from his rounds, but Mrs. McAuley was sure she could get hold of him. He rang up the local ambulance, Hertford Hospital and Giacinta's son to bring his mother back. George appeared and had to be told to be very good and go upstairs: Mama was not well. He crouched beside Judith, wiping her face from time to time as the sweat poured off it. He spoke to her because he found the sound of his voice seemed to calm her. Every minute seemed an hour.

At last McAuley arrived. "Well, that is most unexpected," he said in a matter-of-fact way. "But there does not seem to be much wrong. I wonder how it happened? Go and get me a large basin, a bucket full of luke-warm water, half a dozen kitchen cloths and two good white linen napkins. Then go and give George something to eat and put him to bed; I hear him crying. I'll give you a call when I want you."

Edmund obeyed. It was a relief to look after George and give to his little boy the love he felt for his mother. He heard the ambulance drive up. George had just gone off to sleep when McAuley called him.

"It's a little girl. When I say little, I mean minute. She seems perfectly all right, but at that size I think you ought to baptize her for safety's sake."

Both Richard and George had been premature, but nothing like as small as this. Edmund's mind was in a whirl. He could not think of any other name but Judith, so another Judith the little creature was.

"And how's my wife?"

"I simply don't know. It is some form of hysteria which has fired the whole mechanism. But, as I said before, she has no reserves. Your wife is just about as weak as your daughter is wee. Well, we had better pack up now. Judith I will be in hospital for just about as long as Judith II will be in an incubator — say four weeks. One cannot let babies face the world at less than five pounds, you know. I have not weighed the little thing, but I suspect that she will nearly have to double her size. Now we shall put up the two Judiths into the ambulance and off they go to

Hertford Hospital. Mr. Jenkins (a man who had come with the ambulance) will clear things up. In the meantime you can give him, me and yourself a generous swig of your excellent brandy, so that we can drink to the health of the two Judiths. And you can cut me a large slice of cake if you can find one."

When Giacinta returned, her son drove Mr. Jenkins home. McAuley stayed until after midnight, consuming large quantities of cake and brandy. He was a real friend. "You can go to the hospital now if you like," he had said, "but I am against. There is nothing you can do except give your wife a rest. Ring up the hospital tomorrow morning. Go to the Treasury as usual. Leave after lunch so as to get to the hospital at about 3:30 p.m. — probably the best time."

That was the evening of Wednesday, July 24th.

When Edmund visited the hospital on Thursday afternoon, Judith was asleep. The nurse woke her at four to give her some medicine. She smiled at Edmund and asked him to kiss her. She laid her hand out for him to hold. "I haven't seen the little creature yet. I am told she is tiny but perfectly all right — thank God! They are bringing her in tomorrow."

The sister explained: "Your wife is very heavily sedated. It was her nervous condition which gave Mr. Edwards (the consultant) a little anxiety. Early in the morning she was very agitated and kept calling for a Mrs. Larkin. Is she a relative?"

"No, just a friend."

"Well, we shall see how she is tomorrow. If Mrs. Rougham is more settled, perhaps you could ask Mrs. Larkin to visit her on Saturday. Mr. Edwards feels that it might go a long way to calming her."

Edmund was told to return a little later — at 5 p.m. on Friday.

He did. Judith was bolstered up with a head-rest and pillows. She looked absolutely beautiful, with her wonderful deep-brown hair falling in cascades on the pillows and her naked arms lying on top of the bed-clothes. She was completely in her right mind.

"I've seen her. Isn't she wonderful, poor pathetic little creature. And to think that she has got an immortal soul! You are an ass, Edmund; fancy baptizing her Judith. One cannot have

two Judiths in the same family. When the ceremonies are supplied we shall have to add another name. What about Ruth? It
will sound absolutely awful, 'Judith Ruth,' but that cannot be
helped. I haven't a clue what Ruth means in Hebrew, but in
English it means 'mercy' or 'pity.' She is God's ruth to me. Oh,
Edmund! It's so stupid but you have no idea how much I wanted
a little girl. God is so kind. Now I have one. And as we are immortal, I shall have one for all eternity. Isn't it marvelous? They
will be rolling the incubator in again at six so that we can both
see her. We are not allowed to touch her, which is a bit mortify-
ing. I'm sure you can get round Sister so that I can touch her tiny
hand with the tip of my finger."

In fact, it was all wonderful. Judith I was perfectly normal.

Edmund had seen Mr. Edwards before going in to Judith. He
had indeed met him at the McAuleys' and he seemed a competent
fellow. "Your wife, Mr. Rougham, is both physically delicate
and nervously very high-strung. I imagine that she is quite
brilliantly intelligent. Unfortunately, one has to pay for one's
gifts. I notice from her file that she has suffered from toxaemia in
both her previous pregnancies. There is no sign of that now. But
there is a nervous obsession centred round a Mrs. Larkin. Can
you throw any light on this?"

Edmund had to admit that he could not. She was the ex-
postman's wife at home, whom Judith held in high esteem.

"Very well, ask your wife. I have tried, but she clamps down
like a — like a clamp. And, if necessary, get this lady to visit Mrs.
Rougham. The best way to exorcise ghosts is to produce them in
flesh and blood."

Judith seemed so perfectly natural and normal that Edmund
broached the subject after the incubator had been removed.
"Judith, darling, I have seen Edwards, who tells me that you
want to see Mrs. Larkin. Shall I bring her over tomorrow?"

The result was frightening. Her arms began twitching upwards,
her jaw dropped and her eyes became glazed. Edmund was on the
point of calling for help when she clicked back into normality. But
there was a change: she had become very tired and rather sad. "Ah,
yes, Edmund! Thank you so much for reminding me. I was so

preoccupied with Ruth that I forgot to tell you. Yes, be a dear and bring Mrs. Larkin over tomorrow, along with her eldest daughter, Mrs. Rainbird, if possible."

It was then that Judith told Edmund what had happened on Wednesday afternoon. "Poor little Todson, I nearly killed him. I hope he forgives me. Do you know if he ever found his *béret*? It went soaring away over the bushes. It is the last thing I remember before I woke up in hospital."

On Saturday Judith had more visitors than was good for her. At 11 a.m. the Brig and Lucy turned up. They were sensible and only stayed five minutes. They inundated the whole hospital with Rougham Roses. At 12 noon Lady Milden arrived. Unfortunately, she had run a hospital during the war and had decided views as to how it should be done. However, she was sweet with Judith although she put all the nurses' backs up. John and Joan Milden came at 3:30 p.m. They were sensible and brief. But at 4:30 came the busload: Edmund, Richard and George; Mrs. Cacciacapri; Mr. and Mrs. Larkin; Mr. and Mrs. Rainbird; and Mr. Tom Larkin representing the rest of the clan.

Edmund managed it all perfectly. Richard and George were pushed under the bed to play games. Giacinta was sent to inspect Ruth in the incubator; her shrieks of joy could be heard all over the hospital. The Larkin males were relegated to the hospital grounds to smoke their pipes. Only Edmund and the ladies Larkin and Rainbird remained.

"Thank you so much for coming," Judith said to Mrs. Larkin, "but there is something I want to tell you. On Wednesday Father Todson asked me to attend a meeting on family planning and contraception. I want you to let every other woman in the parish know that I refused and beg them to do likewise. That is really all that I have to say to you, Mrs. Larkin, except that I love you dearly and admire the way in which you have raised your children, especially you, Mrs. Rainbird. You will not go far wrong if you bring up your beautiful children as your mother did you. Kiss me, both of you; then Edmund will take you along to see what is in the incubator."

Tears were shed. "We knew you'd give us the right answer,

Mrs. Rougham, Ma'm," said Mrs. Larkin. "We cannot trust the priests any more but we knew we could trust you."

On Sunday Edmund went to the hospital fairly early in the afternoon. Judith was fine. She had enjoyed the great concourse of people on Saturday. She was also very relieved to have got Mrs. Larkin off her mind. Edwards had been quite right; it had made a different woman of her. She was as gay as a lark.

They played "memories" together. This was a game in which a place or event in their lives was pinpointed and they had to remember all they could about it. It was tremendous fun, as nobody ever remembers quite the same things. Judith usually won in spite of Edmund cheating whenever he could. Apart from having a woman's eye for detail, Judith was a bit of an extrovert; she remembered things, objects, far better than did Edmund. Edmund was a bit of an introvert and remembered his reaction to things far more clearly than the things themselves. What lovely memories they had! What happiness they had enjoyed together! Yes, Judith was perfectly all right. There was certainly nothing wrong with her memory. Edmund went home with his confidence completely restored. Judith would be home in ten days instead of four weeks. Little Ruth, of course, would have to incubate for her allotted time.

On Monday, July 29th, Edmund managed to leave the Treasury early and arrived at 4 o'clock. He had not been there half an hour when the nurse came in: "There is a Father Todson who wishes to see you. He is not on the list, but can he come up?" The "list" was of people who were to be allowed to visit Judith. As a matter of fact, they had all been on Saturday. The answer to those not on the list was to be a firm "No." But a priest, the nurse thought, that was different.

"No," said Edmund.

"Yes," said Judith. "There is something I want to tell him. It won't take long. And be nice to him, Edmund. He's a poor little thing, really. He is a sort of ugly beetle: although unattractive, there is no reason why one should stamp on it."

So Father Todson was shown up. It must be remembered that in his own eyes Father Todson was as innocent as Judith's newborn babe. When he heard of the premature birth, it explained Mrs. Rougham's unexpected behaviour. The assault with the poker and the misadventure of his *béret* were manifestations of hysteria connected with childbirth. It had nothing to do with him. Tommy Todson had done no wrong. He noticed, however, that the so-called educated classes had a streak of violence in them which was fortunately lacking among people in humbler circumstances. In the whole of his life he had only twice been assaulted: once when Mr. Rougham had shaken him out of his wits and once when Mrs. Rougham had attacked him with a poker. However, he forgave them. It was doubtless part and parcel of "bourgeois culture." He entered Judith's room as replete with charity as he was with innocence.

Judith sensed this and acted accordingly. To Edmund, however, Todson was the little brute who had nearly killed his wife and child. He stood silent and erect the other side of Judith's bed so as to keep Todson beyond arm's length and out of harm's way.

Todson chatted aimlessly about Judith's health and the baby. Judith interrupted him: "I am grateful to you, Father, for calling. I wanted to see you. I wish to apologize for bashing you with the poker. It was instinctive. Unbeknown to yourself you happened to touch on a subject to which I am particularly sensitive. I should have said or done nothing had you implicated nobody but myself. But the criticism of Mrs. Larkin and her children, particularly Mrs. Rainbird, was beyond my endurance."

At this point Todson attempted to open a dialogue but met with so peremptory a "Shut up" from Edmund that he did so.

Judith continued. "Anyway, Father, Mrs. Larkin and Mrs. Rainbird were kind enough to call on me two days ago. I told them under no circumstances to join your discussion group and to warn the other ladies of the parish not to do so either."

Aghast, Father Todson again tried to interrupt, but to no avail. Judith raised her voice until she almost shouted: "I do not believe in Tommy Todson being the controller of creation. And you, teach sacrifice to your girls. And get Butterworth to teach heroism to his boys..."

It was obvious to Edmund that Judith's temperature was rising. Her arms were beginning to twitch, as they had on Friday. "Keep calm, Judith," he said, and then to Todson: "Come along, Father, and bless our little girl." He practically pushed Todson out of the room and took him to where the incubators were, a few yards down the corridor. He showed Todson the baby and left him to it.

He came out of the incubator room. There, in the corridor, gesticulating wildly and jabbering incoherently, was Judith. He tried to lead her back to her room but to no avail. He lifted her in his arms. She was difficult to hold, she jerked so frantically. He managed to turn the handle of the door without losing his grip on her. As he did so, she made a strange noise, between a hiccup and a sob, three or four times. She fell limp in his arms. He laid her on the bed, kissed her on the forehead and rushed to the sister's office. "My wife has had another attack of hysteria and has fainted."

The sister came along and felt Judith's pulse. "Yes, Mr. Rougham, she is in a hysterical coma. I shall get the house physician straight away. Please go down to Waiting Room Number Two on the ground floor." Edmund obeyed.

It was quite a nice little waiting room, presumably for VIP's. He was alone, thank God! He had no illusions. He knew that Judith had died in his arms. He took the rosary out of his pocket and looked at the little crucifix. "Jesus, Jesus, I cannot express my gratitude. Thank you. Thank you so much for Judith. What happiness we shared! I thank you, too, for Milli and when I lapsed. It made me realize how much I needed both you and Judith...And fancy inspiring us to play 'memories' the day before she died! There is no courtesy so gentle, so considerate as yours...And then to let her die in my arms...No, I cannot express my gratitude...I suppose I should feel sorry but I don't. I feel so happy — and so grateful..."

It was over an hour later that Mr. Edwards came in. "I have sad news to bring you, Mr. Rougham. Your wife is dead."

"I know; she died in my arms."

"We did everything we could to revive her. We have all the

apparatus here. There was absolutely no response." He gave some sort of medical explanation for the death: "It means that she did not die as a result of childbirth, but from total nervous exhaustion."

"I am sure you did everything you could, for which I thank you. Can I see her? I loved her tenderly when she was alive; I should like to see her dead. I was not able to have a good look at her when she was in my arms."

"Well, she is still in the theatre surrounded by all the apparatus."

"It does not matter. I shall get the undertakers to drop her home for a night. I shall just go up to say goodnight to my little girl. I doubt if I shall see her again until after the funeral. There is so much to do at death. Good night, Mr. Edwards; and thank you again."

He went up to see his baby. There some fifteen in the room, but he never had difficulty recognizing his own: she was the tiniest and pinkest of them all. "You were Ruth to your mother," he said to himself, "but you are Judith to me. I was right to baptize you Judith. There are not two Judiths in the family. There is only one; and now it is you. Giacinta will care for you as the apple of her eye. Goodnight, my tiny Judith, God bless you." He kissed the lid of the incubator and left his rosary on it. "I shall swap it for your mother's when I come back."

Yes, there is so much to be done at death. Edmund's first reaction was to bury Judith privately at Rougham with just the family. No, that would never do; it was funking it. She should be buried from Holy Cross, the church she had built. Inevitably it would then be a very big affair. Apart from parishioners and relatives and connections from both sides of the family, there would be people from the Rougham Estate and from the Milden boards, from societies and committees with which Judith had been connected, from the recusant families into which she had married. The chancellor and his wife would certainly be there, as would the permanent undersecretary, the local authorities and crowds of friends. He would have to persuade Todson to move his table back into the sanctuary or there simply would not be room.

And who would be the celebrant? He knew several decent priests. He was standing in the bedroom and looked up at the crucifix. No, a strange priest was neither what Judith would have wished nor what the crucifix said. One must drink the chalice to the dregs. The celebrant should be the murderer.

So it was done.

Judith Rougham, née Milden, died on July 29th, 1968. It was the day on which Pope Paul VI promulgated *Humanae Vitae*, the encyclical condemning artificial contraception. It came four years too late. It was accompanied by a statement to say that it was not an infallible pronouncement. Neither bishops nor priests payed the slightest attention to it.

On Friday, August 2nd, Edmund buried Judith, the frail marriage convert who died for her faith.

It was several weeks later that Edmund began to feel the grief of loss and misery of loneliness. Yet, even they were mitigated by his gratitude for having possessed Judith. Her last words ever re-echoed in his memory: "Teach sacrifice to your girls and heroism to your boys." It was she who had been heroic; it was up to him to offer the sacrifice. As he knelt each evening in front of his crucifix, he felt, rather than understood, the truth of Pius XII's strange blessing: "Those arms will ever be outstretched in suffering and in mercy over you." Yes, and Judith had had singularly delicate and lovely arms...

Edmund Rougham has not remarried.

THE END

Printed in Great Britain
by Amazon

53427291R00138